SELLOUT

James W. Lewis

The Pantheon Collective (TPC)

www.pantheoncollective.com

The Pantheon Collective (TPC)
P.O. Box 799
Santa Cruz, CA 95061

ISBN: 978-0-9827193-0-5 (Paperback)
ISBN: 978-0-9827193-1-2 (Ebook)

Printed in United States of America
Cover: Designed by Marion Designs
Interior: Designed by The Writer's Assistant
www.thewritersassistant.com

"*Sellout* is a book that takes interracial dating to another level. It has unexpected twists that readers will not see coming and suspense that is out of this world. The author's creative way of linking these individuals and couples made for an exciting book. Sellout is very entertaining and will keep readers on the edge of their seats."

– APOOO Reviews

"*Sellout* was an awesome debut novel by James W. Lewis. Mr. Lewis had me laughing out loud at some points and had me really thinking at others. Mr. Lewis does an excellent job in showing both sides of the color spectrum. If you are looking for an enjoyable read, this book is for you. Sellout would also make an excellent novel for a book club discussion."

– Urban Reviews

"A true writer can bring a powerful story line to your backyard. The book dealt with real-life taboo situations that evoke deep rooted emotions. The book was just amazing."

– Sisters United Book Club

"It takes a turn that I did not expect and actually has you on edge."

– Urban Divas

"This book has Drama, Hope and Healing. It will have readers wanting more. It is a terrific conversation piece. This novel will have extended and heated discussion. Job well done."

– Savvy Book Club

"The characters are well developed and likeable. They help you understand the reality - joy and pain of love relationships... some work and some don't. Love makes the relationship last, not our likenesses. James Lewis makes us see that true love is not colorblind."

– Atlanta Literary League

"Race is always a touchy subject. When a person truly falls in love, race is not important. The author did a great job with his first book and I look forward to reading others."

– Circle of Color Book Club

Dedicated to Mommy
Thank you for your unique form of
"punishment" that led to this!

Acknowledgments

It's been a long time coming! I started on this rocky road toward book publication nine years ago, steady creeping and crawling up that long ladder to attain the revered status of "novelist." Got short stories and essays published here and there, some online, some in print.

Read umpteen writer magazines, attended writer conferences, participated in writers groups—everything possible to prepare me for writing a novel. I've learned a lot, but I still have *much* more to learn about this writing thing.

Writing is such a solitary profession, where it's just you, a computer (or notepad), and all the ideas in your brain itching to get out. But even though a writer may write the book, *no* writer can do it alone. From the first word on the page to the final product, each process requires a helping hand along the way. On that note, I'd like to acknowledge the following peeps:

Of course, the Man upstairs for blessing me with this talent. I will cherish the gift He's given me and take it as high as I can. It's sad to waste talent, and J-Dub won't waste any of it!

My mother Phyllis for making me write a story every day for punishment when I was still a snot-nosed hard-headed youngster. Look at what you've done! :-) To my brothers Kenny and Quen; and nephews Tyrone and Miguel. You are my inspirations. To my cuzzo Brian: Thanks for all those nights on the couch!

To Patty: You will always have a special place in my heart. Thank you for everything.

To my "circle," the usual suspects: Oscar, Debra, Mark, Erika, Mike, Michelle, Troy, Chelsey, Bobbie, Ralph, Lori, BJ, Mo, Sonja, "T-Bear," Mac, and Cindy. Thanks to Walter Trent for all you did my last year in the Navy. Appreciate you guys for your friendship and support! You may not know it, but you've all helped me through some tough times.

To the Garrards of the family: My grandmother Gertraude, all my aunts, uncles, first, second, third, fourth-to-the-third power cousins—all ya'll! I'll always be "Junior" to you!

Thanks to all the Cashers, my new Bay Area fambamily!

To my industry friends who've helped me along the way: Literary Agents Mondella Jones and Claudia Menza; Editors Tia Ross, Kimberly Hines, Deatri King-Bey, and Stephanie Casher (more on her below); Law Professor Tonya M. Evans; Author Jessica Tilles; and Keith Saunders at Marion Designs. I am a much better writer because of you.

To the male authors who've helped me say "yes, I can!": Eric Jerome Dickey (the man!); Travis Hunter; Marcus Major; Eric Pete; Omar Tyree; E. Lynn Harris (RIP); Alvin Romer; C. Kelly Robinson; Stephen King; and Relentless Aaron. I would daydream about being in your shoes one day. Thanks for blazing the trail.

When I needed information on writing, these sites never let me down: Timbooktu.com (my first publishing credit!); AALBC.com; Blackmeninamerica.com; Writers.net; RAWSISTAZ.com; Blackwriters. org; Blogginginblack.com; and Book-Remarks.com. To my online writer groups: BlackExpressions; FictionFolks; AAMBC; Writersrx; Readers In Motion (RIM); and Self Publishing. And big shout outs to all the TPC fans and my Facebook friends!

Thanks to all the book clubs. Without you, independent publishers and writers would never get the exposure they deserve. Can't wait to meet you!

To all my fellow veterans (retired and active): Thanks for fighting the good fight. My heart will always be with you.

To my TPC partner Omar: Without hesitation you decided to take me on as not only a business partner, but as TPC's debut author, even before you read this book. I'm extremely grateful for that. Your drive, commitment, and "outside-the-boxness" greatly inspire and influence me to aim higher with no fear.

And to my *other* TPC partner Stephanie: You are a partner in every sense of the word. Without you the past few years, I would've been a 747 flying through turbulence with only one wing. But with your guidance, love, and friendship, you have become the other wing that has helped this "plane" fly and land safely countless times, even on days when I thought it would crash. You are an irreplaceable part of me, and together, I truly feel we will always soar. DWK loves you!

And to anyone I've forgotten, hopefully I'll get you in the next one! :-)

I love feedback, so hit me up anytime at james_wil_lew@yahoo.com. Also, you can visit me at www.jameswlewis.com and www.pantheoncollective.com.

Thank you for purchasing SELLOUT. I hope you enjoy!

Peace and love,

James W. Lewis
The Pantheon Collective (TPC)
25 May 2010

Chapter 1

Tammy

Another so-called man bit the dust.

I cannot believe I stayed with Craig's sorry ass for so long. After the string of zeros I'd run through—including I-still-suck-on-my-mama's-tit Andre and wife beater Simon—I thought I'd completed all the on-the-job training necessary to pick one out from a line-up. But somehow, Craig slipped under the radar. At the end of the day, he was no different than the others—just another sorry example of underdeveloped male sperm.

The actors changed, but the same tired script never did. Well, I pressed the pause button on that low-budget flick. I was done with men. Especially *black* men.

It took a small piece of paper to break the proverbial camel's back. It was a Saturday morning and like a good "wifey," I was sorting laundry while Craig played basketball. At the start of our so-called courtship, I didn't mind serving up the king's treatment, but I noticed after a month of cohabitation, cooking and cleaning had become the routine for me.

As I separated darks from whites, I checked the pockets. Craig always left a trail—change, pens, receipts. Inside the back pocket of his jeans—the same baggy pair from the night before—a piece of paper brushed my finger.

I almost threw it away, but the cursive style caught my eye. When I flipped it over, my jaw dropped, ringed glasses slipping down my nose as I digested the bitter taste of betrayal:

Craig, you knocked it out the park last night! Grand Slam! Call me anytime. Tracy.

I felt my insides turn, a volcano on the verge of vomiting lava on Craig and anyone around him. A tick formed in my cheeks, then somehow shot to both hands. I stood seconds away from smashing something against the wall. Such a damn *fool!*

To ward off the demon in me, I clutched the heart-shaped gold pendant around my neck, channeling my father. It'd been seven years since my number one fan left me for Heaven. Moments like these made me miss him even more. Daddy had always been the antidote to a jacked-up situation, but thanks to pancreatic cancer, I had to fend for myself. My mother died in a car accident when I was three.

I traced a finger across the smooth texture of my pendant before I opened it to gaze at my father's handsome face. In the photo, Daddy's little girl sat atop his broad shoulders. He wore fatigues, an Army vet after twenty-four years. Our wide smiles and chocolate dimples were so alike it looked as if someone had stamped his facial impression on me.

Taking a deep breath, I tried to draw strength from my father's memory. As I shook the cobwebs from my eyes, I experienced a long overdue moment of clarity. Craig and I had been together four months, the last month in my apartment. Two weeks after moving in, Craig's job at a local plant laid him off—or so he said.

I worked as a mortgage loan officer, but thanks to the housing bubble bursting, I spent most of my days navigating through the tangled web of short sales and foreclosures. Despite the long hours I put in at the bank, I still found time to play Craig's wing while he "searched" for another job. I became the Whitney to his Bobby, *always* on the lookout for gigs. I even brought home classifieds from just about every Dallas newspaper.

But I never found evidence of a job search. The classifieds I'd placed around the house never gave me the impression of someone searching for a nine-to-five—no highlighted sections, no pen marks, crumpled pages. Can't say the same about the umpteen rap magazines with big-booty hoochies on the front page.

A friend even emailed me asking why Craig hadn't called him back about a position at an airplane parts factory, a job that I, the naive "ride-or-die chick," tried to hook up. When I confronted Craig, he invoked his inner ten-year-old:

"I forgot."

He *forgot*. Whatever. Just like his dumb ass forgot the note in his pocket. Who leaves a damn note in a pants pocket anyway? So stupid.

I stood up from the bed. Oh yeah, the blinders came off. No more blind love—I was *done*.

Cuss words and basketball thumps pierced my thoughts. Craig's cackle echoed through the hallway outside my apartment. "Bitch this, nigga that." I told that boy about his nasty mouth. Who wants to hear that mess?

The front door opened and foul-mouthed chatter permeated the living room. Slipping Tracy's secret message into the pocket of my sweatpants, I turned back to the clothes, a new agenda on my plate.

"Tammy?" Craig yelled. "Where you at, girl?"

I picked up a stack of his clothes and started a pile by the door. He entered the bedroom a moment later. "Hey, shawty?"

He got no reply. In the past, my heart would jump when he'd come home from playing basketball, his body shiny from sweat. Sexy as hell, especially with cornrows and a neatly trimmed goatee. His bad boy swagga always pushed my buttons, but not today. Not anymore.

"Laundry, huh? Cool, cool." He pointed at the sweat suit on top of the pile by the door. "Ima wear that after I shower."

"You're going to wear baggy pants while looking for a job?"

He didn't respond to the question, just chuckled a little. Instead, he said, "Say, baby, before you wash these clothes, can you whip up some of dem apple cinnamon pancakes?"

Wow, he's got some nerve, I thought.

Words sounded off in my head, reminding me of Craig's vitals. Liar. Cheater. Lazy. Unemployed. He didn't want a partner; he wanted a mother.

My new path became billboard clear. I didn't need extra mess in my life, *especially* from someone four years younger than me.

I threw up a smile as fake as Joan Rivers' plastic face. "You want pancakes, huh?"

"Yeah, whip 'em up for me and Grip. And later on, Ima whip on this ass." He slapped my butt.

A loud rattle drew my attention toward the living room. His homeboy Grip pulling out that damn Xbox, I bet.

"You can make your own damn pancakes," I said, as Craig headed back toward the living room.

Craig braked in his tracks as if he'd slammed into a wall. "Huh?

Whatchu mean?"

"I mean, I'm not cooking you anything," I replied, my back to him. "Not anymore."

He said something, but I zoned it out. My nonchalant sweep around the room for anything Craig-related held top priority. I grabbed his gym bag and shoved his junk into it.

"Baby, wha-wha-whatchu doin'?"

Ah, yes, the stuttering. Craig always stuttered when flustered.

I picked up the bag and stomped in front of him, nudging his chest with my elbow. "Excuse me."

Craig followed me into the living room. My focus switched to Grip and that damn Xbox *I* bought for Craig's twenty-sixth birthday.

"Baby!" Craig cried, touching my wrist.

I pulled my hand back, then swung the bag at the front door. Grip turned, eyes rolling from my feet to my face.

Grip was also twenty-six years old and like his friend, no direction, no employment, no future. Grip and Craig had played basketball in 80-degree weather, but did that stop him from propping his sweaty dark-chocolate legs up on my table? Hell no. Not only that, his sweaty ass dripped all over my leather couch.

Grip held the joystick, its cord stretched beside a Gatorade bottle on the table. Had he bothered to put the bottle on a coaster? Nope. The way he made himself at home, you would've thought he paid rent up in here.

Grip's chapped lips slit into something that I think was a smile. "What up, shawt—"

"Turn it off," I cut in.

15

Grip's jaw dropped. Three gold teeth flashed me. "Why?"

Craig stepped to my side. "You ain't got to turn it off, dawg. My girl trippin'."

Trying to show up in front of his boy. Typical. "I've been a fool, but not anymore. You need to get your nasty clothes out my place and take Grip with you."

"Girl, I ain't goin' no where!" Craig plopped down on the couch. "I don't know who you think you talkin' to. Grip, hand me the other joysti—"

"'You knocked it out the park last night,' " I said in a phony high voice. "'Call me.' "

I balled up the note and flung it at Craig. It bumped the bridge of his nose. "I can't believe you left behind the smoking gun. Why don't you take your triflin' ass to Tracy's house?"

Bus-ted.

Except for audience cheer from the game and Grip whispering a cuss word, I didn't hear anything else. Craig's eyes swelled so much I thought they'd pop and drop to the carpet.

"T-turn off the game, d-dawg," Craig said. Funny how fast the stutters came back.

Grip shifted his eyes to Craig with the how-you-let-her-catch-you look. He removed his legs from the table, grabbed his Gatorade, then stood.

"Aw'ight, then," Grip said. "I gotta roll, anyway." He slapped hands with Craig, angled around the table and pressed the Xbox power button. "I'll, uh, see ya'll lata."

Grip closed the door. I tapped my fingers on the kitchen counter, watching Craig. Part of me couldn't wait to hear his last words before he stepped the hell out my life.

Craig scratched the side of his neck. "D-d-did Tra—"

"You need to get your funky ass off my couch."

He stood up. "Did Tracy call here?"

"Here? Why would...ooooh." I slapped my forehead. "You gave that bitch my house number, too? I bet you two stayed in here a few times while I was at work, right? When *your* sorry butt was supposed to be looking for a job."

His shin banged the table. "No-ow! Shhhhhh. Baby...we never stayed here! You sure Tr-Tracy didn't call?"

What the hell? He made his priorities quite clear.

"Craig, take your bag, your ball and your ass out my face. You are so worried about this Tracy bitch, you can't even see I'm kicking you out."

He reached for my hand, but I didn't give him the luxury. "Baby, look. Tracy's n-nothin', aw'ight? It only happened one—"

"Didn't I say get out of here? It's over!"

We stared at each other, but no words passed between us. My heartbeats felt like a hundred horse hooves galloping against my chest. An emotional breakdown neared, but I refused to let my big woman composure waver.

"Aw'ight, aw'ight." Craig picked up the basketball and slung the bag over his shoulder. "Look, Ima call you lata, okay? And, um, b-baby? If...if you hear any rumors about me—"

"I don't want to hear anything except that door closing."

He stood for a second or two, then did just that. Gone.

Steam in my lungs drained through my lips, caving in my chest. "Rumors about me...the hell? Damn, he got some nerve."

I placed my elbows on the counter. A dull ache ballooned inside my chest, spread to my belly and swirled hunger into nausea. Seconds later, I grabbed my cell phone and hit up my girl Miki.

17

Five rings later, she answered. "Tammy, what's up, girl?"

"Nothin'." I sighed. "Well...some mess just went down with Craig. I kicked him out."

"*What?*"

"Yeah. He's gone."

Miki didn't hide what she felt. "About time! I told you he was sorry!"

"Miki, I'm really not trying to hear that right now."

"I'm sorry, girl, I didn't mean to sound all insensitive. You wanna come over and vent?"

Venting sounded like a good idea. I looked at the clock on the microwave. It said ten thirty-five. "Yeah. Give me an hour."

愈 愈 愈

"Hi, Aunty Tammy!"

My "nephew" sprinted toward me, bumping into my leg. "Hey, little man." I hugged him. "What 'cha doin'?"

"Watchin' cartoons."

"Really? Any good ones?"

"Yeah! I'm gonna watch Spidaman! Wanna watch with me?"

"Aunty Tammy and Mommy are gonna talk first, baby," Miki said, walking in from the living room. "Go on to your room."

I said, "I'll come back there in a little while, okay?"

"Okay!" He gave me a missing-toothed smile that warmed my heart. Then Jumping Jack Flash trotted off to his room.

I sat down at the kitchen table and crossed my legs. "Damn, that boy's getting big."

"Yes, he is." Miki opened the fridge. "Smart, too. You know, the other day he asked me where his daddy was."

"Oh boy." My mood crash-landed at the mention of Kevin's sperm donor. "What did you tell him?"

"The truth—that I didn't know." Miki grabbed a bottle of OJ and poured herself a glass. "Five years and that nigga still hasn't seen his son."

As much as Miki tried to play the bulletproof diva, I could see the hurt in her face. I knew that pain. The kind of pain that pulverizes a woman's spirit and kills trust. The kind of pain that cuts you when a man lets you down.

Thoughts of her sperm donor fed my anger. Such a coward. I wouldn't mind initiating a beatdown on the "boy" that planted Kevin's seed. Rip his little "yang" off, throw it to the dogs.

The baby business had become so cliche: Black man shows up, makes baby, disappears, then starts the cycle over again with another open-legged fool. I knew way too many women who had fallen into that trap, left behind to don a Superwoman cape and raise their kids solo.

Before Miki closed the fridge, a bottle in the door caught my eye. "Is that hard lemonade?"

"Um-hum. You don't want no orange juice?"

"No, I need *that*."

She frowned. "Girl, it's not even noon. I thought you said you hadn't eaten, yet?"

"I don't care. I need a real drink."

"I heard that." She grabbed the bottle, then sat next to me. I popped off the cap, tilted the bottle up and gulped some down. The carbonated stream burned my throat.

"Well...I don't wanna say I told you so, but..."

I rolled my eyes. "You just couldn't resist."

Miki smiled. "Hey, it's not often that I'm right, now. Let a sista bask in the moment."

We chuckled. Just what I needed, a few laughs.

"Before he left," I said, pushing my glasses back up my nose, "he said 'if you hear any rumors 'bout me.' "

"What did he mean by that?"

"Girl, I don't know. I didn't wait around to find out."

Miki nodded. "Good. I'm glad you found that bitch's number. And I know his ass wasn't tryin' to find another job, either, especially with Grip dealin'. Craig was probably dealin', too."

"Probably."

Turning my head, a magnet picture on the fridge of Miki, Sheryl and me caught my eye, an old snapshot from our high school varsity basketball days. Sheryl moved to San Diego about a year ago, where her younger brother Dedrick stayed. Whenever Sheryl and I talked, conversation wouldn't end without her saying something about me and Miki moving out there.

"Craig ain't about nothin', just like the rest of these niggas 'round here," Miki ranted while gesturing for her purse hanging from my chair. I handed it to her.

She said, "I told your bachelor-degree havin' ass you could do better than Mr. I-barely-graduated-high-school."

"Damn, Miki! Enough with the 'I told you so'!"

"Sorry. But you need to hear it."

"Pssst, whatever."

Miki dug around in her purse for cigarettes. Her shoulder-length waves no longer hid the cut on her neck. With her high-yellow complexion, the scar resembled a thin red line from a felt-tip pen. A permanent engraving from a dead man named Stanley, another ex on Miki's longer list of zeros.

Three years ago, strung out on crack, Stanley kneed her to the kitchen floor, grabbed a steak knife and sliced a 6-inch loop in her throat. It took two of his crackhead buddies to pull him off.

I'll never forget the sea of blood surrounding Miki as she lay on the floor, just a few feet from where we sat. Stanley got his, though. Two stolen vials of crack got him two bullets. He became another statistic, one that didn't bother me at all.

I took my glasses off and set them on the table. Resting my head on the chair's curved iron backside, I closed my eyes and tried to sip away the pain. Didn't want to talk anymore.

Good thing my girl knows me well because she got the hint. Her chair tapped the floor, and then her arms wrapped around me from behind. I smiled and rubbed her hand.

"You gonna be okay, girl. Forget Craig. No good, anyway."

"Thanks, Mik."

She stood up. As she walked away, I heard her light the cigarette. "Listen, I have leftover chicken and biscuits in the fridge. Help yourself. I'm gonna check on Kevin."

I took another sip of hard lemonade, my head still leaning over the chair. "Okay. Thanks."

She left the room. I sat alone, my thoughts my only companion, the chair's iron bars poking my spine and shoulder blades. But I ignored the discomfort because boys posing as men smothered my brain...all of them...trash. Craig. Stanley. Kevin's "father." Andre. Simon. The losers that stood around the street corners near my apartment. Down low bastards...*trash*! And they all held a common thread.

I took another sip, fueling more gasoline on top of an internal flame. *We shall overcome, my ass. Black men are the reason we're not overcoming a damn thing.*

The iron bars against my spine took their toll, but I didn't budge from the chair. A bubble stung the corner of my eye, and tears finally fell.

"*Niggas,*" I whispered. "*Damn niggas.*"

I'd never used the N-word that way before. Actually, I hated that word. But it's easy to say when you feel hate.

I knew Daddy wouldn't like this new attitude, so I took off my pendant and placed it in my purse. I didn't want his picture anywhere near the hate nipping at my heart. The moment the pendant left my neck, I vowed a black man wouldn't touch this body again for a *long* time. If ever.

Ready to break away from it all and start anew, I pulled my cell phone from my purse and dialed Sheryl's number.

"Hello?" Her voice was groggy.

"Sheryl, it's Tammy—oh!" I looked at my watch. I had forgotten the two-hour time difference. "I'm sorry. I woke you?"

"Don't worry about it. I needed to get my ass up anyway. Went to some nightclub last night, out all late thinking I'm still twenty-one years old."

I sniffled. "Oh. That...sounds like fun."

"Well, it was...are you crying, girl?"

"No, no." I wiped tears from my cheek. "Hey, you still want me to move out there?"

Chapter 2

Terrell

I love black women.

I repeat: I *love* black women. Dated black women most of my adult life. Butterscotch, caramel, dark-chocolate—I've sampled all the different brown colors and flavors.

But too much of the same flavor gave me headaches. After years of applying my brown women-only rule, I had to put sistas on hold for a minute. My mental health depended on it.

I used to wonder why TV always showed a deep-pocket black man sporting a white woman, especially a blonde. Maybe the whole "trophy" thing had something to do with it, since white folks declared blondes the apple pies of American beauty. When I was younger, we used to call those brothas "sellouts."

But after my friend Dedrick crossed over with a few of them, then settled down with a *fine* white girl named Penelope, I realized looks had nothing to do with it; maintaining sanity *did*. The last few women I'd dated stretched the limits of my sane mind, especially my ex Tasha. She brought too much baggage to the party, trying to make me her personal bellboy.

As a single thirty-five-year-old optometrist with no kids, I admit—I'm a catch. I'm the *only* black optometrist in the city and women push up on me all the time. I had my pick of San Diego's finest, but I stayed true to Tasha, trying to play the good man role that women complain don't exist. But even on my best behavior, I still had to put up with drama queen theatrics.

I tolerated Tasha's occasional flare-ups. Thought I could handle them, but they just wore me down, you know, got on my nerves. Stupid, kindergarten nonsense, too. Arguing just for the sake of arguing, it seemed. One night, she *really* acted the fool, and I had to fire her ass. For good.

On our weekly date night, Tasha and I made plans for dinner and a movie. I wore a cream-colored short-sleeved shirt and khaki pants, showing off my toned, 6'0", 190-lb frame. Yeah, I hit the gym on the regular.

Tasha rocked a halter-top and skirt on her guitar-shaped figure. When she walked, cuts in her thighs and calves flexed. I'd always loved her toned legs, especially when I would wrap them around my lower back.

After a nice steak dinner, we hit the movie theater, hoping for a gang of action and laughs. The new Will Smith movie delivered the goods, at least for me. Tasha seemed to have a good time, but once we left, somebody pressed her mute button. Blind-sided by silent treatment again; it happened so many times.

Moonlight, summer breeze, stars scattered like diamonds in the sky...a perfect Friday night for a lover's prowl. But my code of conduct—somehow, somewhere—sabotaged romance.

I tried to hold her hand as we walked to my ride, converse with her, continue the good time I *thought* we had, you know. No go. Folded arms and a frown revealed a woman on the verge.

But why? I had no idea. Attitude reared its hideous head for the billionth time.

Aw man, here we go again, I thought. *What did I do now?*

I tried to hold the door for her. "I got it!" she snapped.

She slid her leg in, slammed the door, went back to arm folding. Confused, I stood for a second outside the car. Then I got into the driver's seat and popped in a mix CD, pretending everything was kosher.

Can't do that for long, though. Stay quiet and you risk stirring up an emotional earthquake because your girl will think you don't care. Try to talk, you risk saying something stupid that might unload a flurry of "bitch bombs." You can't win.

I considered my odds better with the latter, so I tried to soothe the tension with conversation. Turning down the music, I said, "Baby, you ok?"

Her cast-iron gaze fixed on the windshield. She smacked her tongue and said, "I'm fine."

"You sure? You don't look—"

"I said I'm fine!"

Damn. At-ti-tude. Sistas should own the copyright on it.

But, hey, at least I tried. That should've counted for something, right? Wrong.

My music sounded better than Tasha's jagged tone, so I pumped it up. *I guess no booty for me tonight.*

We arrived at her apartment ten minutes later. Summoning my last attempt at chivalry, I stepped out to open the door for her. That's when my hope for peace buckled under pressure.

She saw me walking around the front toward her, but no, Ms. Attitude still stepped out on her own. Not only that, she slammed the door and marched away from me!

25

"Pissed" is a few levels below what I felt. I don't give a damn who you are. *Nobody* slams the doors of my Lexus IS 300, aka "Lexy." Crazy ass.

I placed a hand on the hood. "Woman, what the hell is wrong with you?"

Nothing. Not a word. Tasha disappeared inside the building, her heels pounding the steps. The B-word jammed between my tongue and lips. I'd never called Tasha that word before, but she came damn close to a ricochet of B-words.

I told myself not to run after her, but instead of heading home, I followed Tasha up the stairs. I caught her at the front door, her cheeks moist from tears. She didn't slam the door this time, so I followed her into the apartment.

Tasha turned on a lamp. I stood in the small entrance area where vinyl meets carpet while she plopped on the leather sofa. Still no open communication.

Did I need to buy a vowel up in here?

A blank TV screen seized Tasha's demonic stare. She sat with arms folded and legs crossed, red-coated nails tapping her biceps. Her leg bobbed, foot inches from the glass table.

"All right, Tasha. What did I do now?"

"You got some nerve." She wiped her cheek. "You think I didn't see you?"

"See me what?"

"You know what. Don't play stupid."

I do? I thought. Oh, boy. Time for twenty-one questions.

A carved wooden mask of an African queen drew my gaze toward the wall. Her Highness held no answers for me, so I turned to the mahogany desk and Dell computer. The African violets on the desk didn't hip me to any secrets, either.

I calculated new formulas on my mental chalkboard. The answer lay somewhere between dinner and the movie:

Ok, I opened all doors for her...bought her popcorn...drink...um...let's see...is it that time of the month, again? No, she got off two weeks ago. What then?

Tasha's heel banged the table. "How can you not know what I'm pissed about?"

"What kind of question is that? Just tell me!"

She shook her head. Her lips moved and words came out, but I couldn't understand a damn thing.

I leaned against the wall, folded my arms. "Stop mumbling, please."

The second time, her words came out loud and clear. "I saw you staring at that white woman!"

Aw hell. Caught. The bitch storm cometh.

Tasha despised two things: Me gawking at other women and black men dating *white* women. Well, she had caught me peeling the clothes off a peach-skinned, long-haired blonde with my stare. That's double trouble.

Blame it on hormones. Or that ass. A *swollen* ass. This girl had crazy back like a sista. An oxymoron for a Caucasian female, but she worked it.

Tasha had dipped into the bathroom while I stood in line for popcorn and drinks. As I grabbed the snack tray, the blonde walked by with another female.

"*Dayum*," I whispered. About twenty-four years old, around the time a woman's luscious figure ripens. Booty so thick I could set my tray on it. Shape of a heart turned upside down.

When I walked off, my head still leaned ninety degrees her way. I broke my trance because I almost bumped into an elderly lady. I excused myself, then saw Tasha angling around a group of teenagers. Thought she didn't see me, but obviously she did.

"All right, Tasha," I said, palms showing. "Yeah, I was looking at her. I didn't know you saw me. You know I wouldn't disrespect you like that."

"You wanted that girl! Shhhhh. Dreamin' about them, too!"

"What?"

"Don't play dumb! I'm talking about what happened this morning. Who was the bitch you were dreaming about?"

"What the...oh, *hell* no! You can't be mad about that!"

"Don't tell me what I can't be mad about!" Damn, if looks could kill.

I lowered my eyes. Somehow, I held back an eruption of laughter. Unbelievable. How could she be mad about a wet dream?

Tasha leaned forward and placed her elbows on her knees. "Well, who was she?"

"I don't know! Baby, it was a dream."

"How could you not know?"

Again with the questions. I took in a deep breath and exhaled, purging the smirks.

"Baby," I said, trying to stay calm, "it was a dream. Do you understand? I had a dream about a woman I've never seen before, that's all."

I moved toward the sofa with slow footsteps, as if showing extreme caution to a wild animal. With Tasha's pouty lips and flared nostrils, my approach seemed appropriate.

She smacked her tongue. "No, it wasn't just a dream. I tried not to let it bother me, but with this stunt you pulled tonight…shhhh." The tears kept coming.

"Baby, I—"

"That mess was all over my new sheets, too!" she cried, cutting me off. "Probably jackin' off while I was asleep, thinkin' 'bout some white bitch, huh?"

I slammed my hands on the sofa's armrest. "It-was-a-wet-dream!" I lowered my voice. "Men have them all the time. It's no different than when you had that dream and woke up crying."

"But I wasn't sleepin' with nobody! It was a nightmare!"

I threw my hands up. I couldn't win. She had a jacked up comeback for everything I said. We went from arguing about a woman at the theater to a wet dream.

As Tasha said, I'd squirted on her thigh and bed sheets while asleep. Waking up to hot syrupy liquid on her, she wanted to know the W-T-F details. Like a super supreme idiot, I told her I dreamt about riding a train with some woman riding *me*. No idea of the woman's identity, but I swear I'd reenacted a scene out of the movie *Risky Business*.

I told Tasha the truth, something she always stressed in our relationship. Thought I did the right thing.

But then Tasha asked, "What color was she?"

With idiot mode in high gear, I said, "I don't know. Some white girl, I think."

I'm surprised I didn't win a Darwin Award that night.

It's one thing to admit dreaming about another woman *to* your woman. It's another to reveal a color you know damn well could set off a racist like Tasha. I had done both.

Call me a highly educated man with "lowly" common sense.

Tasha didn't go off on me when I first told her, but apparently she'd bottled up that hot steam—until now.

I couldn't respond to Tasha's bitching at first; the stupidity of it all seized my tongue. The no-name white woman lived in a fantasy land. Figment of my overactive imagination, a dream. In other words, *fake*.

I asked, "Are you telling me you're jealous about a white girl in my dreams?"

"Oh, so, *now* she's the girl of your dreams, huh? I knew it! You just like all these other tired brothas trying to screw white women! I catch you staring at them all the time!"

"Stop turning my words around, *please*!" I stepped away from the sofa and stood in front of the TV. The table separated us, which, I believe, was a good thing. "And stop accusing me of stuff! Look, I could've lied about the dream, right?"

"But you had a reason for that dream!"

"I...you...uggh!" I curled my fingers. This time, I heard bones pop.

We faced off across the room. A temporary cease-fire helped calm the storm a little. I searched for evidence of the occasionally fun, always intelligent woman I'd dated the past few months. Nowhere in sight. Outta there.

I rested my hand on the TV stand. "Damn, look at us. I thought we'd have a nice night at the movies and come home to some all-night 'healing'." I shook my head. "But here we are arguing, *not* about a real-life girl, but some *fake* girl in a dream. Man, you're acting stupid."

Like I said, no common sense.

30

"Oh, so now I'm stupid?"

"I didn't say you were stupid! I said—"

"I heard you! Just 'cause you a eye doctor, you think you all that. I've seen this before. The higher up the ladder a brotha climbs, the lighter the women get until they become white!"

Boy, boy, boy. I thought I could fend off the verbal jabs, but she had stepped up to another level.

"What the...where the hell is this coming from?" I asked. "What, you'd rather me get with a sis..." I swatted my hand in front of me. "You know what, forget it. You need help."

I unleashed the hounds of hell when I said that. Tasha shot back, flailing her arms and screaming, but I no longer acknowledged her tirade. Seeing Tasha through new eyes, I decided homegirl had issues. Never really knew how deep until a damn dream killed that fickle love thing between us.

For a moment, I wondered if her head dancing would rip the skin around her neck. Ridiculous. Tasha was clearly a straight up fatal-attraction psycho who had reached her expiration date.

"...so if you want a white woman, go 'head! You dreaming about them! I can—hey! You ignoring me?"

I blinked. "Huh? Oh, I was—"

Tasha rose from the couch, her Damian eyes laser beaming my way. Can you believe this second-coming-of-the-Exorcist pushed me? I stumbled back, nearly bumping into the TV. Again, I somehow restrained the monstrous urge to retaliate.

Tasha stomped toward the bedroom. "Get out!"

Another door slam cut through the air. She wanted me out and that's what I did—for good.

As I started Lexy's engine, I glanced at a picture of Tasha and me dangling from my rear-view mirror, vowing to never see that face again. I ripped the mini-pic off, crumpled it up and pushed it in my cup holder.

Like I said, I'd been loyal to sistas. Except for one or two one-night wham-bams that don't really count, I'd never actually *dated* white women. Obviously Dedrick knew something I didn't know. Maybe hidden treasures lay in the world of "vanillas," as Dedrick called them.

So I decided to branch out, go on a few dates. I thought a little one-on-one with some "snow whites" would give me a taste of what I'd been missing.

Chapter 3

Penelope

They say, "Once you go black, you never go back." I really haven't been back since.

How the daughter of an old racist redneck from a small hick town called Starkdale got involved with black men, I don't know.

All right, all right, I lied. I *do* know.

His name was Jamal. Lean, tall and toned like a basketball player. We met at a sports bar in downtown San Diego. Jamal was so different from the guys I hung around with in Mississippi—mainly his color, of course. Even today, my home city has a black side and a white side, a divided lower-class population that works together during the day but rarely mingles at night.

But California was a long way from Starkdale, so when Jamal asked me to dance, I figured what the hell? As we angled toward the dance floor, it occurred to me I'd never danced with a black guy before, despite some interaction with them in high school and eight years in the Navy. Kinda weird, considering I'd harbored many secret crushes on black guys. You just don't find them in country bars though, which is where I usually hung out.

At first Jamal and I kept a safe distance as we danced, about a foot or two apart. He had this two-step, finger-snap thing going that was so cute, but nothing that outshined my little side-to-side, on beat, off beat dance—if you can call it a "dance." At that time, I didn't listen to much Rap music.

Then the DJ played "It's Gettin' Hot In Here" by the rapper Nelly. Couples swallowed floor space, assuming all kinds of inappropriate postures. I was determined to keep things innocent, but a few seconds into the song, Jamal turned into a little devil.

Jamal's hips pumped harder, arms and legs moving faster. Then he pushed his hands in the air. I gasped every time he did that. I think it had something to do with those rock-hard biceps, not to mention nice, juicy lips. I'd noticed him swiping his tongue across them as he lip-synced the lyrics.

My friend Jen danced with Jamal's friend, Brandon, a hot white guy. She pushed her hands together, egging me on to close the space between me and Jamal. As I pumped my hips toward him, Jamal bent his knees and spread his legs. For a few seconds, he stood the same height as me, his face inches from mine. I stared into his eyes...just for a moment. Bushy eyebrows, thick lips, super smile. Very cute.

I tried to pick up the rhythm. He placed his hands on my waist; I did the same. Our hips kissed for the first time as dribbles of sweat tickled my inner thighs.

I noticed some stares from a few white guys at the bar, but tried to ignore them. I was trying to concentrate on my crash course in Hip Gyration 101, courtesy of Jamal and his magic pelvis. I thought I was getting the hang of it, but then I dipped my body and banged my knee against his thigh, bumping into a guy behind me.

Good going, Pen.

Jamal leaned toward my ear and said, "Don't worry about it." I tilted my head; his lips grazed my earlobe. "I love the way you move."

He sparked my hormones so fast. I'm sure the margaritas helped, but when his breath brushed my neck and sexy voice dripped through me, he stirred enough heat to blister my jugular vein. Scary.

Our bodies became a vanilla and chocolate swirl. Jamal could shift his hips from 5ᵗʰ to 1ˢᵗ gear in a snap, but I loved 1ˢᵗ gear, with his slow circles and swift bumps against my pelvis. I mirrored his moves and went along for the ride, like two boats rocking against a gentle wave.

It didn't take long to realize his boat had a concrete "anchor" attached. I felt it poking me, sandwiched between my private spot and his hips. My nature responded. How could it not?

I wonder if what they say is true? Are black guys really that big? He's soooo hot. If Jamal can move like this on the dance floor, I wonder what he's like in bed...

The DJ said a few words, then mixed in a Techno song. With a thin film of sweat covering me and raw throat, I needed a break and some water.

I swiped hair off my drenched cheek and placed my hands on his shoulders. "C'mon," I said on my toes, "let's sit down."

We stepped off the dance floor while Jen and her guy stayed. She shot me a look; I stuck out my tongue.

Before I reached the chair, Jamal pulled it out for me. How sweet. When Jamal sat down across from me in the light, he looked two times better.

He folded his arms on the table. "Damn, Penelope, you worked me out, girl!"

The corners of my lips crept up. He remembered my name. "I was just trying to keep up with you, Mr. Dance Fever!"

"I heard that," he said. "Hey, you got a lil' twang in your voice. Where you from?"

"Place called Starkdale." I dabbed a napkin on my forehead. "Small town in Mississippi. I'm really sorry I bumped your leg, by the way."

"It's cool. You was doin' your thing!"

"Yeah, right. Whatever I was doing, I sure do need the exercise. My butt is getting huge!"

"You say that like it's a bad thing."

"What, it's not? You don't think I'm too big?"

"Big? You are not big at all. You thick!"

"*Thick?*"

He licked his lips. "Yeah. Brothas love females with thickness." He scooted his chair back and stared under the table at my legs. He was a cocky little sucker, but I liked that.

"Love your thighs, too!" he said. "Matta' fact, if not for the long blond hair, you could pass for a light-skinned sista. You got an onion, girl!"

I laughed so hard I almost slipped off the chair. Never heard a behind called an "onion" before. Our conversation fascinated me, though, learning more about this thing black men have with big butts and all. I'd always hated my pear shape, but Jamal said why hate what my mother gave me? He praised my shape with words that turned my cheeks red. Called me a classic figure eight, a brick house. A Caucasian hottie with a bangin' body.

"All right, all right," I said, fanning my face. "That's enough. I've met my quota on compliments!"

Jamal pushed his chair back. "I just keep it real. You fine as hell." He stood up and stretched. "You want a drink?"

"Some bottled water would be great."

He flashed his mega-watt smile. "Be right back."

I slumped further into the chair. I swear ever since I saw a shirtless LL Cool J licking his lips in a music video, I've had a secret fetish for black men. For silly reasons, I guess, like the way they walked, talked and especially the way they danced. But even though I'd spent a decent amount of time daydreaming about a taste of chocolate, I'd never gotten this close before.

Jamal had me aching to take my curiosity to the next level. With his bronze skin, fleshy lips and cut physique, I was barreling down a road to the taboo motherland and didn't want to stop. Even though my father would feed me to the hounds for dirty dancing with him...for speaking to him.

For that itchy tingle burning between my sweaty thighs.

"Wake up!" Jen cried, slapping my chair. "Where'd the black Adonis go?"

"He's at the bar," I said. "Where's his friend?"

Jen sat in Jamal's chair. "In the restroom. How's it goin' with him?"

Before I could respond, Jamal reappeared with four bottles of water. He set them down on the table and extended a hand to Jen. "Hey, I'm Jamal."

"Nice to meet you. I'm Jen. Brandon went to the restroom."

Jamal flashed his hi-beam smile. "I saw you coming over and thought you might be thirsty, too, so I got water for all of us. Help yourself."

"That's so thoughtful of you, Jamal," I said.

Jamal grabbed a chair from a table next to us and sat beside me. "Well, you know, I gotta take care of the best lookin' females up in here."

And right there, Jamal sucked us into a hailstorm of charm. Brandon came to the table and the four of us got better acquainted, talking about everything and laughing up a storm. We eventually introduced more margaritas.

Brandon and Jamal were in the Air Force, stationed four hours north of San Diego. That gave us a lot in common since Jen and I were old Navy buddies. After active duty, we'd taken jobs as functional analysts at a naval facility called SpaNet.

Jamal and Brandon had come to San Diego for the weekend. The following Monday, they were scheduled to fly out to Sheppard Air Force base under new orders. Jen and I whined upon hearing the news. As the clock ticked down on my time with Jamal, my body fever jumped, intensifying my "itch."

We danced a few more times. Tired and burning up, I took Jamal's hand and looked at his watch. It was 1:27 A.M.

"It's getting late. I think I wanna go."

"Yeah, me too. Let's roll."

I tapped Jen's shoulder and we vacated the floor. As we headed toward the exit I cuffed Jamal's arm, causing this scruffy-faced white guy to fix me with the evil eye. He stood by the entrance, holding a Corona beer and shaking his head. I recognized him as one of the guys that gave me dirty looks earlier.

I stopped in front of him. "Why do you keep staring at me? Do you have a problem?"

The guy took another sip, but didn't say anything. Just walked away. Must have been intimidated by our two personal "bodyguards."

"Seems like dude don't like you, Penelope," Brandon said. "Or maybe you, Jamal."

"That's cool." Jamal wrapped his arms under my breasts from behind. "Say, man! Don't worry! She's in the good hands of a black man!"

I threw the back of my head against Jamal's chest and laughed. We all did.

Jamal nudged me outside. Early morning air cooled my hot skin.

"Damn, girl," Jamal said, "I didn't expect that! Thought you was 'bout to beat ol' boy down!"

"Yeah," Jen said, walking behind us. "Penny's a firecracker."

I locked my arms around Jamal's arm. "That guy's an ignorant ass."

"All righty, then," Jamal said. "Calm down, killer."

We stepped off the curb and walked through the parking lot. "Hope my evil side didn't scare you, Jamal."

"Scared, no. Surprised, yes." He leaned toward my ear and whispered, "*I love a woman with spark, though.*"

I forgot all about that guy.

We wandered around several cars. Brandon and Jen held their own conversation a few steps behind us.

"So, um," I cleared my throat, "are we...*you* heading back to the motel?"

He nodded. "Yeah, that's the plan. You wanna hang for a while? We can pick up sumn' to eat and chill in the room."

"Um...sure. I'm kinda hungry." I found my Civic and turned to Jen. "Jen, you wanna get something to eat? We can bring it back to their rooms."

"We were just talking about that," she said. "How about you guys ride together? I'll ride with Brandon."

I smiled. Music to my ears.

ଔ   ଔ   ଔ

Brandon and Jen disappeared into a room a few doors down while Jamal and I set up a picnic on his motel bed. We lay with shoes off and legs stretched out, backs against the headboard. The TV offered the only light in the room. We conversed and laughed about this and that, even touched hands a few times.

Though Taco Bell hit the spot, I was aching to tame my *real* appetite.

We finished our food and put away the cartons. We glanced, then stared, edging closer to each other, our faces only a breath apart. His eyes...those *lips*! I could taste them without even touching him.

Gunfire from the TV phased out, my mind now wasted away from margaritas and a hunger for flesh. I wanted him *bad*.

When we kissed, tingles rode the curves in my spine. We stripped off our clothes and made them room ornaments; my bra and panties soon followed. Jamal's lips traveled my cheeks, my shoulders, naked chest. He slipped two fingers inside me. I gasped, digging my nails into the mattress. My back arched so, so high.

He maneuvered toward the end of the bed, placing his knees on the floor. With his hands locked on my thighs, he pulled me closer and spread my legs in a wide V angle, my wet walls like the Florida Everglades.

But then something made my face burn. Waves of panic rippled inside.

As Jamal toured my inner thighs, I struggled with the conflict between desire and guilt. What was I doing in a motel room with a black man? Was my physical famine so strong that I could commit an interracial felony with someone I'd just *met*?

The image of my father popped in my head. Great timing, huh? I closed my eyes and tried to erase memories that haunt me to this day...

I was twelve years old, sitting on the floor watching a movie. Larry sat next to me while my mother washed dishes in the kitchen. In the movie, a pretty dark-haired white girl ran into the arms of her high school star athlete boyfriend. Seeing that black boy's lips touch hers sparked a rage in my father I'll never forget.

Impaired from his usual Jim Beam, my father threw the empty bottle at the TV. "Damn niggers! Stay with your own kind!"

Glass shattered inches from my bare feet, causing me to jump back. Accustomed to my father's outbursts, Larry didn't move.

I tried to step away from the mess, but my father's cold hand wrapped around my elbow and yanked me forward. I stumbled against the living room table and stubbed my big toe on a piece of glass. Pain shot through my foot, but my cries fell on deaf ears. The same hate my dad harnessed for black men bored into me from dark blue eyes.

"If you ever give your body to a monkey," he said, pink face twisted, "I'll kill ya. And if I can't do it, I'll make sher somebody else does, ya hear me?"

His firm tone froze me. I nodded because I believed him.

He let go of my arm and I limped toward my mother, staining the hardwood floor with blood. Mom placed a hand on my shoulder and walked me toward the bathroom. Years of my dad's outbursts had worn her down, and my mother was as timid as I was.

My brother Larry patted my shoulder. "It'll be okay, Pen. You know how he gets when he's drunk."

Dad was like the devil to me as a little girl, especially when liquored up. Besides him, I could think of a million other reasons to stop my coffee-colored pipe dreams. For one, the last time I shared a dark space with a black guy...well...let's just say the outcome wasn't very pretty.

But that was then. What's done is done. I'm not a little girl anymore; I am a twenty-eight-year-old woman with a strong body and mind, and I no longer felt black men were taboo. I owned this night and damn it, I could indulge in whatever I wanted.

And I wanted Jamal.

Jamal's strong hands split my legs. I smothered my fear and gave in to lust. He buried his head between my thighs and circled his tongue in and out of me, tasting natural honeydew that had seeped hours ago.

"Damn, you sexy as hell, girl." He ran his tongue along my sticky thighs. "Taste good, too."

So many pleasant surprises in one night. I didn't think black men took trips down south.

After a few laps around my center, Jamal slithered between my legs...pecking my belly, licking my nipples, nibbling my neck... tasting my tongue. Before I could catch my breath, he stole it away when he entered me. My God. He filled me up, made me howl to a fake moon. Nothing mattered anymore except that piece of him inside of me.

My warped mind blurred guilt. He wore no condom, but I didn't care. I know, I *know*. Dumb move Pen. What can I say? I just didn't friggin' care.

His deep, hard strokes tapped a primal core. Cries erupted from the pit of my stomach, my nails raking skin off his thick back. I screamed so loud; came so hard. The harder he pumped, the deeper he plunged, the more I transformed into something...animal. Like a creature of the night.

Within minutes, my body rode an endless tremor and I thought I would puke all the margaritas out of me.

I had done it. Crossed over with Jamal and tasted the forbidden fruit. And it was *sooooooo* good. Why did the Air Force transfer Jamal away? It just didn't seem fair that I wouldn't get a chance for seconds.

But it wasn't long before another black man took his place.

With the chains of fear shattered, I felt bold enough to act on the crush I had on my co-worker Dedrick. I'd liked him for awhile, but his dark brown skin kept me at a distance. That stupid stuff was over, though. Once Jamal popped my black cherry, I was ready to get to know Dedrick a whole lot better.

What my dad didn't know wouldn't hurt him. Or me.

Chapter 4

Tammy
Nine Months Later

"Hey, Hot Chocolate, just wanted to let you know I'm coming in tonight."

"Dale, you only told me forty-five times via email."

"Did I? Then you know this white boy wants a date, right?"

"A date? I don't know about all that!"

"C'mon! We can go to a club or something. Don't you want to see me pop my thizang?"

I exploded in laughter. This Ivy League white boy was always trying to show how "down" he was. "*Thizang?*" I cried. "What the hell is a *thizang?* You've been watching too much BET."

"Don't hate. I'm just spittin' game, shorty."

"Whatever. I may have to rain check that date."

"Oh, brushing me off, huh? Why you gots to be playa hatin'? You needs to be concentratin' and fixatin' on Dale datin'!"

Again, I rolled. "Dale!" I cried, struggling to speak. "Boy, shut up! You're gonna make me pee myself."

"Okay, okay." He chuckled. "I'll leave you alone. Bye, Hot Chocolate. See you soon."

"Okay, sweetie. Bye."

I hung up the phone, shaking my head. Though he had more cheese than an extra-large pizza, Dale sure did know how to inject a ton of smiles. He cracked me up every time. I even liked his corny pet names, especially "Hot Chocolate."

Dale was also a loan officer, but based in Jacksonville, Florida. He flew to the West Coast on business quite a bit, and during my six months working here at a too-big-to-fail bank in downtown San Diego, we had run into each other three or four times at various work functions. The first time I caught him staring at me, I could tell he wouldn't mind a sample. He was cute, too, with dirty blond hair and a big-toothed smile.

After a few hours of work, I decided to break for lunch. I dialed Sheryl to see if she wanted to join me for a quick bite. She was free, so we chose Horton Plaza, an outdoor mall.

Sheryl and I met at the 4th and B club, a venue for comedy shows and live music. We strolled down 4th avenue, the San Diego weather a comfortable seventy degrees, even in the middle of winter. We crossed the trolley tracks and in less than two minutes, stepped onto an escalator toward the plaza.

I felt like Italian food; so did Sheryl. We bought calzones from a pizza place, then found seats in the shade.

Sheryl set her tray on the table. "Hey, what happened to your pendant? I've known you all these years and never seen you go anywhere without it on. Did you lose it?"

"Nope. Just decided not to wear it for awhile."

"Why not?"

I shrugged. "I really don't want to talk about it."

"Not even with me?"

"No, not even with you. Sorry."

Sheryl stared at me for a moment, trying to gain top-secret access to my thoughts. Some things I didn't want to reveal, though, even to a best friend.

"Fair enough. I'll leave it at that." She grabbed her fork. "So... now that you're all settled into your new place and job, how do you like San Diego? It's been, what, damn near a year since you moved here?"

"Yeah, time sure does fly, doesn't it? I like San Diego a lot, though. Nice, laid back city."

"That's one of the...aw hell." Sheryl shook her head. "There goes another one."

I took a sip of Pepsi. "Another what?"

Sheryl nodded toward the litter of winter shoppers behind me. "See him?"

I scanned the area. Didn't see anything unusual, just people dipping in and out of the plaza stores.

I turned back to her. "Girl, who?"

"That dread-locked boy with the snow bunny. Another brotha fiendin' for vanilla." She frowned. "That's one thing I *don't* like about this city."

As soon as she said vanilla, a tall, Rasta brotha with locks walked by us. He had a golden haired Britney Spears clone under his arm, her pink-colored lips stretched from ear to ear.

Sheryl's gaze followed them. The couple obviously didn't sense the heat she generated because they went about their business, laughing and carrying on.

I tore off a crust. "Why do you look all mad?"

She gave me the thousand-wrinkles-on-her-forehead look. "*Why?* You should be mad, too."

"For what? That's his business."

"Well, I'm tired of it." Sheryl stuffed her mouth. "Dedrick keeps screwin' these white bitches, too."

Damn sure the truth. I hadn't once seen Dedrick with a sista since I moved to rainbow California. When we lived in Dallas, Dedrick used to wear holes in his sneakers chasing after me, but I'd always viewed him as a kid brother, so I never gave him the time of day. Then baby boy grew up, became some kind of computer network guy and went from awkward teen to *da-yum*! He could have his pick of women now, and was clearly expanding his horizons.

While part of me understood why Sheryl was upset, how could I be mad about Dedrick only dating white girls when I had built my own brick wall that barred brothas? Since the break-up with Craig, the only man I'd allowed to "chip my bricks" was Dale, a white man who lived a thousand miles away. Black men could do their own thing for all I cared. The word "statistic" and Tammy would never ride in the same sentence. After my past experiences, I felt if I kept messing with black men, somehow, someway, I'd end up a statistic, too.

Sheryl sipped her soda. "I can't believe that boy. Always sellin' out. And, oh, he's been hanging around this *nice*-looking brotha, too. An optometrist."

I crossed my legs, pulling my skirt to my knee. "For real?"

"Yeah. But whenever you meet him don't bother trying to push up. From what I can see, he collects white women like baseball cards."

I chuckled, then we sat quiet for a second. As I ate, I watched people out and about.

Out of nowhere, Sheryl said, "This is crazy. White women are stealing our men!"

"Damn, girl, quiet down!" I glanced around, looking for eyes our way. "Don't you think you're being a bit melodramatic? You make it sound like some kind of conspiracy or something."

"It's worse than a conspiracy, Tammy. It's an epidemic." Sheryl picked up a napkin. "If your skin tone is any darker than this napkin, a brotha's not trying to talk to you."

I shook my head. "Girl, shut up! What about the men you've hooked up with since you got here?"

"You mean *boys*? I haven't had one relationship that lasted three months. I actually saw one of my exes with a white woman the other day. I'm telling you it's an epidemic."

"Come on, it can't be that bad."

"Oh, no? I bet before Tomi gets here we'll see at least two more Oreo couples."

As soon as she said that, I spotted a brotha with a short brunette who looked like she just woke up. Girl had the nerve to roll up in the same pizza place, knowing damn well she stood a slice away from crushing a weight scale.

I nodded toward them. "There's one."

Sheryl turned. "Ugh! Damn shame." She leaned toward me, cuffing her hands over her lips. "Brothaman hooked up with a whale, didn't he?"

I laughed. "Girl, you wrong!"

I scanned the food court. Picking out white-black couples had become a game.

"So," Sheryl said, "don't you think it's time to get out of that funk? You've been sulking since you got to California."

"Oh, stop it. Always exaggerating. I haven't been sulking."

"Yes, you have. Damn, do you even like men anymore? Seems like all you do is work, go to the gym and study."

"Listen to you. What is the point of me dating if, as you say, all the brothas are busy chasing white girls?"

Sheryl changed her tune. "True...but...well, there are *some* good brothas out there. I'm sure a few have tried to get with you, especially once they see your cutey-booty dimples."

"Oh, hush. I don't have time for men."

"*What?* You could at least get some hump action!" Sheryl gave me an odd look. "Girl, you're not over Craig, yet? Forget that fool! He's...damn, there's *another* one!" She switched gears, pointing over my shoulder. Back to the "snow bunny" rant.

A light-skinned boy about nineteen walked alongside a bony, curly-haired girl, her skin a pale beige color.

"She doesn't look white," I said. "Probably Mexican."

"She counts, too! See, not only do sistas have to compete with white girls, but Mex'cans, Indians, uh...uh...Asians!"

"Well, maybe we should give 'em a taste of their own medicine and start stepping out with *their* men."

Sheryl sucked her teeth. "You know what? I thought about it, but...I really don't want their men. A white guy? I just couldn't do it."

Dale's name edged to the tip of my tongue, but I held back. I hadn't convinced myself *I* could cross over, either.

While searching for another subject change, I noticed a guy runway-walking toward us, his booty popping. Jet-black hair so wavy it could make you seasick. Definitely a black guy with a queer eye.

I tilted my head toward him, still looking at Sheryl. *"Look at this boy sashaying like a fashion model,"* I whispered.

Sheryl smiled. Without turning, she said, "That's Tomi."

My bottom lip hung. "*That's* Tomi? Your new girlfriend you've been dying for me to meet?"

"Yup. Pretty, huh? That boy's so hot we'll need an AC when he sits down."

"I thought he was a *she*?" I said in a low voice. "Why did you call him your girlfriend?" I peeked at Tomi's booty-sway stroll. "Never mind. Dumb question."

Sheryl waved Tomi over. "Hey, Tomi. About time your ass got here."

Tomi swatted his hand near his face. "Shhh! Please. I was on the phone with Deshawn's ig'nant ass."

"Oh, yeah? Tomi, this is my girl Tammy."

I was about to extend my hand but Tomi bent down, stretched his arms and hugged me.

Tomi said, "Been wanting to meet you. This girl talks 'bout you all the damn time."

"Nice to meet you, too." I tried to hug up from a seated position. A little awkward. Tomi sat down.

Sheryl pointed at a leftover piece of calzone, but Tomi waved it off. "I ate in the back of the store while I was talkin' to Deshawn."

"What's going on with him?" Sheryl asked.

"Tsssk!" Tomi rolled his eyes. "He wanna get back wit me, talkin' 'bout he miss me. Damn, he confused. I'm like, 'boy, get yo' ass out the closet and stop experimentin' with me!' "

I dropped my jaw. That boy put it out there without a care in the world. I liked him already.

Curious, I asked, "So he's creepin' on the down-low?"

Tomi crossed his legs. "Yeah, girl. You'd be surprised how many black men out there just *actin'* straight. I been wit a few of 'em, talkin' 'bout they ain't gay. This guy Paul called himself 'try-sexual.' "

"Trisexual?" I asked.

"Yeah, as in t-r-y. Said he likes to *try* anything freaky with a man or woman, but he don't call himself gay. Can you believe that? I'm like 'whatever.' Keep thinking that lie while rammin' that thing in my booty hole, *o-kay?*"

No, he did not just say that!

Sheryl and I blew up. I laughed so hard I thought my vocal cord would collapse. People turned our way, but I don't think they heard our A-B-C conversation. Security probably would have kicked us out if they had.

Tears watered my eyes. I dabbed my moist cheeks with a napkin.

Sheryl tapped my hand. "And after Paul realized he wasn't gay, who did he leave you for?"

"Some white bitch."

My head shook. "What? No, he didn't!"

Tomi nodded. "I ain't lyin', girl. Saw 'em kissin' in a club. Soon as he saw me, that fool 'bout ta knock people over tryna get out."

I folded my arms against my chest. "Damn."

"Told you, girl," Sheryl said. "White women are like flies at a picnic. Just everywhere."

We laughed. Damn, it felt good to smear happy tears against my cheeks for a change. But the laughs didn't stop there.

Tomi looked up and whispered, "*No, she didn't walk out here in dem flip-flops.*"

Sheryl and I turned to see a bowling ball-shaped woman in a T-shirt and sweatpants wobble by with two rug rats. Poor woman needed half-a-day of pedicure work and half-a-year at Jenny Craig.

Tomi slapped Sheryl's knee. "You see dem toes, girl? How you gon' have toenails lookin' like pitch forks?"

I covered my mouth. It took all my cheek muscles to restrain the piece of calzone I had just chewed. I thought my skull would crack trying to hold back a rumble of laughs. Tears bubbled in Sheryl's eyes.

I pushed my plate away. Smart idea because Tomi didn't stop.

"Yeah, girl," he said. "These fools out here be—would you look at this parakeet lookin' heifa right 'chea?"

Damn, that boy took people-watching to another level. Had me covering my stomach, pretty much having a fit.

I finally saw the young girl he joked about. Typical teenager except she had green and red spiked hair.

Tomi shook his head. "That child look like she should be on somebody's shoulder, talkin' 'bout 'Polly wanna cracker?' "

And that's how the rest of lunch went. I can't remember the last time I laughed out loud and acted the fool in a public place. I thought Dale pushed my funny bone hard, but Tomi played on it like a joystick. Tomi became my new best friend within fifteen minutes of meeting him.

Felt good to break out of my shell for a while.

છ   છ   છ

I opened my apartment door and ran a hand over sore belly ripples. I didn't need to do my nightly stomach crunches; Tomi had worked my abdominal muscles enough. And that was over four hours ago.

I kicked off my heels. The bright red "2" flashing on my answering machine drew me toward the small glass table next to the sofa. I pressed the Play button and sat down. Sheryl's silly butt came first:

> *"What's up, girl? Didn't I tell you about that fool? Crazy, huh? Ha! Hey, me and Tomi was talkin' 'bout going to the club on Friday. You need to bring your butt, too! Call me back."*

I hadn't been to a club in months, but Sheryl never gave up trying to get me out. I wasn't lying about being busy, though. Homework took up most of my free time during the week and I had a writing class on Saturday mornings. I reserved Sundays for "me" time. I'd discovered it was easier to maintain a brick wall with a packed schedule.

The machine beeped. Miki's voice came next:

> *"Hey, girl. Call me back. Got some dirt."*

I picked up the phone and dialed Miki's line. A tender sting throbbed around my kneecap, so I gave it a deep massage.

Miki picked up after the second ring. "Hey. Just get home from work?"

"Yeah. You should've seen me and Sheryl today. Acting a straight fool at lunch. This new gay friend of hers had us rollin'."

53

"For real?" Miki paused. "I miss you heifas."

"Well, you can always come out here and live with me for a while like I did with Sheryl."

She sighed. "Maybe one day. Since all ya'll just got up and left me. I don't have anyone here except Kevin."

"Girl, we didn't leave you. Stop the guilt trip."

"Whatever. So, you want to hear the dirt or what?"

"Spill it."

"Grip is dead."

"What?" Blood rushed my cheeks. I rose from the sofa. "What happened?"

"Shot five times. Some kids found his body next to a dumpster in an alley. Looks like a dope deal gone bad."

The phone almost slipped through my hand. Of course. That's one of the reasons I never cared for Craig's childhood friend— the drug mess. Craig once swore he wanted no part of it. Since I left him, I could only wonder if he had sold his soul to the dope devil—or if he sold all along while with me. I suspect the latter.

"What about Craig?"

"Don't know. Haven't seen or heard about him. I wouldn't be surprised if he was involved, though."

"I...um...let me call you back. Trying to digest this."

"Okay. Talk to you soon."

We hung up. A short wind breezed through my lips as I rested my head against the sofa, eyelids at half-mast. I was stunned to hear the news, but the iron shield around my heart barred any sympathy for Grip. Why have any? Grip chose that path, so the nigga got what he deserved. And I bet Craig followed that grimy road, too.

On impulse, I reached for my pendant, but forgot it wasn't there. My father hadn't touched my heart since I left Dallas. I thought the pendant would be better off zipped up in my purse. Too much hate still in me, I guess.

I thought again about my conversation with Sheryl. Maybe black men really were an endangered species. If most black men were either dead, in jail, gay, or jumping ship with white women, why shouldn't sistas jump ship, too?

Dale's blue eyes and dirty blond hair popped in my head again.

Chapter 5

Terrell

"Check you out," Dedrick said, holding my retinoscope a few inches from his face. He handed it back to me. "This place is nice. You da man."

I shifted my gaze around my cozy 20-by-12 exam room, the perfect size for a doctor and patient. The door to the left led to my office, while the door to my right opened into the short hallway that led to the waiting room. Near the front desk was an inventory room, not much bigger than a closet, but big enough to store a variety of supplies. Two above-average female assistants were the cherries on top.

Yeah, I'd done pretty well the last few months. Up and running in my own practice. I guess I *am* "da man."

"Thanks," I said, strapped with a proud grin. "Rent is a bitch, but I'm doing ok."

Dedrick ran a finger along the oak frame of my Doctor of Optometry degree on the wall. "You think you a Dr. Huxtable?"

"Yeah, you can say that," I replied, chuckling. "The Dr. Huxtable of eyeballs."

Like a nosy kid with the need to get his fingers on every gadget in sight, Dedrick turned to my patient chair and tweaked the trial frames mounted over the seat.

"Don't mess up my equipment, now," I said. "That stuff isn't cheap."

Despite my feigned annoyance, I was happy to have my partner-in-crime back. Dedrick had been in Japan on government business the last few months and things hadn't been the same without my wingman.

"So, how's business so far?" Dedrick asked, sliding his six-foot frame into the patient's chair. He set his Nikes on the footrest, got comfortable.

"Not bad. Got my name in the phone book and word-of-mouth has picked up. Definitely getting a lot of black folks. Nobody's ever seen a black optometrist before."

"A lot of females?"

"Oh, yeah." I pressed Play on the iPod mounted between two small speakers. "A few sistas definitely tried to get their flirt on."

"Nice." Dedrick bobbed his head. "Tight mix, man. With all the CDs you sent me in Japan, I can tell you gettin' good at this DJ thing. Damn, you 'bout to quit your day job to be the next Funkmaster Flex, Dr. Eyeball?"

I took off my lab coat and laid it on the back of my chair. "Naw, bro. Optometry pays the bills. I made this mix for Lisa."

Dedrick's eyelids drooped, dark-brown pupils targeting me. Gum pops cracked inside his mouth.

"You staring at me?" I asked.

He tapped his fingers on the armrest. "Lisa, huh? The short-haired brunette?"

"Yeah. Her friend is dropping her off in about twenty minutes. While you and I lift weights, she'll be...man, what's up with that goofy look?"

"Nothin'," he said, stroking the peach fuzz on his chin. "Just can't believe how far you've jumped over."

"Dee, what are you talking about?"

"You know what. You drownin' in a sea of vanilla wafers, big dawg."

I erupted in laughs. Dedrick never called them white women, just names like "vanilla wafers" or "Barbies." He told me his sister Sheryl called them "snow bunnies." Shoot, *I* even had pet names. Whatever the label, I'd been OD-ing on them for months.

"You hit the skins, yet?"

I turned the music down. "Of course. Last night."

"Damn, you done jumped *waaaaaay* over!"

"Man, I'm just experimenting. Booty is booty, though. It's all the same. Well...I take that back. I think white girls are freakier than sistas."

"Told ya, man," Dedrick said, reaching out to give me a pound. "Some Barbies have Mandingo fantasies and wanna test the stereotypes, so they take freaky-nasty to the next level. No wonder I haven't been back to black in a while."

"You're crazy, fool. But to be honest, dating marshmallows has definitely been...interesting."

"Marshmallows? Yo' ass sounding like me now."

"What can I say? You've rubbed off on me in more ways than one."

"Well, tell me about it, black man. I've been gone for a minute, so I don't know the extent of your crossover."

I exhaled. Time for a heart-to-heart between men. I stopped the iPod and leaned my chair back.

"Well, it's definitely different. I've dated what...five of them since I dumped Tasha? Whole new world."

"No attitudes, either, huh?"

"I haven't stuck around long enough to find out. Still in date mode."

Dedrick nodded. "Well, I haven't seen nearly as much attitude in Barbies as in sistas. What I like most about them is you don't have to feel like you're on guard all the time."

"Yeah, I had to be on my P's and Q's with Tasha."

"It's called baggage. Black women carry around *too* much of it. A lot of them don't even know what to do with a *good* brotha."

"True, true," I replied.

Dedrick twisted his lips. "When I lived with Nicki, I can't remember a day when I didn't come home to a battlefield! Just arguing over nothin', you know what I'm sayin'?"

We slapped hands. "Tasha was the same way. A few sistas before her had similar issues."

"Yeah, but Barbies? They're more bubbly: 'How was your day?' or 'would you like a back rub, babe?' "

"The way it should be!" I cried, cosigning with him.

"Sistas be claimin' they fed up with us, but brothas can't be fed up? Sistas need to get a clue. Get an attitude adjustment, cater to your man, stop looking for basketball player height, go to the gym, stop—"

"Damn, bro, slow down!" I laughed. "What 'cha mean by 'go to the gym,' anyway?"

"You know what I mean. Besides Nicki bitchin' about money or whatever else, she was gettin' fat!"

That must have been the last straw for Dedrick. I'd known him for about a year and the man hit the gym for two hours *every day*. A female wouldn't stand a chance with him if she couldn't meet his minimum four-days-a-week fitness requirement.

"I've seen sistas up in the gym," I said, feeling a sudden need to defend them.

"But not as much as Barbies. They all up in the gym. Step classes, Yoga, Pilates."

I nodded. "I hear you."

An old *JET* magazine on my desk swayed my thoughts a little. Gabrielle Union blessed the cover. "I won't lie," I said, staring at her perfect white teeth and coke bottle frame, "I still love a nice ass and pretty brown face. Most marshmallows can't touch that."

You would've thought I said something dumber than your typical politician the way Dedrick warped his face.

"Fool, you crazy!" he cried. "I'll take legs over ass any day. I've never been into the thick thing. I like that long, sleek, leggy shape."

"Riiiight. What about Penelope?"

Dedrick's lips parted, but only a cluck sound came out. Round cheeks softened into a smile.

"Aw'ight," he said, nodding. "You have a point. She does have back."

"Not just back—she's *thick*. I was like *daaayum* when I first met her. Reminds me of Ice T's wife a little."

"Yeah," he said. "Long blond hair, pretty pink lips, ass...damn. I noticed her right away when she starting working at SpaNet. You know I had to push up on it. On the low-low, of course."

I nodded. Can't have fraternization on a government job.

"At first she was playing hard to get, but after a while we started talking more and hit it off." He blew out a breath. Something on the tile floor caught his gaze and his voice withered away. "Half the dudes in the company tried to holla, but she eventually chose me."

"So, what's up with you two? You guys have been official about three months, right?"

"Yeah. But because of my time in Japan, I haven't seen her in damn near two months. Our schedules are crazy. I pick her up from the airport tomorrow. She's in Norfolk now."

"Don't you guys travel together sometimes?"

Dedrick shook his head. "Different travel times for each team. I'm leaving again next week for Meridian, Mississippi to upgrade the computer networks for the tech schools on the naval base. I wish she could join me 'cause her family lives near there. I think her dad is sick."

"Damn, you already at the 'meet the family' stage?"

"Naw. She doesn't talk about her family much, but I get the feeling they're a little on the redneck side. Who knows what they'd do if she brought my black ass home."

"It's like that? Damn."

Dedrick scratched the back of his fade. "She told me she'd been with a brotha before, but I'm the first she's been serious about."

"And what about *you*?"

Dedrick shrugged, but didn't answer. I could see it in his eyes, though. He'd fallen for her. Don't know how far, but Penelope had worked his heart.

A tap on the door interrupted us. "Come in."

Luna, my curly-haired Latina assistant, popped her head in. "Hi," she said to Dedrick, puffy lips curved. She turned to me. "I put away all the patient files, Dr. Jackson. Shaundra is still working on inventory. You have anything else for me?"

"No, Luna. I'll see you tomorrow." I smiled. "Thanks for all your hard work."

"You're welcome." She waved, smiling. Dedrick threw up two fingers. The door closed.

Dedrick said, "She's not bad looking. I like Latinas, but they got attitude, too."

"It's white or nothing for you, huh, OJ?"

"Naw, man. I'm not saying I'll never go back to black. I just prefer snow bunnies right now." Dedrick stood, then stretched. "What about *your* Jungle Fever, playa? *You* ready to go back to black? I can hook you up with Sheryl's friend Tammy. Man, I had a huge crush on her back in the day."

"She fine?"

"Oh, yeah. Want me to set something up?"

"Naw, that's all right."

"You sure?"

"I don't need a hook-up. Dr. Huxtable of Eyeballs is doing okay with the ladies."

"All right, Doctor Pimp. Well, I'm outta here. I'll meet you and ol' girl at the spot."

"Cool. Lisa should be here, soon." I unbuttoned my shirt to change into my gym clothes. "Saw this nice dark-haired Demi Moore lookin' female on the biceps machine the other day."

"Yeah?"

"Yup. I might need to stock up on more peaches."

We laughed. No doubt—I *had* jumped way over.

ଓ   ଓ   ଓ

As I closed my office door, Shaundra stepped out of the inventory room. She locked the door and flashed a wide smile. I spread my lips an inch or two, then pretended to zip up the gym bag strapped around my shoulder.

Patients weren't the only ones trying to "holla" at me; sometimes, subordinates want a slice of the boss, too.

I leaned against the front desk. "Hey, Shaundra. You all done?"

"Yes." She removed her lab coat. Wavy reddish-brown tresses framed her face and brushed her shoulders. Her hair complimented Noxzema-smooth skin the color of nutmeg. Slick shifts in her gaze hiked up my arms to my face.

I broke her look of lust by saying, "If you're ready to go, I can walk you down."

She reached for her purse. "What a gentleman. Thank you."

As I held the door for her, her hooded eyes beamed one-way lasers with a message any hot-blooded male could read. Lovely young sista. Definitely knew how to stroke the ego of the head Negro. If I wanted, I could seize that opportunity. But since I wrote her checks, she was *way* off limits.

After locking up, we strolled toward the stairs. As we descended, Shaundra rained hints on me, talking about how good she looked in the black mini she wore to some nightclub a week before. She definitely didn't mind toying with the supervisor-employee red zone. I knew I needed to remind her I'm Bossman and not a potential hook-up.

When we exited the building, I realized I didn't need to halt Shaundra's flirts. Lisa took care of that for me.

"Hey, Terrell!" Lisa said, bouncing toward me in a sports bra and red biker shorts. "Are you ready?"

I gave her a peck and a hug. "Yup. Watch me bench-press seven-hundred today."

Lisa rolled her doe eyes. "Whatever."

I turned to Shaundra. Two minutes ago, Saturday morning sunrays sparkled from her face. The moment Lisa's pale skin and green eyes came into view—dark clouds and thunderstorms.

I pulled Lisa close. "Shaundra, this is Lisa. Lisa, this is one of my assistants, Shaundra."

Lisa extended her hand. "Nice to meet you."

Shaundra's eyes shifted to me and I felt the blaze from her three-second glare. Typical black woman reaction.

Shaundra shook Lisa's hand. "Nice to meet you, too," she replied, her tone dry. She walked away. "See you tomorrow."

Lisa frowned, eyes searching for answers. "*Is she okay?*" she whispered.

"I'm sure it's nothing," I lied.

We walked toward my ride. Shaundra drove off—no wave goodbye, nothing. And I guess, no more sucking up to the boss.

I held the passenger door for Lisa. "Thank you," she said, pink lips raised. She didn't stop smiling even after I closed the door.

My pearly whites shined, too. Something about Barbies made me want to step up the chivalry. Maybe their perky reception to my gentlemanly ways got me. Don't know. Whatever the case, I always felt appreciated.

As I made my way around to the driver's side, a black Nissan Sentra with two females inside murdered my smile. *Aw hell.*

The Sentra parked next to my ride, facing the opposite direction. The dark-skinned sista behind the wheel turned down the radio. I didn't know her, but I knew the passenger well.

"Told ya, girl," the driver said, wrinkles mangling her forehead. "Look at her."

Tasha stepped out of the passenger side, shaking her head. "I knew it. You are so sorry."

Despite the put-down, my initial thought was *damn, she looking good.* Attitude smears a pretty face, though.

"Tasha," I said, hand on the door handle, "what are you doing here?"

"No, the question should be what is *she* doing *there*?"

I turned to Lisa. Her bottom lip lay open, eyes wide.

"Don't worry about it," I said, trying to ease Lisa's shell shock. "That's the ex I told you about."

Tasha and her nameless cohort blabbed behind my back. "White bitch" and "fake ass nigga" were the last straw.

"Look, Tasha, you have no business here. I don't appreciate you barging in on me and my—"

"Your what? Your *girl*?" She shook her head. "You're nothing but a damn sellout!"

"Oh, so you drove all the way down here just to tell me...never mind. Bye, Tasha."

I got into the car and slammed the door. Once I started the engine, my subwoofer drowned out Tasha's insults.

Driving off, I didn't speak. Neither did Lisa.

Despite the boom in my ride, Tasha's last word mushroomed in my head: *Sellout.* A name I used to call other black men.

Well, if I had become a sellout, I blame black women for placing my stock up for sale on the white women market.

Chapter 6

Penelope

"We're leaving in about ten minutes," my co-worker Bill said, poking his head over the cubicle partition. "You almost ready?"

"Yeah, just going through some email. I'll meet you guys in the lobby in ten."

"Okay." Bill ducked back into his foxhole. I heard him gather his things and shut down the computer.

I clicked on my email inbox. My heart skipped when I noticed Dedrick's email address in bold black letters.

"What in the world?" Pressing a hand over my mouth, I smothered away laughter. The subject line asked, *Ready to ride this train 2morrow?* Such a goofball.

I read his message. He planned to take off work early so he could pick me up at the airport. Then we'd go back to his "crib" for a weekend of home-cooked meals, DVDs and "waterbed romp shakes" as he called it. It had been so long; I couldn't wait.

Before closing the email, I noticed an attachment he had titled *The Train.* I tilted my head. "Hmmmm."

I had no idea whether or not the attachment was safe for work, so I turned the monitor toward me. Opening the picture, my jaw fell, inner furnace firing up. I would need to wipe sticky juices off my seat when I stood.

My honey had sent me a shirtless pic, his gap-toothed smile high and wide, hands on his waist. Mr. Muscle Fitness looked yummy and he knew it. I caressed my thighs, easing a soft sigh through my lips. Fading into a fantasy, I saw myself taking a long ride on the Dedrick Express, my nails digging into his dark-brown pecs. Yes, a long, bumpy ride. I could feel it. Damn, I could *feel* it.

Before falling victim to my own combustion, I shook away my X-rated thoughts and blew Dedrick a kiss. I shut the computer down, but Dedrick had booted me up.

Because of our criss-cross travel schedules, I hadn't seen him in almost two months—unless you count webcams. It seemed the deeper we stepped into each other's lives, the more our teams deployed to opposite ends of the earth. Like some conspiracy to keep us apart or something. It really sucked.

Yes, absence made my heart grow fonder, but I also starved for his nourishment. Instant messenger chats, emails and phone calls helped bridge the divide, but it wasn't the same. Nothing could replace a lover's touch.

Thankfully I could retire all that technology for a little while because I'd see Dedrick in less than twenty-four hours. The thought triggered shivers in all regions of my body.

Again, I shook away my fantasies. Grabbing my purse, I said goodbye to my East Coast SpaNet counterparts and made my way toward the elevator. I hurried past Mark's desk, the database programmer. The Joe Smooth wannabe had been hitting on me for weeks.

I pressed the elevator call button, hoping to escape before Mark noticed me. No such luck. He grabbed the elevator door before it closed and stepped inside. "Now, how you gonna leave without saying goodbye to Marky Mark?"

The door closed. Just me and him. Cologne dusted the air around me. *Great.*

"Guess I'm just anxious to get home," I said with a shrug.

"Yeah, but damn, not even a goodbye? My feelings are hurt."

"Sorry." *Third floor...second floor. C'mon!*

A deep twinge throbbed in my neck. I stroked the small patch of skin between the bones in my spine. Mark picked up on my obvious sign of pain.

"Neck sore?"

"Yes," I said, circling my neck, "from staring at that monitor all day. But it's not too bad. I'm okay."

"I can massage it for—"

"No, no. I'm fine. Thanks."

The "ding" sound saved me, but Mark decided to take one last chance at seizing the moment. "So, what are you doing tonight?"

"Not a whole lot." The elevator doors slid open and I stepped out, Mark chained to my side. "I'm leaving tomorrow, so I'll probably wash clothes and pack."

"Oh, yeah? Damn, that's too bad."

I removed the visitor badge from my jacket and handed it to the receptionist behind the front counter. Mark faced me and I caught the I-want-you twinkle in his eye.

"You know," he said, "you should let me take you out before you leave."

Swiping strands of hair behind my ear, I said, "I don't think my boyfriend would like that very much." I bee-lined toward the exit, heels clicking against the marble tile.

Mark put pep in his step. "Oh, your 'boyfriend', huh? Oh, okay. Well…it's your last night. Let me show you a good time. I promise I'll be a gentleman."

Yeah, right. "Can't. My flight's at eight tomorrow morning. I need to get there early so I can drop off the rental car."

Thin lines formed in his forehead, wrinkling the smoothest baby-bottom skin I'd ever seen. Teeth as white as a blank sheet of paper. Although a cutie, his pick-up lines had grown tiresome the last few weeks.

I heard another "ding." Bill and Randall stepped out of the elevator. Finally.

"Well, it's been nice working with you, Mark," I said, as they walked up. "Take care."

Mark stepped back. He looked like he wanted to kick them for blocking his last attempt at me.

After dropping the guys off, I stopped at Roses department store to buy laundry detergent, a *Cosmo* mag and a few packs of gum. After that, I picked up dinner from Shoney's. Although it was my last night in Norfolk, I intended to keep it low key. Besides, I needed to call home to check on Dad.

My dad had been diagnosed with cirrhosis two months ago, and to tell you the truth, the results didn't surprise me. I watched my father consume tons of whiskey my whole life, changing from ok-dad to psychopath at the drop of a hat. I hated him for that. When I was growing up, my mother hardly said anything about his drinking or the verbal abuse. She never spoke up for herself or us. I was so desperate to escape that I joined the Navy, just to get away from them and Starkdale's small town mentality.

But now Dad was too sick to hurt anyone anymore. Unfortunately my brother Larry had become a clone of my father—an alcohol-inhaling, white trash racist. I don't know why they insisted on clinging to their Segregation-era way of thinking. That's one of the reasons I avoided going home the past few years.

But I couldn't avoid the family any longer, not with Dad getting worse. I didn't really have money for a flight out there, but as fate would have it, Dedrick's team was scheduled to travel to Mississippi next week. If I could trade places with someone on his team, I'd be able to fly home for free, not to mention spend more quality time with my guy.

I wrapped my hair in a bun, changed into sweats and flipped on the television. I tried to get lost in some reality TV, but not even the train wrecks on *Rock of Love* could distract me from the battleground in my head—going home, my sick father, Larry, Mom.

Dedrick.

I admit, after my one night with Jamal, I targeted Dedrick. A little undercover flirting on the job led to a movie, a few dinner dates, then apartment stay-overs. Days, then weeks crept by. Before Dedrick, I didn't know I could smile or laugh so much, and it wasn't long before he gripped the reins of my heart. My whole time here in Virginia, Dedrick had been a twenty-four hour matinee in my head. Whatever hold he had on me, I didn't want him to release those precious strings strapped to my soul.

A smile blossomed while I recycled images of Dedrick. I slid down the bed until my head rested on the pillow. Yup, I'd fallen pretty hard. Too bad my father and Larry threatened to kill my joy.

Before I left Starkdale, I remember telling Larry about a woman we knew who was dating a black guy. Larry took a long swig of

Jack Daniels and said, "Nigger lover. You'd better not even think about it."

Stunned, I replied, "Why, what would you do?"

"You wanna know?" His eyes reminded me so much of Dad's. "I'd kill you and your nigger boyfriend. Couldn't take it, sis."

Like I believed my father, I believed him, too. With that cold threat haunting me, I felt I had no choice. Before I left for Norfolk, I started distancing myself from Dedrick. But it didn't work. I missed him too much. I was sprung. And totally screwed.

Sitting up, I grabbed the phone to dial home, something I should've done before my mind detained me. Larry picked up after the third ring.

"Hey, Larry."

"Sis, how are ya?"

"Fine. What 'cha doin'?"

"Nothin' much. Came by the house to pick up some things from ma old bedroom."

I smiled. That deep home-grown southern drawl flavored his scruffy voice. I could feel mine making a reappearance.

"Oh, okay. Where's Mom?"

"At the hospital with Dad, doin' a follow-up. I just left there. Ain't lookin' too good, Nel."

"How's Mom holding up?"

"Hard to say. She's been walking around like a zombie." He paused. "So, uh, you're in Norfolk, are ya?"

"Yes. Leavin' tomorrow."

"When ya comin' back to your *real* home, sis?"

"Well, if everything works out, very soon. Another group from my company is flying to Meridian. I'm gonna try and switch to that team so I can come home for a quick visit."

"Good idea. Get away from them niggers and wetbacks for a minute. You ain't messin' with any of 'em, are ya?"

I just knew the N-word would rear its ugly head sooner or later. "Shut up."

"Jokin', lil' sis. I know I taught ya better than that."

I nibbled my bottom lip. Larry and Dad had tried to instill their lethal brand of hatred in me, especially since I'm a "deadly scoop of southern, blue-eyed kryptonite for black men," as Larry had once said. But obviously brainwashing me hadn't worked.

"Well, um," I said, my heart beating faster, "I'll call back later to talk to Mom. I hope to be home soon."

"All right. Talk to you later."

"K. Tell Mom and Dad I love 'em."

"Will do. Bye, baby sis. Love ya."

I smiled. "Love you, too, big bro. Bye."

When I hung up, I realized I missed my older brother, despite the KKK in him. When we were growing up, Larry had been my fiercest protector, especially during our teenage years when certain parts of my body ballooned. With his fists and Dad's rifle, Larry scared away a beehive of horny toads, mostly dirty old white men in their 30's and 40's who were always chasing after me. He even shot at one fella he caught peeping outside my bedroom window.

Luckily, Larry missed. But he would've gotten him if he could. That's how my brother is when provoked, a time bomb seconds away from wiping out anyone in his path.

ଔ   ଔ   ଔ

It felt good to finally touch down in San Diego. I'd been on the East Coast for about six weeks and was aching for home. My own bed. Dedrick.

I checked my watch. The rest of my team would arrive in two hours. To prevent exposing my whatever-you-call-it with Dedrick, I had booked an earlier flight behind their backs.

As I made my way through the airport terminal, I speed-dialed Dedrick. He picked up after the third ring.

I smiled. "Hey, stranger."

"Hey, girl, where are you?"

I stepped on the escalator, a familiar itch sprinkling between my inner thighs. Knowing Dedrick was in the vicinity had awakened my hormones. "I'm heading toward baggage claim. Are you here?"

"I just got on Harbor Drive. Be there in 'bout 5-10 minutes."

"All right." I stepped off the escalator. "I'll see you soon. Can't wait."

"Me neither, babe. See you soon." We hung up.

I bet I wore a smile that stretched the length of the Coronado Bridge. He'd never called me "babe" before.

As I waited for my bags, I scanned the area around me, half-hoping Dedrick would appear from the crowd with open arms, the way I'd fantasized on the plane. But other than the usual airport hustle-and-bustle, no Dedrick.

Then I heard, "Nel!"

I turned to see Dedrick step from behind a Starbucks stand. My lips curled up. Sneaky little liar.

Belly gnats swirled into a large lump, then spread warmth throughout my body. The itch between my thighs erupted into a thousand tingles that raked down to my toes.

"What's up, gorgeous?" he said. "Long time no see."

I walked to him, my gaze stuck in a tunnel with Dedrick as my salvation. I paid no attention to the older white couple shaking their heads out the corner of my eye.

Once Dedrick wrapped me up, I knew I would do whatever it took to switch to his team. And when his lips found mine, for a second my plot wasn't motivated by my need to secure a free flight home. I just didn't want to be away from him again.

Damn the fraternization policy.

Chapter 7

Terrell

"Man, San Diego's not going to the playoffs this year!" Dedrick cried. He steered his Range Rover down a short hill, then made a left. "They messed that up *last* year!"

"Don't knock the Super Chargers, now," I said. "We *will* win the Super Bowl."

"Ain't gonna happen. Dallas will do the damn thing this year. Watch."

"We'll see."

We sped past Balboa Naval Medical Center en route to Dedrick's sister Sheryl's house. She'd been holding his "The Hangover" DVD hostage for about a month and we'd come to rescue it. I knew Sheryl had major issues with brothas dating Barbies, so to avoid a confrontation, I decided to wait in the Rover while Dedrick retrieved his property. Besides, we had to be at Dedrick's crib in less than an hour. Penelope was coming over with one of her Barbie friends to watch the movie on Dedrick's new 53-inch Sony flat screen.

I studied the dark-gray clouds muddled in the California sky like a field of dirty cotton balls, a thunderstorm threatening to rain havoc on us. "So everything's cool with you and Penelope, huh?"

"Oh, *heyell* yeah!" Dedrick said, punching the accelerator to push the Rover up a steep embankment. "After I picked her up on Friday and got back to the Pimp Shack? Bruh! We stayed in the house the whole weekend! Man, I smacked so much booty I—"

"Hold up, fool!" I cried, hands up. "I don't need to know all that! I just wanted to know if things were cool, not how hard you hit it!"

We laughed. "My bad," he said.

I took a sip of Powerade. "Naw, that's good, man. You didn't even mess around while you two were apart, huh?"

"Naw, I sure didn't. Two months, too, and I was in Japan, a black man's paradise. That's the longest I've been away from booty since what...*97*? We're all right, though. Nel is my girl."

His long fingers tapped the wheel. While sitting quiet for a few seconds, I noticed a faraway shadow masking his face. I knew that look—the crooked grin, the eye twinkle. Clearly Penelope's mental image had road-blocked his mind.

"Thinking about taking her to the club this Friday before I leave for Mississippi," Dedrick said, coming back to life. "Wanna roll?"

"Can't. Me and Christy going out."

"Christy? *Another* Barbie?"

I smiled. "Oh, yeah. Had to replace Lisa since Tasha scared the piss out of that girl."

"Yeah, good thing you dropped that psyche-ho. I bet you won't have to worry about Christy goin' off on you for no damn reason."

I nodded. "*No* worries over here."

Dedrick turned onto Pershing Ave, where Sheryl rented a small house. Rows of single-family homes built in the twenties lined the street. Two youngsters swerved their BMX bikes to the side of the road to avoid the Rover.

Dedrick pulled into Sheryl's driveway. A black Acura was parked in front.

"Hmmm," Dedrick said, "Tammy's here."

I stroked my chin. Dedrick talked about Tammy's looks a lot, and I finally had a chance to see for myself. I'd never told him, but I'd wanted to peep her out for a while. I'm still a hot-blooded man, despite my black-woman hiatus.

"So, Playboy," Dedrick asked, reading my mind. "You wanna meet her?"

I exhaled a breath as if I had no choice. An act, of course. "Yeah, damn."

He opened the door. "Aw'ight, then. And be careful with my sister. She might start some mess if she finds out about our plans tonight."

I nodded, then stepped out. Because I wore a sleeveless gym shirt and shorts, the fifty-degree air felt good against my bare arms and legs. A welcome change from year-round summer weather.

I followed Dedrick up the stairs. My heart jumped a notch. For some reason, nerves got nutty the closer we got.

Dedrick raised his fist to knock, but Sheryl opened the door. "Hey, punk," she said. She turned to me, her cherry-painted lips raised. "Hey, Terrell. Nice to see you again."

"What's up, Sheryl? Same here."

Though Dedrick bitched about his sister a lot, Sheryl didn't hurt my vision at all. With large round eyes and dark-brown bubble cheeks like her bro, I'm sure brothas kicked it to her all the time.

Before the cream puffs, I probably would've been one of them—if she wasn't Dedrick's sister.

Dedrick stepped inside. "Where's my DVD?"

"What DVD?"

"Girl, stop playin'!" They went back and forth.

"Hey, boy," a voice said, interrupting their brother-sister nitpicking.

As I stepped from behind Dedrick, the leaf of a large plant slapped my temple. I ignored it because the sista sitting cross-legged on the brown leather sofa slapped me, too. And she didn't even touch me.

"What's up, girl?" Dedrick said, stepping to her. "You lookin' all good." He leaned down and kissed her cheek. "Tammy, Terrell. Terrell, Tammy."

I waved. "Hello, Tammy. Nice to meet you."

She smiled. "Nice to meet you, too."

Damn. My boy didn't lie. Cute as *hell*. When Tammy smiled, dimples peek-a-booed from high cheekbones. Like small incisions in smooth hot cocoa skin.

She wore a long-sleeved button-down blouse and jeans—casual wear that revealed a *King* magazine figure. Nice cleavage, too. Hair touching her shoulders. I wanted her to stand so I could inspect the back.

A classy woman—or at least it seemed that way. Damn, she could've been Gabrielle Union's sister. I turned to the TV because my short glances almost became a long stare.

I heard a toilet flush. A door opened and a pencil-thin woman disguised as a man sashayed in. He shook when he saw Dedrick

79

standing near the sofa. Dedrick looked ready to throw up on homeboy's shoes.

Dude wore a black shirt that said "It's raining men!" in white letters across the chest, with "and I'm drowning in 'em" in small letters underneath. Moms poured too much sugar in that fool's tank.

"Oh," he said, finger waves rippling his hair, "girl, I didn't know you had company up in here. Hey, y'all."

Dedrick sat on the sofa arm. "Sup."

"Terrell," Sheryl said, now standing next to him, "this is my friend Tomi. That's T-O-M-I."

Tomi? I thought. *Figures.* Dedrick had mentioned Sheryl's flame-boy friend, but not the name.

"How you doin', Tomi?"

He waved a limp hand. "Hey."

Tomi turned to Sheryl, snickering, as if swapping coded messages at each other. Tammy cuffed a hand over her lips. Dedrick and I frowned, clearly not in on the joke.

After a few moments of uncomfortable silence, Tomi said, "Well, I need to get on outta here. We on for Friday, right?"

Sheryl gave he-she a hug. "Yeah. Call me."

"All right." Tomi hugged Tammy goodbye, then curled around the glass table toward the door. Homeboy walked like he popped his pelvic bone with each step. I stepped back so he could reach the door. His gaze held on me a second too long.

"Bye, y'all." Tomi left the room, leaving behind a cologne cloud that could obliterate nostril hairs.

"Damn, y'all pitiful," Sheryl said. "I saw your faces."

"You okay, Terrell?" Tammy asked, her full lips curved, dimples creasing her doll face. "You look sick."

I waved away the strong scent. Guess I *did* look sick. "Uh...I'm fine. Interesting cat."

"Yeah, that's Flame Boy," Dedrick said, face twisted. "That fool gets on my last nerve. But enough of Queer as Folk." He slapped his sister's butt. "Girl, get my DVD. Me and Terrell gotta be at my crib by four."

"Why? You guys got snow bunnies to get back to?"

"You can say that," Dedrick said. "Now go."

Before shifting my focus toward a home decorating show, I noticed Sheryl roll her eyes. Her mood spiraled as fast as the temperature outside.

"Whatever," she mumbled as she disappeared into her room.

Dedrick strolled toward the kitchen. "Want sumn' to drink?"

"I'm cool, Dee," I said, leaning against the wall next to another Jurassic plant. Caught Tammy's eyes again. She smiled. For a second, tunnel vision struck. I turned back to the tube. Felt like a damn fourteen-year-old.

"So," Tammy said, "you're the optometrist, huh?"

"Yes."

"I think Sheryl said your practice is off Highway 163?"

"Yeah, on Balboa Ave. You need an eye exam?"

"Well..."

"Woman, you know good and well you need an exam," Dedrick said with a Sprite in hand. "Can't even read letters two inches from your nose without glasses."

"Shut up, boy. Don't forget, you were as blind as me once."

"Key word—*were*. You know I got LASIK eye surgery. You need to get out of those glasses and contacts and get it, too."

Tammy shook her head. "Uh-uh. I don't want any laser beams anywhere near these eyes."

I smiled. Dipping a hand in my pocket, I grabbed my wallet. "Well, if you haven't had an exam in over a year, you should definitely get one." I handed her my business card. "Check us out."

"Thanks." She took the card and flipped it from front to back. I noticed her pretty red nails. Hands looked silky smooth. No scars or blemishes. Nice.

Sheryl marched into the room. "Here's your funky DVD." She slapped the DVD case against Dedrick's chest and almost knocked the soda out of his hand.

"'Bout time, damn." He flipped the lid to make sure the DVD lay inside. "Learn how to return stuff, nucca."

"Shut up, fool." Sheryl turned to Tammy. "And here's that magazine I told you about."

I glanced at the *Newsweek* magazine with Beyonce Knowles, Star Jones and a woman I didn't recognize gracing the cover. It read "Black Women" in bold white letters. Sheryl sat down next to Tammy while Tammy flipped through several pages.

"Yeah, girl," Sheryl said, crossing her legs, "this article will definitely open your eyes. It's pretty sad. Did you know black women are five times *less* likely to marry by age forty than white women?" She turned to Dedrick. "Hmmph. I wonder why?"

I blinked. Another three-second glare scorched in dark eyes. Yeah, I saw it. A look of contempt that makes some brothas hang their heads to avoid a verbal lynching. It's a black woman thing. Since I started my "boycott," I felt the heat often.

"Aw'ight, aw'ight. We need to roll," Dedrick said, tapping my arm. "I know what's coming." He leaned toward his sister and kissed her cheek.

"What's coming?" Sheryl asked, her forehead crumpled from phony surprise. "I'm just sayin'."

"And I'm just leavin'," Dedrick said, hugging Tammy goodbye. He flashed a look of doom at me and nodded toward the door.

"Well," I said, "nice to meet you, Tammy. See ya, Sheryl."

Tammy smiled. Damn, those dimples. "You, too."

"What about you, Terrell?" Sheryl asked, unwilling to give up the fight.

"What?"

Dedrick tapped my arm again. "Let's go, man. You 'bout to get drilled."

Sheryl asked, "Did you know the marriage statistics of black women?"

"No," I said.

"*No?*" Sheryl asked. "Interesting. Why do you think that is?"

I sighed as the police-type interrogation threatened to drown me. Why Sheryl still fired questions at a man leaving the premises, I had no idea. Tammy sat with her arms folded, no doubt set to chime in and unload some bitch bombs of her own.

Dedrick opened the door. "Sheryl, you need to cut it out. Don't you see us leaving?"

"Let the man answer first."

"*Yo* ass." Dedrick tapped my arm for the gazillionth time. "We out."

Dedrick stepped out, but I stayed. Maintaining composure, I said, "Sheryl, I really don't see what's wrong with—"

"Brothas dissin' sistas?" she asked, jacking my statement as her own. Sheryl obviously didn't give a damn about decapitating my response. "Or...oh, I don't know...sellin' out for a piece of the pie with the *white* Cool Whip on top?"

I dropped my head. She just *had* to go there. Even emphasized the word "white."

I turned to Sheryl, twisting my lips to muffle cuss words. "Aw'ight, Sheryl. Yes, I date white women. But I'm not tryin' to go there with you, so—"

"Maybe somebody *needs* to take you there. All you lost brothas, including Dedrick's funky ass."

A flow of air eased past my lips. Cut me off *again*. Mouth like a Samurai sword, chopping up all my comebacks in mid-air. Sheryl reminded me why I flew the Caucasian Express.

While shaking my head, I heard Dedrick yell, "C'mon, man!" I didn't budge, though; I had words for the Tasha-clone. Tammy sat quiet, apparently enjoying a brotha on the hot seat.

"Somebody needs to take me there, huh?" I asked, restraining an outbreak of B-words. "First of all, I don't know where you come off talking to me like you know me—"

"Terrell, you're no different than these other brothas walking around with white wom—"

"Stop cuttin' me off!" I yelled. Sheryl shook, but Tammy didn't flinch.

But I wasn't done. I said, "You sound just like my ex. See, this is the reason I quit sistas! All that attitude!"

The two women glared at me, their eyes on fire. I knew the hounds of hell were about to unload from every which-a-way, but I didn't care. I had to check Sheryl's ass.

Dedrick about-faced and approached the steps. Sheryl, bottom lip hanging, forehead wrinkled like a raisin, sat still. Stuck somewhere between shock and pissed-offness, no doubt. To my surprise, Tammy never shifted. No hailstorm of bitchy retorts, no fingers tugging at her earrings, no head shaking. Still sat with a leg crossed over her thigh, arms folded under her breasts.

Dedrick stepped back inside, just in time to hear Sheryl snap, "Ignorant thing to say for such an educated man, don't you think? Well, you can—"

Tammy raised her palm. Did it slow and smooth like a Mafia crime boss, but kept me in sight. Once Sheryl noticed Tammy's stop sign hand signal, her lips braked. Sheryl snickered, then slammed back against the couch.

Not bad. Shut Sheryl's ass up in a way I couldn't.

"You quit sistas, huh?" Tammy asked. "That's funny. Black women have *never* quit on our men the way you guys have on us."

Tammy's cool response tripped me up. My lips hungered to snap back, but I couldn't find the words.

Dedrick grabbed my arm. "Man, let's go. Told you to come on. I knew this would happen."

No use arguing with the unarguable. I shot out the door quick, as if the house had ejaculated me to freedom. Sprays of rain mixed in a chilly breeze kissed my face and brushed off thick layers of tension. I hauled in a ton of air to extinguish 100-degree heat.

As we approached the Rover, Sheryl cried, "Mama's rollin' in her grave right now because of you, Dedrick! You just like Daddy!" She slammed the door.

Huh? What the hell did that mean? I knew their mother had passed a few years ago from cancer, but Dedrick never spoke of his dad. Only thing I knew about him was he had dipped out when Dedrick and Sheryl were teenagers. I turned to Dedrick and saw the look of a man ready to punch something.

Opening the passenger door, I said, "Sorry, man. Should've left when you called."

Dedrick shook his head. "Told you my sister is California's number one instigator. Bringing up my parents like that. Bitch."

He backed up, then sped off toward the highway. A Hip-Hop jam bumped from the radio, but my mind rocked to its own rhythm.

Intrigued by Sheryl's comment, I asked, "What did your sister mean by that?"

"What?"

"You know, what she said about your parents?"

He tapped the wheel, stared ahead. I thought he would hip me to the secret, but instead he replied, "Ain't nothin', man. No thing."

Obviously classified information, so I didn't press. "Oh, okay."

We sat quiet, cleaning up the residue of anger in our own private ways. With my head against the reclined seat, I switched my thoughts to Tammy, replaying her last statement. It stuck to me, too.

Maybe brothas *did* give up quicker. And with me and Dedrick's current stance on not dating sistas, we had proven her point. There we were, two above average-looking brothas driving away from two fine sistas to kick it with white women. Gave up on chocolate for a buffet of peach-flavored delights.

Granted, Sheryl is Dedrick's sister, but our retreat from her house symbolized what thousands of black men had done—and were *still* doing. Running away. From black women.

Yeah, maybe Tammy had a point. But what could I do? Sheryl's outburst was a prime example of why I'd traded sistas in. Who needed that kind of abuse? I sure didn't.

Dedrick stopped at a streetlight. "You okay, man?"

"I'm good. You?"

"Yeah, I'm straight."

"Kinda wish I hadn't blown up like that."

"I hear you. Swear my sister loves drama."

I sighed. "Yeah."

Light turned green and Dedrick sped off. Potholes in the crusty road rattled the Rover.

"But enough of that, Playboy!" Dedrick cried, slapping my knee. "We don't have to worry about her ass. Why? 'Cause we gon' hook up with the honeys tonight, check out that movie, then stir up some vanilla yogurt!"

I exploded in laughter. "Vanilla yogurt, huh?"

Dedrick knew the deal. A few drinks, a good movie and some vanilla yogurt—especially new, untested yogurt—sounded like what the doctor ordered. Just had to keep the Mack skills up so I could dip my spoon all night.

Thoughts of dessert finally pushed Tammy out of my mind.

Chapter 8

Tammy

With his ignorant ass, I screamed in my head more than once.

Luckily for Terrell, I'm not one to go off on a person I've known for less than ten minutes. If I'd allowed my composure to untangle, Sheryl and I would've ripped his ass to shreds.

Sheryl definitely said her piece after Dedrick and Terrell retreated to their "snow bunnies." She cussed them the hell out, but Terrell had more than earned the tongue-whipping. I cannot believe that fool had the nerve to say he "quit sistas." Was he trying to get the black slapped out of him?

Damn, the man is *foine*, too. And an eye doctor at that? I'm not gonna lie, I had the flicker of a naughty thought when he walked in. But after witnessing the true ass in him, I decided Dr. Terrell D. Jackson would *never* examine these eyes. Or anything else for that matter.

I didn't want a downpour to cage me in Sheryl's house, so I left shortly after Dedrick and Terrell. Light sprinkles smacked my face when I stepped out the door. I hopped into my Acura, the *Newsweek* magazine in the passenger seat.

I stopped at Target on the way home. While picking up bottled water, I saw a bronze-skinned brotha grabbing a carton of Red Bull. Couldn't believe it. *Another* one.

Brotherman had apparently sold-out, too, just like Dedrick and Terrell. To what else? A skinny-ass brunette. One more brotha who had caught the disease, as Sheryl would say.

The woman pushed a basket with a little light-skinned boy inside. He slapped his tiny hands against the plastic push handle, testing his lungs with baby talk.

"Can you grab some water, too, babe?" she asked.

The man stopped beside me and picked up two cases of Aquafina. Barely even acknowledged a sista, and I *know* I looked good.

A few seconds later, brothaman and his trophy wife walked out of my line of sight—and not a moment too soon. After that scene with Terrell, it seemed fate was taunting me, and I was *not* in the mood.

Outside, showers battered the pavement. Bad enough Terrell rained on my parade; now Mother Nature had joined in. I grabbed a newspaper, covered my perm and trotted to my car. Once I got home, I lost the wet clothes, replaced the contacts with specks and donned comfy sweatpants and a T-shirt.

Settling on the couch with the *Newsweek* magazine, I engrossed myself in an article that discussed the dismal outlook of Fortune 500 black women in today's society. Apparently we were scaring off brothas too many levels down the tax bracket.

Shoot, no need to scare brothas off. I'd seen three runaways in the past hour alone.

I shook my head and sighed. Sad reading, that's for damn sure. The article portrayed hard-driven black women as sabotaging their bond with black men, mainly because brothas lagged too far behind. A man's ego is already a fragile thing; add a confident woman with more dollar signs and their egos shrivel up like prunes. *Especially* brothas.

Hmmph. Blame *us* for the state of black men? So ridiculous. Really, why should a sista apologize for busting her butt up the corporate ladder and being recognized for her efforts?

"Enough of this," I said, tossing the magazine aside. I was still ticked off after leaving Sheryl's house and the article didn't help at all. To get my mind somewhere else, I grabbed the remote and flicked on the TV. Big mistake.

Another low-budget music video on BET with some deluded, thinking-he-fine dirty-south idiot rapped about "candy paint" and an "iced-out grill" worth more than my annual salary. He attacked the screen, arms and hands all over the damn place, mumbling bleeped-out junk. Same old tired formula—a wannabe thug-pimp-balla with basketball-sized titties smacking him upside his head.

Now what exactly was I supposed to find entertaining about this ignorant fool jumping around like a foul-mouthed clown? Was I not supposed to notice the blatant degradation of black women? Ugh, sometimes BET was bad for my blood pressure.

And to top it off, on that rare occasion when you *do* stumble across a black man who not only has it together but is upwardly mobile, a pale-skinned, golden-haired airhead chained to his side reminds you he "quit sistas." My blood pressure shot up higher as Dedrick and Terrell jumped to the forefront yet again.

The nerve of those two, shunning the race of females that birthed their brown melanin. Ever since Sheryl first bitched about brothas flaunting yellow and peach-skinned women, I'd been seeing them everywhere—in magazines, TV, movies, on the street. Why were black men running away from sistas as if we had Mad Cow Disease or something?

I flipped to CNN and saw a well-known basketball player's peanut-shaped head plastered on the right side of the screen.

Here we go again. Figures.

Dumb ass had a starting position on a championship team and still found a way to tarnish the silver spoon he'd created. At the prime of his career, this fool pulled a knife on a teammate in the locker room of all places. He'd probably be kicked out of the league and into prison. I swear, sometimes it seemed like prison was a black man's rite-of-passage. *Stupid!*

Somehow, amid the barrage of niggerant brothas, the image of my father broke through.

When I was about eleven, my I-hate-boys facade shifted. Daddy noticed and he would tease me about the crushes I thought I'd kept secret. A cute boy would pass me in a store or on the sidewalk, and Daddy would catch the glow in my eyes. He'd dig a finger in my dimples and say, "You know you like him!" I'd wrinkle my face and cry, "Eeewww! No I don't!"

Daddy used to tell me a prince would come and sweep me off my feet one day, and I believed him. Even as a little girl, I created an ideal man in my head—a dark-skinned brotha with a smile as bright as Atlantic City after midnight. In other words, Blair Underwood.

But Craig was no Prince Charming. Neither were the men before him. Nope. Too busy trying to be thugs, playas, ballas, niggas, stunnas—and any other word that ends with an "uh" sound.

My future with a black prince didn't look so rosy anymore, much less realistic. The three sistas on the cover of *Newsweek* caught my gaze again. Funny, those sunshine faces didn't represent the article's hard reality. I damn sure didn't smile like that when I read statistics that said sistas were more likely to divorce and less likely to marry than white women. How could I smile about that?

The article didn't even attempt to provide a solution. No, just rehashing the same tired script with the same sad inevitability.

I channel-surfed my way down to MTV. Yet *another* pimp-balla-stunna rapped about hoochies in thongs, blinged out with ice on his wrist-slash-teeth. Damn. How the hell can we upgrade our marital status with fools like him creating the template for black men to follow?

I had no clear answers. The outlook looked like one big thunderstorm with no sun in sight.

I stood up, stretched, then walked toward the kitchen. A business card on the counter caught my eye.

My nails tapped the counter. "Hmmm."

I'd been tiptoeing around that card since Dale gave it to me months ago. I thought about calling the number a few times, but never did.

Until now.

"I need to quit this nonsense." I grabbed the phone. "Why not give it a try?"

Card in hand, I dialed. Dale picked up after the second ring.

That fool said, "I *knew* you would call Big Daddy!"

I laughed. Dale aka "Big Daddy" had that kind of magic. "Oh, you *knew*, huh? Right, you silly butt. How are you?"

"I'm good. Happy to be back on the West Cizoast."

I stepped back into the living room and grabbed the remote, muting the thug on the screen. "Good to have you back." I swallowed, heart rattling. *Here goes.* "Soooo...what did you say about a date?"

There. I'd done it, broadened my horizons, or at least, opened myself to the possibility. Brothas just weren't making the grade. And the ones that did passed us over for a lighter shade. *Way* lighter. I couldn't compete with that. Didn't even want to try anymore. I was done. *Done.*

If black men could cross over, I could, too.

Before I knew it, I was lying on the couch laughing my butt off at Dale's corny jokes. Our verbal bond broke me out my no-man shell and within minutes, I stirred an image of us exploring the true meaning of ebony and ivory. I'd never even kissed a white boy before. Thin lips. Uh-uh, didn't think it would work for me.

But the more Dale and I conversed, the more a bridge toward our private lives grew closer. Possibility became curiosity. Curiosity became fantasy.

I guess I sold out, too.

Chapter 9

Penelope

"Well, our weekend rendez-screw has ended," Dedrick said, turning into my apartment complex.

Laughter tightened my belly. "*Rendez-screw?* You and your made-up words."

Dedrick flashed his million-watt smile. "You have a good time with King Dingaling?"

"Of course I did, Mr. Dingaling." I stroked his leg. "I don't think I'll be able to walk straight for at least a week."

He slowed to roll over a speed bump. "Right about that. Dr. Long Stroke was puttin' in work!"

"Oh, stop it."

He had some truth to that statement, though. Actually, a *lot* of truth. It had been a nonstop sex-fest from the moment we set foot in his apartment. Two months of no contact will do that to ya. Besides, it just felt too damn good to stop. I'd recently gone on the pill, so no more condoms—just one-on-one carnal chaos in pure form. It'd been a while since raw male flesh made me crawl up the walls, but Dedrick's magic wand made me crawl, scream, moan and then some.

A chill made my thighs quiver. Flashbacks.

Dedrick parked next to my car. "Well, it's Monday morning," he said, yawning. "Back to the nine-to-five and acting like co-workers."

I nodded, looking out my window. "Yeah. But at least I get to see you in a few."

"True. Damn, I've never dated a co-worker before. I'm breaking *all* the rules!"

"What rules, mister?" I asked, slapping his arm.

He leaned toward me and answered with a kiss, his lips muffling my words. As his tongue fed off mine, he shut down all mindless chit-chat. Soon my body wanted to indulge in "deep" conversation with him again.

"All right, girl," Dedrick said, coming up for air. "Gotta go."

I checked the dashboard again. We had to be at work in half an hour. "You're right. Better stop before I have an accident on your seat."

Dedrick grabbed my bag out of the back seat. "So, you're gonna drop off your stuff real quick, then roll?"

"Pretty much. Gotta use the restroom, too, ya know. Female stuff."

"Right, right. Well, let me take your bag up."

"No, no. I got it." I took my bag and waved him away. "You go on. I'll see you at work."

"You sure?"

"Yeah. We shouldn't come in at the same time, anyway. We may raise eyebrows. I think some people already suspect us."

"Oh, well. That's our bidness." He checked his watch. "All right. We can continue this after work."

"Can't wait."

He wrapped me up, then gave me a see-you-later peck. No goodbye.

I watched my black Adonis drive off. Right then, I understood what they meant by "once you go black, you never go back." After sampling loads of yummy chocolate, I *really* didn't see myself going back anytime soon. Maybe never. Besides, white guys seemed so dopey to me now.

I dropped my bag on the couch. Since I showered at Dedrick's, I didn't need to do much until I noticed the strawberry on my neck. Dedrick had marked his territory pretty good with a hickey the size of a quarter, darker than the day before. I rummaged around in my drawers for a turtleneck to cover it.

In about twenty minutes, I was at work walking toward my desk. Dedrick was in the back room working on the computer network, so I avoided that area. Instead, I took my time greeting folks I hadn't seen in a while before tackling the hundred-plus emails in my inbox.

Mid-morning, I went to the lounge for a soda. I ran into Margarette, an analyst on Dedrick's team. We'd been chatting for a few minutes when Dedrick walked in. "Hello, ladies."

"Hey, Dedrick," Margarette said.

"Dedrick, how are you?" I asked, as he dropped some coins into the vending machine.

"Cool, cool. How was Norfolk?" Dedrick played our little game well.

"Oh, it was, uh, nice." I popped open my Sprite. "Good to be home, though."

"I'm sure it is." He shot me a quick wink and naughty smile. Then he headed back to his computer room hideaway. No reason for anyone to be suspicious. We kept it short and sweet.

I turned back to Margarette. "You all ready for that trip to Mississippi?"

Margarette ran a hand through her thick gray hair. "Not really. My mother wants to visit that week, but I won't be here. Besides, we just got back from Japan. So much traveling." She sighed. "I'm burnt out from all of it."

A bell went off in my head. Opportunity was knocking.

"Well, today is your lucky day, Margarette. I might be able to work something out with you."

"Really? How?"

I gave her the scoop about my father's illness and my desire to visit him. It didn't take much to convince her to switch teams with me so I could travel to Mississippi in her place. Of course, we had to clear it through our team leaders, not to mention the head honcho of our department, but to my surprise, our request moved up the chain of command with no problems. Once I explained my father's situation, my supervisor pretty much sealed the deal for me. So even though I had just returned from Norfolk, I'd be heading out again next week to Meridian. It worked out perfectly. Now I could devote more time to my family *and* Dedrick.

While riding a slice of Cloud Nine, Bill walked in with a vase of long-stemmed red roses. All eyes turned to me as Bill set the flowers on my desk.

"Got this from the receptionist at the front counter," Bill said. "Special delivery for Penelope Miller."

"Are you sure?" I asked, my mouth like a large hole.

"Yup."

Nosy eyes surrounded me, spying in on the new joy six red roses had injected. So beautiful.

At first I thought Mr. Joe Smooth from Norfolk sent them, but then I read the note: "Welcome back, babe. I missed you. Love K.D."

Words clogged in my throat. I felt as if sprinkles from a warm Hawaiian waterfall peppered my skin. The message was so simple, but strong enough to tug at the corner of my eyes. I smiled at the secret initials only I knew. K.D. King Dingaling.

"From your boyfriend?" Margarette asked, prodding me for details.

"Yes." My eyes watered.

"Very nice. Lucky woman."

I nodded. *Yes, I am.*

As I took a whiff, I glanced at the back of the office, just in time to see Dedrick appear in the server room doorway. He smiled at me, then disappeared inside.

Yes, we were definitely in it hot and heavy, but part of me knew we would have to cool our affair once we arrived in my neck of the woods. As much as I wanted him by my side 24/7, our little fling thing wouldn't fly well in Starkdale.

ᑕ ᑕ ᑕ

I glanced at the roses on my nightstand. "Did I thank you for the flowers, yet?"

Dedrick caressed his lips against my cheek. "Only a million times."

Adjusting my neck inside the cradle of his arm, I said, "Babe? Um...you know we'll need to keep all this kissy stuff under wraps when we travel together."

"Don't worry, I know how to keep things on the down low. When we get to Mississippi, I'll sneak to your room for late night snacks."

"Late night snacks, huh? Silly. Well, if we're as good at sneaking around there as we are here, we should be fine. Maybe we can give each other room keys."

"Good idea. Meridian's boring as hell, too. Not much to do except slap skins all day, anyway."

"Oh, be quiet."

Dedrick's head tapped the headboard. "Seriously though, I'm actually looking forward to the trip now. I really didn't think you'd be able to switch teams 'cause of budget issues. Glad you did. Now you can see your father."

My warmth cooled a tad. "Yeah."

"I can meet your Mama and brother and we can hang out. He'll teach me to hunt; I'll teach him Dominoes."

"Uh, I don't think it'll happen like that, deary."

"I'm just playin'," he said, pecking my forehead. "I *do* know where I'm going. I'm not dumb."

I moved a strand of hair that had stuck to my sweaty temple. "What do you mean?"

"Girl, you know what I mean. You never really said it, but I can tell you don't want me to meet your family. They'd probably run for the ol' rope as soon as my black ass walked in."

I blew a short breath. Dedrick had connected the dots.

"Well," I grazed his calf muscle with my nails, "I don't know about rope, but my dad and brother are kinda...redneck-ish."

Dedrick tilted my head toward him. "I hear you and trust me, I'm not even thinking about taking you to some Hobo restaurant

99

in the wrong part of town. A black man with a fine white woman? Down there? Hell naw, the good ol' boys would be dustin' off the white sheets just for me!"

I frowned. "I admit, growing up, I knew a few people like that. My dad's friends, pretty much."

"Your dad had friends in the KKK?"

"You can say that." I lowered my eyes. "My brother isn't much different."

I flashed back to a black boy I knew from high school. What Larry and Rick did to him...

"Damn," Dedrick said, interrupting my thoughts. "We'll just be extra careful. You'll probably spend most of the time with your family, anyway. Don't worry, babe. It'll be cool."

His brown eyes and soft voice paralyzed the world around me. I'd been so afraid he'd hold my background against me, but instead I felt closer to him than ever. Since we were in sharing mode, I found myself wanting to know more about his family history.

"What about *your* dad?" I asked. "How come you never talk about him?"

He rested his head against the headboard, staring up at the ceiling. "Not much to say. Divorced my moms when I was 'bout sixteen, then bounced. Don't really know where he is and don't care. He was in and out of the family, anyway."

"You never tried to look for him?"

"Nope."

"What about your sis—"

"I really don't want to talk about it, Nel. It'll just get me in a bad mood. Let's drop it."

"Oh." I ran my nails around his hand, looking away. "I'm sorry. Didn't know it was such a sore subject."

"Don't worry about it. Maybe one day I'll let you know what's up. Just...not right now."

"Ok."

We sat quiet. I understood secrets, so I left it alone. I even had a few of my own that I definitely didn't want Dedrick to know about. Guess we all have bones buried in the closet.

"Hey, Nel," Dedrick said, "I would like to do something before we fly out next week. Busy on Friday night?"

"No. What's up?"

"Thinking about going to the club, the one off Rosecrans. We haven't done the nightclub thing together yet, and I wanna show my woman off. Wouldn't mind seeing that body in a mini."

My woman, he said.

Even if I tried, I couldn't stop the corners of my lips from rising, but an army of jumpy nerves formed, smudging my natural high. I knew the club well, but never went in...for good reason.

Jen and I used to hang out at Spurs & Saddles, a country and western spot just outside the Marine base and about a mile down the road from "The Jungle." Well, that's what we called it. It seemed a weekend wouldn't pass without a fight in *their* club. We'd drive by and see blacks standing in long lines. I could never see myself in that same line, despite my secret lust for black men. Figured I'd look like a white speck on a black chalkboard.

"Ya won't see me on the dark side," I'd joke to my country friends. "No way."

Oh, how things changed.

"Um...you sure you wanna see me dance?" I asked.

"Hell, yeah! I know we still have to front at work, but not anywhere else. And you know what? I don't care if any of our co-workers see us together."

I felt those same shivers again. He had this way of melting me with only a few words.

"Well?" Dedrick asked.

"I'll go," I said, grabbing his wrist. "But...you have to do something for *me* first."

I guided his hand toward the wet fleshy folds between my legs. Two fingers slipped inside. My lips spread, a soft hum creeping up my throat. I slid my other leg up so he could part my seas and dip in restricted waters where only *he* had access. Nibbling my bottom lip, I closed my eyes.

But before I floated to paradise, I prayed that our first night out as a couple would take our relationship to the next level and not the other way around.

Chapter 10

Penelope

I'd never been a minority before. Not like this, anyway. Now I know a little bit about how African-Americans must feel.

Dedrick and I arrived at the nightclub around midnight after grabbing a late-night bite at Denny's. I loved the way he opened the door for me and held my hand as I stepped out of the car. Such a gentlemen.

A chill breeze brushed over me. Dedrick and I wrapped jackets around us, then we strolled through the parking lot. I noticed major differences between the people heading to the country bar down the street and those standing in line where I was going. Skin-tight denim vs. baggy jeans. Ball caps vs. cowboy hats. Black vs. White.

But I was walking toward the wrong side. The "jungle" side.

Keenly aware of my status, my grip around Dedrick's arm tightened. Blacks walked beside us, behind us and in front of us. I heard bits and pieces of chatter and wondered if Dedrick and I were the main topic. I felt stares sticking to me from all sides.

Dedrick slid his arm down my back and took my hand. "You aw'ight, Nel?"

I watched the steps because I didn't want to introduce my face to the cement. Walking in stilettos didn't make things any easier.

Still, I replied, "I'm fine."

Dedrick paid twenty dollars to a black woman behind a window. As we turned away, I noticed her shaking her head. Dedrick didn't seem bothered at all by her obvious disapproval, acting cool and calm. Proud even. He made my body warm, stripping scales of anxiety off me.

We walked down a short hallway. Rap music thundered the walls. A song I liked by Kanye West, I think. The closer we got, the more my chest thumped, like someone performing CPR on me.

After dropping off our jackets at the coat check, we made our grand entrance. As we stepped through a cluster of people just standing around, more eyes followed me the moment my pale skin became visible. My nerves flared up again; I really felt like an intruder on foreign turf.

Although rap music attacked my eardrums, I still heard a guy say, "Damn, white girl got a fat ass." Was that a compliment?

I turned to the dance floor and saw a mix of white, black and Asian females. Even though it felt like it, I *wasn't* the only "foreigner." My shoulders loosened and I felt nervous energy fading.

Dedrick pressed his lips against my ear. "What do you want to drink?"

"A Long Island, please."

"You got it."

As we waited for the bartender, Dedrick pulled me in front of him and cuffed his arms under my breasts. He nudged his mouth against my hair until his lips found my neck. I placed my head against his chest and held his hands. His embrace made me feel so secure. Wanted.

The music's hard beat finally gripped me. My butt moved to the rhythm against Dedrick's groin.

His lips grazed my ear. "You know you the finest female up in here, right?"

Sweet talk planted a smile. He knew exactly what to say.

After we got our drinks, we maneuvered to a corner table by the DJ booth. I set my purse on the table while Dedrick pulled my seat. *Always* the gentleman. And they said chivalry was dead.

The DJ switched to a song by that guy Timbaland, one I liked. I lip-synced the lyrics, feet tapping the floor. The stress that followed me inside finally disappeared.

I finished my Long Island, turned to Dedrick and gestured toward the dance floor. He took my hand and with a few twists and turns, we stole ownership in a small corner. Inner vibes drove me. The DJ mixed in a new tune, one I'd never heard before, but still commanded my hips to move. I turned my butt to Dedrick and tried to ride the vibrations within the bend in his body. I loved the way he circled against me. *Loved it.* As for me, well, you definitely couldn't mistake me for some video chick, but dang it, this white girl was gettin' down!

We danced to a few more songs, then sat down again, this time near the entrance. The breeze blowing in from outside relieved us from the heat wave of meshed bodies on and around the dance floor.

While Dedrick went to the bar for another dose of liquid refreshment, I pulled a compact from my purse. After disappointing a handsome Latino guy who asked for a dance, I inspected my face and hair.

"Girl, you know you look good." Dedrick set a bottle of water in front of me. "With your sexy self."

I grinned. "You're not so bad, either."

He leaned toward me. "Dayum, Nel! You was out there salt shakin'! You have fun?"

"Sure did."

And that was the truth. I had a blast. Even better than my first dance lesson with Jamal way back when.

The DJ said a few words before spinning a slow song. The stares did nothing to me now. Maybe Dedrick's cool, calm nature was contagious. Or the Long Islands were finally kicking in. Whatever the reason, I wasn't the same person that walked in not too long ago.

I decided to visit the ladies room to freshen up. I was about to excuse myself when I noticed a dark cloud color Dedrick's expression.

"Ain't this a bitch?" he said.

I followed his gaze. He was staring at a skinny guy who had just walked in with a pretty dark-skinned woman. They seemed to have a good time together, laughing and slapping hands. When they saw us, they waved. I heard Dedrick mutter something under his breath, but he painted on a happy face and waved back. I kept my poise, but I'd already guessed ex-girlfriend. Hopefully not a *current* girlfriend I didn't know about.

The skinny guy sauntered over to our table with the girl in tow. He seemed more interested in men than the women who paraded in front of them. The black woman stood behind Dedrick and placed her hand on his shoulder. Staking her claim, I guess.

"What 'chall doin' here?" Dedrick asked.

"Boy, you know why we here." The woman looked me up and down. "How long y'all been here?"

"'Bout half an hour," Dedrick replied. He turned to me. "Nel, this is my sister, Sheryl. That's her friend...um...Tomi." Tomi waved at us.

The dreaded Sheryl. I admit I hadn't expected such a pretty face considering all the ugly things I'd heard about her. Apparently she had an intense dislike for women like me.

I forced a smile. "Hello, Sheryl. Nice to meet you."

She shook my hand, which surprised me. "Nice to meet you, too. Having a good time?"

"Yes. I was just trying to keep up with your brother on the dance floor."

She chuckled. "Well, I taught him everything he knows." She winked at him. Dedrick's face went flat.

"All right, then," Sheryl said, "I'm 'bout to get somethin' to drink. Talk to y'all later."

"Bye, Sheryl." Again, Tomi waved. I waved back.

I noticed Dedrick clenching his jaw. "You ok?"

"Yeah, I'm aw'ight. Can't believe she brought Flame Boy up in here." He finished his drink. "I'm still pissed at her."

"About what? She seemed nice."

"She and Terrell got into...aw, never mind. It's nothing."

I wanted to push for more information, but my bladder wouldn't let me. "All right, babe. I'm going to the ladies room. Be right back." I kissed his cheek and snaked through the wolf pack, rejecting at least three guys along the way.

When I located the bathroom, I didn't see an assembly line of females smearing lipstick and makeup in front of mirrors. An empty women's bathroom; I couldn't imagine the odds.

After I finished, I exited the stall. Right then, the bathroom door swung open and in marched Sheryl, with Tomi right behind her.

Tomi caught my stunned expression. "Oh, girl, don't mind me. I don't use the boy's bathroom." He leaned against the radiator by the bathroom door. "I don't even remember the last time I was in one."

I giggled. "No worries."

I honestly didn't mind. He sounded so much like a woman I couldn't imagine him in a men's bathroom anyhow.

As I fumbled in my purse for some lip-gloss, Sheryl joined me at the mirror. She turned her head to the side, finger-combing the back of her hair.

"So, you really like my brother, huh?"

"Yes." I swiped gloss on my lips. My smile gleamed in the mirror. "A lot."

"Uh-huh. And why is that?"

My smile turned into a frown. What a strange question. "Because I think he's...ya know...a great guy. A very good man."

"You're right. He *is* a good man. A good, buh-*lack* man."

Oh, boy, there she is. The real Sheryl.

Sheryl shook her head. "I've been trying to figure it out, but I don't get it. What do you white girls have that's so damn special?" She looked down. "Well, I can see with you and that bubble butt of yours. You must have the bomb coochie, too."

"Excuse me?"

"She said, *bomb coo-chie*," Tomi replied. He loved this; I could tell.

I checked the door. Tomi crossed his arms, eyes daring me to make a move.

Sheryl giggled. "You know, brothas flock to snow bunnies like—"

"Snow bunnies?"

"Yeah, *snow bun-nies*." She pointed at me. "Like you."

I wrapped my purse around my shoulder. "I don't need to listen to this."

"Oh, yes, you do."

I tried to step to her left; she stepped with me, blocking my advance. We stood face to face.

"Black women just can't win," Sheryl said. "Once some white ho throws fake titties and long blond hair in a brotha's face, it's a wrap. No more black women. It's like..." She tilted her head, a finger on her bottom lip. "It's like ya'll are a disease."

"Whatever." My breathing sped up. Time to go.

I tried to angle around her again, but she snatched my arm. When I yanked my arm back, a scratch marked my elbow.

"Aw, watch out, now!" Tomi cried, laughing. "Baywatch 'bout to get in yo' ass, girl!"

"I ain't skurred," Sheryl said. She turned to me. "So, snow bunny, what should black women do? How do we...oh, how do I say this... *cure* our brothas of this widespread, pasty disease?"

I didn't reply. Again, I tried to step away. Again, she grabbed my arm. And again, I pulled back—but this time, *I* stepped in *her* face. I don't know how many white girls the demonic duo had tested in the past, but this time they picked the wrong friggin' one.

"Okay, bitch," I said, "that's the last time you touch me."

Sheryl's eyeballs widened so much I could see veins circling her pupils. At this point, I reckoned either her or me would catch a face full of fingernails and a trip to the floor.

She turned to Tomi. "Did this bitch just call me *bitch*?"

I thought Tomi would pass out from laughing so hard. I didn't budge.

"Tomi," Sheryl repeated, looking his way again, "did this bitch just call me—"

"A *bitch*? That's exactly what I said." I stood in front of her. *My turn to block, now.* "Want me to say it again?"

Sheryl didn't reply. Hard to show off when you can't see your sidekick.

I held my ground. I wanted to rearrange Sheryl's nose and lips so bad. A shred of the hate that had infested my father—the same hate I had tried my whole life to avoid—pumped through my veins.

Our stare down lasted a few more seconds. Sheryl exhaled, then said, "All right. My brother will be pissed about me whipping that ass, but I can handle him." She reached for her loopy earrings.

I reached for my earrings as well. This was it. With my back to Tomi, I prayed he wouldn't snatch my arms from behind.

Instead, Tomi cut between us. "All right, now, girl," he said to Sheryl, "you paid too much for that damn perm. Forget this ho."

He backed Sheryl against the wall, holding her back. Big Badass didn't keep her trap shut, though.

"This ain't over, bitch," she yelled. "Stay your white ass away from my brother!"

I didn't entertain them any longer. When I reached the door, three females rushed in. What timing. Where were they a minute ago?

I stormed past them down the short hallway, zig-zagging around people in my path, my feet not moving fast enough.

Black bitch, I said in my head. *She's got a lot of nerve.*

Loud music hammered my ears and stuffy air burned inside my chest. I wiped my damp cheeks with the back of my hand, my vision hazy. The space around me felt so small, caging me in, suffocating me. I had to get out.

As I rushed outside, an icy draft stung my bare arms. In my rush to escape, I had forgotten my jacket—and Dedrick. I didn't turn around, though. I had to get far away from that place. Far away from...those people.

"Nel!" Dedrick cried, skipping down the stairs with my jacket in hand. I kept my stride through the parking lot.

"Nel! Hold up, girl!"

I still didn't reply. I didn't want to face Dedrick, didn't feel like talking, didn't want to go back inside. The only thing Dedrick could do for me was stay quiet and take me home.

Chapter 11

Tammy

"What am I doing?"

I *thought* I was ready to test the blue-eyed waters. But a thousand butterflies nibbling my stomach said, "*Hell* no."

I caught my face in the rear-view mirror. Hmmm, a sista didn't look half-bad tonight. My hair was relaxed, caressing the sides of my cheeks. I wore little make-up, just a soft touch of lipstick. A long-sleeved red blouse and jeans spun a casual but sexy look. I would definitely turn a few heads.

I could see the Marriott up ahead on the right side of the highway. I wanted to call Dale and tell him I was only a few minutes away, but I forgot my damn cell phone.

My airbrushed fingernails tapped the steering wheel. Alicia Keys screamed through the radio waves, but my mind shut her out. Had it really come to this? Me, Sheryl and Miki used to swear we'd never "cross the fence." Now look at me. No wonder I hadn't told Sheryl about my date with Dale. She and Tomi tried to drag me out to a nightclub tonight, but I lied and said I had too much homework.

Don't get me wrong, Dale's not bad on the eyes, but I'd never pictured myself with a white stand-in. Only black and Puerto Rican men lit this fire, never a white guy. Not even Brad Pitt.

But still...had I given up on my own race too quickly, like Terrell and Dedrick?

Damn it, brothas forced me into this. If the grass is greener on the other side, why not lie in it? Maybe Dedrick and Terrell were onto something. Besides, it felt good to have verbal intercourse with a man; I missed that. Felt good to laugh, too. And I hadn't had any of what Sheryl calls "stroke action" in a *long* while, either. Not since Craig months ago. I was definitely overdue for some of that.

But...could I do it with...a white man?

While my hypocrisy and conscience went at it, I pulled into the hotel parking lot. The moment I drove up, Dale came through the glass doors.

Here we go, I thought, my face flushed. *Damn, should I get out and hug him or what? I...shoot, here he comes. He...I...*

"Hi, sexy," he said, stepping off the curb. "I was trying to call you, but kept getting your voice mail."

Let me stop. I put an end to the silly fight within myself and stepped out of the car. "I'm sorry," I said, walking toward him. "I left my cell phone at home."

"Not a problem. I'm just glad you came. I was prepared to cry all night if you stood me up."

"Oh, boy, hush."

When we embraced, I soaked my nose in the masculine scent of his aftershave and cologne, my cheek pressed against the stubble around his chin. He smelled nice, but while in his arms, I couldn't help checking out the area. Thankfully, I didn't see anyone I knew. None of my "peoples" around to look down on me, either.

He looked really cute, though. Sports coat, nice jeans. Hair spiked out all over his head, but neat. A silver necklace shined as bright as the sparkle from Crest-white teeth.

"So, um," I said, breaking away, "you ready to go?"

"Yes, Hot Chocolate. Thanks for picking me up."

Through the glass doors, I saw an older black couple stepping off the elevator. "No problem. Let's go."

As I turned away, I caught a laser-like stare from Dale. I thought he'd light my ass on fire, eyeing it all hard.

"You look really nice," he said. "*Really* nice. Red looks good on you."

I opened the car door. "Thank you. Now stop staring at my butt."

"Starin' at your butt? Me? I was looking at...that...patch of grass behind you."

I chuckled under my breath. "Whatever."

The black couple came through the glass doors. I sped away before they could ID the sista with one of "them." Damn, with my nerves in the electric chair, I felt like a deserter trying to uphold anonymity.

Turning down the radio, I asked, "So, how was Vegas?"

"Vegas was fun. I wouldn't mind going back. You should've seen me, Tam. Chris and I went out and tore it up on the dance floor."

Chris was a co-worker. "Stop lyin'!"

"I did! I told you I would! Watch!"

No, this fool didn't. Hands above his head, he snapped his fingers and hummed a silly song, moving right to left, almost bumping my arm off the wheel. When he leaned his head back and paused, I damn near swerved into the median.

"Boy, you are so stupid!" I cried.

"Told you. This white boy can dance."

"Is that right?"

He shot me a goofy look, then faced forward. "Um...no. I can't lie. I was out there on the floor, but I bet I looked like I had two broken feet. This white man can't jump *or* dance."

I patted his thigh. "Nothing wrong with that. Do your thing, white boy. Do your thing."

We laughed. Dale had cracked the ice, which helped me exhale. In the shelter of my car, away from the insanity of the world where people judge, humor calmed me down. I saw Dale as "Dale," not some man with peach skin.

I had hoped to stay that way.

Due to its proximity to the theater, we decided to eat at Bennigans. When we arrived, I saw cars clogging the parking lot, the usual on a Friday night. I actually knew people who hung out here, and it dawned on me we might run into one of them.

Jitters made a comeback. I needed to blur my senses with a Martini or something, settle down.

Being the gentleman, Dale stepped out while I fumbled around with my purse. He opened the door for me. I said, "Oh. Thank you, sweetie."

"Any time," he said, his smile a neon light. I doubt he sensed my jumpy nerves.

But then he extended his hand.

For a second, I stared at it. Then I allowed him to help me up. As soon as I stood, I reclaimed my hand, acting like I needed it to strap my purse around my shoulder.

We walked in. The small waiting area was packed, all seats taken. While Dale put his name on the list, I leaned against the wall. I noticed folks of all races everywhere, some already ahead of the game, rubbing shoulders and other body parts with someone from a dissimilar gene pool. That's the California way, like one big U.N. convention of multi-colored people.

But that didn't stop the erratic cadence of my heart.

We watched a basketball game on one of the TVs above the bar. A buff brotha seated across the room glanced my way a few times. Figures. No matter the swirl of colors on display, black-white couples *always* got stares—*especially* fine sistas with white men. Not only from that brotha, but everyone else, too. Hey, all eyes on the sellout black girl! Hmph, no telling the words under their breaths: *How could she? Walking around with someone whose great-great grand daddy raped black women—*

"...name. Ready?"

I shook. "Huh?"

"Hello, earth to Tammy." Dale snapped his fingers in my face. "I said they called my name. Are you ready?"

I didn't like his hands all up in my face like that, but chose not to say anything about it. I peeled myself from the wall and replied, "Sure."

We walked in a line with Dale behind the waitress, me a few steps behind him. She seated us at a secluded spot in the back, away from the bar. Perfect.

"Someone will be with you shortly," the hostess said, big smile strapped.

"Where's the drink menu?" I looked around the table. "I...oh." It was right in front of my face, vertical between salt and pepper bottles. Would've bit my nose if it were a snake.

I surveyed the menu as my heart rate slowed, the all points bulletin on me lifted. From what I could tell, nobody was watching us.

"So, first time out with a white guy, huh?"

I wasn't prepared for that question. "Excuse me?"

"I said, first time out with a white guy, right? You seem kinda nervous."

Damn. I buried my face in the menu. "Is it that obvious?"

"Afraid so, my dear."

I plastered on a brave face and set the menu down. "Well, as a matter of fact, this *is* my first time out with a white man. I don't know why I'm so nervous, though." I rubbed my cheeks. "It's not like I don't know you."

"Well, in a way you don't." For the first time tonight, I saw no smile. All business. "You only know my work side, really."

"That's true."

"Don't worry. This white boy doesn't bite." Smile resurrected.

"I know, I know." I crossed my arms. "But since you brought it up. How about you? First time out with a sista girl?"

"Nope!"

I squinted my eyes. As I maintained the stone-face of a skeptic, Dale changed his tune and said, "Yup!"

I giggled. "That's what I thought. A first for both of us."

Dale ran a hand through his hair. The spikes flipped back in place. "Well, it's okay, right? Just look at me as...a brotha from anotha mutha."

"Oooooookay." I rolled my eyes. "How should you look at me?"

He stroked his chin, staring. "Um...you're a...uh...white boy resista, head twista...butt like a big blista sista."

My hysterics must've rumbled the whole place. Wiping hair from my eyes, I said, "'Butt like a big *blista*?' Boy, you are too much." I waved my finger at him. "Don't be thinkin' tonight you gonna pop this blista. *Mista.*"

He snapped his fingers. "Damn!"

That did it. No more jitters. Mr. Def Comedy Jam killed them all. No reason to distance myself from him. Dale deserved my time *and* attention.

The waitress stopped by and we ordered our food and drinks. After she left, Dale placed his arms on the table, leaned toward me and said, "Tam, I'm curious: Why did you agree to go out with Daley Dale?"

Fair question, but I really didn't want Dale all in my business about the beef I had with black men, Craig especially, so I gave him the short, sanitized version. "Well, to be honest with you, I haven't been out in a while. And I knew I'd have a good time with you, ol' silly butt."

That big smile of his seemed to light up the space around us. "How long is 'a *while*?' "

I glanced at a ceiling fan, my mind floating away for a minute. That's when it *really* hit me—a revelation, I mean. I hadn't had a slice of man steak on my plate in almost a year. Nothing intimate at all, not even close. I'd boarded up my walls pretty tight.

Not that I regretted the solitude; it gave me a chance to get myself together. With a new job, new place *and* new city, I had my hands full. Threw out the garbage of the past, started over, focused only on *me*. If I'd allowed any man inside my shell, I'd probably still be living with Sheryl. Men tend to mess up *eve-ry-thing*.

I placed my elbows on the table, resting my chin in both palms of my hands. "Dale, you probably won't believe this, but it's been like nine months since I've been out with a man. Long time, huh?"

"*Nine months*? Hot Chocolate! What's going on? That's like a, uh, new baby! Were you trying to birth a new man in your life or somethin'?"

I laughed. "Nooooooo, Dale. I just wasn't in the mood for men. Plus with the move from Dallas, it took a while to get situated, you know. New city and all."

He looked away, as if processing what he'd heard. "I hear what you're saying. Part of me feels like you left because of a man, though. Happens to women all the time." Before I could reply, he turned back to me and said, "And if that's the case, he needs his head thoroughly examined because rarely does a woman come better than you in every way."

Whoa. I didn't know what to say. Got me so good a smile shot up a mile high. "Wow, thank you," I said, playing around with my hair and stuff. "That's really sweet."

"Not a problem. Forget all this color business. Any race of man can see you're a beautiful woman inside *and* out."

Beautiful. The only B-word a woman wanted to hear.

Dale was smooth. Definitely not what I expected, being the silly type and all. He helped me downplay skin tone and planted the seeds of wonder. I'd asked myself many ebony and ivory questions before I picked him up tonight, but had no answers. But Dale changed that—with the help of an Apple Martini. Eventually, those questions turned into answers with strong "maybes."

Our food came and we got our grub on. Then we polished off another round of Apple Martinis. Got a little tipsy, emerged a carefree attitude, let loose and just had fun. Those seeds of wonder blossomed as if Dale was a spring rain cultivating my garden of flowers.

After dinner, we headed down the street to the movie theater. Since he bought dinner, I paid for the movie, but he insisted on getting the snacks. While Dale ordered a large popcorn and two-drink combo, I dipped into my purse for saline drops. Damn contacts felt like plastic slits glued to my eyeballs. I gave each eye a drop and wiped away the fake tears with a cloth.

My vision cleared, but I wished it hadn't. Just a few feet away exiting the restroom, I caught sight of someone that froze me in my tracks. Terrell.

I felt my cheeks flush as I cursed under my breath. Terrell walked to the end of the snack counter and stood next to a blond-haired chick who poured liquid butter on popcorn. The closer Dale and I came into their potential view, the more my heart kicked into a stutter-step rhythm. A trillion explosions boomed from one of the TVs mounted above us. I think Dale mentioned something about the movie, but while trying to avoid eye contact with Terrell, I didn't catch a damn thing. My gaze and mind had stuck somewhere else.

Wearing a dark-brown pair of slacks and beige V-neck shirt that looked like a second layer of skin, the label "foine" fit Terrell to a tee. He looked *three* times better in semi-formal attire. What a nice, solid frame on that brotha.

I lowered my head and pretended to dig in my purse. The last thing I wanted was for Terrell to see the woman who had claimed to never "quit on our men" out on a date with one of "them."

But no one can walk straight with their head down for too long. I looked up to find Terrell's stunned eyes on me. *Damn.*

With Terrell and his date a few feet away, we slow-walked side-by-side, but didn't say a word to each other. He didn't know me; I didn't know him. No introductions, no smiles, no signals indicating two people who had met before.

As we migrated toward the movie—the same damn movie, as fate would have it—the image of us struck me as a little sad. Terrell and I paraded Caucasian stand-ins and it seemed we had become poster children for the breakdown in black relationships.

Despite our failure to speak, my short glances clashed with Terrell. The blonde, a green-eyed Gwneyth Paltrow look-a-like with tomatoes for breasts and a big head, almost bumped elbows with me. She cuffed her hand under Terrell's arm, a small sign that screamed a white woman had acquired rights to yet *another* fine-ass black man.

As we approached a corner, Dale held the tray with one hand and placed the other on my back. Terrell caught the obvious gesture of affection and I swear I noticed him smirk.

Dale and I entered the theater a few steps behind Terrell and his trophy. They walked up toward the top, so I found a spot in the middle. I got comfy, threw back popcorn and hoped the new Tom Cruise movie would take me to another place and time.

When the lights darkened, I caught Dale looking around while digging in his jacket pocket. He pulled out a mini bottle of Rum. So silly. Always kept me in stitches.

He poured some in his large Raspberry Iced tea. Leaning toward me, he whispered, "*Gotta keep this party going, you know. Want some?*"

I nodded and let him spike my Coke, giggling like a little girl. For a moment, I wondered if Terrell was playing James Bond, spying on us from rows up. But you know what? I didn't worry about it. I decided if Terrell could toy around with his white plaything, I could do the same with mine.

The movie was so-so, if that. Before the first credit hit the screen, Dale and I became frontrunners ahead of the pack, my hand under his arm. Out the door before anyone else. No Terrell in sight.

Truth be told, I had a wonderful time with Dale. He was the ultimate gentleman and even convinced me to let him drive, knowing my alcohol intake had probably pushed me past the legal limit. I thought that was so sweet.

We chitchatted about the movie, small talk really. But the closer we got to the hotel, the more my body temperature intensified, and I flip-flopped between "maybe" and "yes" in my head. Under the refuge of the early A.M. hours, where the freaks of night played in a circus of sin, I knew I could do anything I wanted undetected. Just me and Dale, two adults—and no one else up in our business. A handsome man sat in my car, a white man, but a *man* nonetheless. A man I maybe wouldn't see for months or even a year after tonight. That brought some comfort because something was bubbling under the surface that needed him *now*.

Dale parked near the front entrance. "So," he said facing me, his arm over the seat, "would you like to walk me up, Hot Chocolate?"

I bit my bottom lip. *Walking may not be the only thing we'll end up doing.*

Chapter 12

Tammy

I didn't have to worry about Dale's lips being too small. Or anything else, for that matter.

It was silly to think our lips wouldn't "fit." Thick on thin, his mouth on mine, we worked it just fine. No problems whatsoever, and let me tell you, it felt so good kissing him, despite the peach fuzz rubbing against my cheek. Call me Sanaa Lathan because I damn sure was on to something new.

It started in the car. A peck turned into a deep kiss, then we were in Dale's room, rolling around under the sheets, skin on skin, hard on soft. A bit of light slipped through the curtains, but with the room lights off, we were pretty much the same color in the dark, anyway.

I saw what he was workin' with while he rolled on a condom. No, not porn star super-sized length. Not really long at all, just thicker than I'd expected. I'd be lying if I said a white boy packin' heat like that didn't shock me a little. Enough to put some black men to shame.

I gasped when he made his "grand entrance," which forced me to wrap my arms around him harder. I raised my head as he slithered deeper, trying to haul in pockets of air while pushing my face into his shoulder and neck. Been so long. *Too* long. Lawd.

Dale worked me slow...just the way I like it. No rush. The midnight storm in physical form. His lips and tongue mapped a trail from my sweaty neck to nipples so pointy I thought they would poke a hole through his skin.

Dale lived up to one particular stereotype, too.

His tongue was like a wet brush, "painting" a masterpiece within the mural of my inner thighs. Absorbed all my natural juices, exploring the flesh that makes me a woman. I grabbed the sheets, arched my back, pelvis twitching from jolts his tongue had fired through my spine.

Then we became one again, like a steady pulse: I was a string instrument, whining my own soprano—a fragmented tune I hadn't heard from these vocal chords in forever. As he choreographed the rhythm of our slow grind, I truly felt he was making love to me.

Dale knew what my body yearned for without even asking, performing double-duty, strumming the tip of my wet triangle with two fingers while tapping a spot that turned up the volume on my solo acapella. Craig never touched me like Dale. He didn't take his time with me *ever*. No black man did, really. Their style of lovemaking was more hardcore Hip-Hop than soft jazz.

But our lazy boogie revved me up way quicker than anything at rabbit speed. Although Dale sped up just a little, the turtle in this race won, and in no time a seismic tremor rumbled my whole body, head to toe. I had to muffle my mouth against Dale's chest to keep from shattering the mirror above the TV.

He lay still on top of me, the both of us heaving in a ton of air. We had climaxed at the same time.

Usually I can't sleep right after a big O, but alcohol is like NyQuil to me, so after a quick trip to the bathroom and some small talk, I rolled over and dozed off with my body folded inside of Dale's, his arm around my hip. Out for the count.

A slight headache woke me up. At first, I didn't know where the hell I was. The alarm clock with its huge red letters in my face startled me. It said a little after six, and for a second I couldn't tell if it was 6pm with the sun going down or 6am and the sun coming up.

The hum of Dale's breathing got my bearings straight, though.

I took a long drink from Dale's bottle of water on the nightstand. Then I laid my head back on the pillow, staring through the curtains, watching cars zip by on Highway 8. Rewinding flashes of the night before, I remembered how much Dale made me laugh and smile. Our convos, sneaking sips of Rum in the movie theater, the Apple Martinis. A nice night...the Perfect 10 of dates.

Then Terrell bumped Dale aside and rooted himself in my flashbacks. The sight of him at the theater knocked me off balance a little, forcing me to recall the emotional disarray I experienced before I picked up Dale. Very awkward. More so than I thought, like he caught me in the process of a crime. And I didn't even know the man!

I don't know why I felt that way, like I'd committed some act of betrayal. But if I was involved in some kind of "offense," Terrell was a co-conspirator because he was damn sure doing the same thing.

Did seeing Terrell push me to go that extra mile with Dale? Sure, the drinks loosened me up, but I only stepped over the edge when I saw Terrell with his little string bean.

When the morning sun sheds light on the world, it can also expose the dirty deeds of the night before. The winds of guilt swept my way again. I couldn't tell if the winds derived from the one-night stand, my exodus to the other side or that "one of them" made me feel so damn good.

Dale was lying on his back, so I slipped out of bed, then back into my panties and pants. I thought standing up would make my head pound, but the water must have helped because I felt my headache fading. I tied my hair up in a ponytail and was fully dressed before he caught me trying to escape.

In a groggy voice, Dale said, "Hey, trying to leave me?"

"Good morning," I replied, slipping into my boots. "Yes, I have some personal business to take care of."

I was lying. I didn't have a writing class today or any other commitment to speak of. I just wanted to get home.

He pulled the covers off his chest. "Aw, man. Well, let me walk you down."

"No, no," I replied, grabbing my purse. "Get some sleep. We can talk later today."

"You sure? I don't mind walk—"

"It's okay." I kissed his forehead. "Thank you for a beautiful night."

"Okay, Hot Chocolate. If you insist." He hugged my old pillow.

I had my hand on the doorknob when he asked, "I'll see you before I leave, right?"

"Of course. If not again this weekend, I'm sure at work."

"Okay. Oh, by the way, *you're* the reason the night was so beautiful."

He revived that little flutter in my belly. I smiled and replied, "Thank you, sweetie. I'll talk to you later."

Within minutes, I was out the door, in my car and on the road again heading home. I raced down the highway, protesting the speed limit with the odometer over eighty. Jazz music helped ease my mind into a catatonic detachment. Still, Terrell played in the background. What was that about? There I was, fresh off an incredible night with Dale, and my thoughts were stuck on Terrell of all people.

Then it hit me.

As I processed the night's events, I finally had my a-ha moment. Like a virus in my conscience that wouldn't go away, always flaring up anything Terrell-related. But I finally knew why.

I still loved me some black men.

Yeah, brothas pissed me off at times, but only brothas had that cultural link that I knew I couldn't find with Dale or, I believe, anyone that looked like him. Dale gave me what I needed as a woman last night. But in the long run, he couldn't give me what I needed and obviously still wanted as a *black* woman.

Bottom line: Black men may have stomped on my last nerve, but I didn't want to give up on them just yet. Seeing Terrell proved that to me. Somewhere in this messed-up head of mine, I guess a part of me was still waiting for my black prince.

But Terrell was still an asshole. Couldn't be him.

Once home, I retrieved my cell phone from the kitchen counter and saw Sheryl and Miki had tried to reach me. I called my voice mail. Sheryl's crazy ass came first:

> *"Girl, you ain't gon' believe what me and Tomi did tonight! Call me back."*

Knowing Sheryl, I could only imagine. Miki came next:

"Hey, Tam. Got dirt on Craig. It's a good thing you left his ass because I think I know what he meant by those 'rumors' he was talkin' about."

Chapter 13

Terrell

For some reason, I was still pissed about seeing Tammy at the movie theater Friday night. With her two-faced ass talking all that mess, claiming she'd "never quit on brothas," and this whole time she was creeping with some *white* dude? Just like a sista talking out the side of her neck.

I sensed her surprise when she saw me with Christy, my Barbie for the night. Seeing her with Mr. Happy Go Lucky shocked the hell out of me, too. The way he had his hands all over her, I could tell he wasn't just some date.

But I will admit one thing: Tammy looked good. *Damn* good. Face cuter than a doll, boy. And those dimples. The booty was just as I'd thought, too—tight, firm and jelly-packed. Couldn't believe she was wasting all that on some white dude. Hypocrite.

I arrived at work and my up-and-at-'em assistant warriors greeted me from behind the counter. Luna was scanning the appointment book while Shaundra prepared new client files.

Luna raised her head. "Good morning, Dr. Jackson," she said, smiling.

"Good morning, Luna. Shaundra."

"Morning," Shaundra said, her head down, voice low. No warmth at all.

I let it go. Since Shaundra saw me with Lisa, a tension hung between us. Minimal conversation, terse remarks, hard looks. Nasty attitude on a steady rise. I dreaded it, but I knew we needed an employer-employee rap session to rectify certain issues.

I entered my office and set my gym bag under my desk. Didn't have my partner in crime to join me for a Monday afternoon routine of Muscle Man fitness. Dedrick was on his way to Mississippi for the next couple of weeks. I talked to him earlier while he was waiting to board his flight. Apparently, something went down at the club between Sheryl, Penelope and that Tomi character Friday night, but he didn't get into details.

Pretty much a typical Monday morning: People needing new frames to replace ones they either sat on, stepped on or lost; happy customers discovering their faces with the help of contact lenses; shocked looks when a black man walks out with a robe and optometrist name-tag, etcetera-etcetera.

The steady stream of clients helped ease the hours along. Around one o'clock, traffic of near and far-sighted individuals finally died down. One young woman sat in the lobby.

Wearing my customary broad smile, I nodded at the curly-haired brunette who sat cross-legged, filling out a form. Not bad on the eyes, either. Another Barbie potential.

As I approached the counter, the front door opened. An older gentleman hobbled in, wearing a thick grey coat. A thin tuft of white hair barely camouflaged his wrinkled reddish scalp. Thick bifocals stretched to the tip of his nose.

I held the door for him. "Good afternoon, sir," I said, my smile a mile high. Nothing like watching fresh income wander in.

"Hello," he replied, his voice scratchy and rough. "I need a new pair of bifocals."

"You've come to the right place, sir." On cue, Shaundra handed me a green folder. "I'll need you to fill out this form regarding your medical history and any vision changes since your last exam."

The man took the folder. A hard frown sprouted more wrinkles in his crumpled brow. I asked, "Would you like to sit down?"

The man didn't budge. His green-eyed gape seemed to burn a hole in my face. *Why the hell is he staring at me?*

He blinked. "Are you...the eye doctor?"

My steady smile became a proud grin. "Yes, sir, I am." I extended my hand. "Dr. Terrell Jackson at your service."

His lips parted. No words followed. Just a blank stare.

With a grunt, the old man shoved the folder against my chest. "I prefer to do my business elsewhere."

I felt the eyes of each female zoom in on us. I stayed calm, but felt the strings of self-control ripping apart. "Is everything all right, sir?"

No response. He wrapped his pale fingers around the knob and pulled.

I tried to get the door for him. "Sir? Can I—"

"I said I prefer to do my business elsewhere!"

A hush swept the room until Shaundra whispered, "*No, he didn't!*"

My body froze. His comment was subtle, and yet, the root of it crystal clear. I restrained the Titanic urge to shove the door and my size eleven in his wrinkly racist ass.

"Well, you have a nice day," I said, somehow managing to remain professional while closing the door. No more "sir" for him, though, especially when he viewed me as "boy."

I sucked in a breath. The whole room seemed to pause, just enough for smoke to waft through my nose and mouth.

"You okay, doctor?" Luna asked.

I waved it off. "I'm fine," I lied. The itch to knuckle up still lingered.

"What an ignorant ass," the young woman in the lobby chair said, frowning.

"Well, you can't please them all, right?" I shrugged, and then turned to Luna. "Anyway, Luna, can you get this young woman settled, please?"

"Sure thing, doctor."

After Luna and the patient left the waiting area, I took a deep breath and counted to ten. Up until two minutes ago, I'd been having a great day.

Shaundra made eye contact with me for the first time in a while. I could see the invisible brick wall she'd built between us crack a little. And I knew why. She and I shared the same hurt when the Grand Wizard wannabe voiced his hate.

I retreated to my office and closed the door. With my head still stuck in war mode, I needed a heavy dose of peace before I could even think about seeing patients. Despite the Degree of Optometry plaque above my head, my own practice and a steady influx of customers, that man still judged my competence with one glance at my skin. And not just *judged* me. Hell no. *Humiliated* me, in front of my assistants and a patient.

Crusty old punk. He can go elsewhere because I damn sure don't want him here. I banged the desk with my fist. *I should've whipped his ass.*

Chapter 14

Tammy

"Girl, where were you? I called Sheryl and she hadn't talked to you, either. I've been trying to get a hold of you for days."

"Calm down, calm down," Miki said. "I did something dumb to my phone."

"What?"

"I was at my mother's house over the weekend. Family I hadn't seen in a while came down from Atlanta. I did a load of laundry and left my phone in the pants pocket."

I merged onto the highway. I'd just left from lunch and had to be back at the office in twenty minutes. "You knucklehead. *Always check the pockets*! Washing Machine 101."

"I did! Missed it somehow. Too damn small. I just got my new phone an hour ago."

"Miss Ann Marie didn't have a phone you could use, heifa?"

"Girl, leave my mother alone," Miki said. "I was with family, having a good time, catchin' up. I was too busy to call you back."

I rolled my eyes. Too busy? After that cryptic message she'd left on my voice mail? I'd been itching to know the 411 on Craig all weekend!

Although I felt a scream struggling to reach high pitch, I held my tongue, calmed myself and gave Miki the benefit of the doubt.

"All right, I know how hectic it is being around family. But they're gone now. What did you hear about Craig?"

"Damn, girl," she said, laughing. "Couldn't wait, huh?"

"Just spill it!"

"Okay, are you sitting down?"

"Yes!"

Miki's breath brushed against the receiver. "Craig is in jail."

"Huh? Why?"

"He was in some kind of arms ring, sellin' guns to niggas fresh outta prison."

"*What?*" I pressed the volume up on my Bluetooth headset. I could not have heard her right.

"Yeah, girl. Feds got him."

"*Feds?*" I replied while exiting the highway. "I can't believe he had all that going on. No wonder he was talking about 'rumors'. And behind my back, too."

"Yup. No telling how long, either. You're lucky as hell, girl. You could've gotten caught up in that mess. Crazy, huh?"

The thought chilled me. "Yeah. That's...a trip. So, how did the cops find out?"

"Okay, check this out: One of the guns Craig sold wound up bein' the one that killed Grip. Fingerprints pointed to some punk kid from the neighborhood. Still in high school. When they caught him, he snitched on *everybody*. That's how they busted the ring."

"*What?*"

"Yeah, girl. What goes around comes around, huh? About twenty of them sitting up in jail, *including* a certain bitch named Tracy Suggs."

"Tracy *Suggs?*" I screamed. "That dumb bitch from our high school basketball team?"

"Yup. *That* bitch."

I stopped at a red light. "Damn. That mutha...I can't believe him. Tracy Suggs of all people. She used to always accuse me of trying to steal her boyfriend."

"I remember that. Apparently she still wanted revenge because she's the same Tracy that Craig was messin' with when ya'll were living together."

"Dayum. I'll be...*day-um*."

Within minutes, I parked my car, then shut down the engine. I replayed the moment I kicked Craig out of my apartment. The Tracy note, his lies, my disgust for him. The anger. A freight train of anger. He was the main reason for my retreat to California.

It all came back to me. That heat I thought I'd suppressed...the hate for him...boiled in me again. Vision blurred from the rebirth of rage. I was so damn naive! Like Miki said, I could've gone down with him!

"You there, girl?"

I readjusted my headset. "Yeah, yeah. Just thinking about that nigga. Fool got—"

"I can't believe you talkin' like that! Don't use that word. It's not you."

"Why not? That's what he is. A nigga that got what he deserved!"

"Stop it, Tammy. You don't even sound right saying it. Just...just be thankful you didn't get caught up."

"Whatever."

"You did the right thing," Miki said. "I didn't see it at first, but... you needed to leave."

"Like I said, you can do it, too. *You* need to leave, Miki."

She didn't answer, but I heard a sigh.

I stepped out the car. "All right, girl," I said, shutting the door. "I'm late for work, so I gotta go. But I'll talk to you later tonight. Kiss Kevin for me."

"All right. Love you."

"Love you, too."

We hung up. Stomping through the parking lot, I'm sure steam rose off my body. I was so lit. *Fuming.* Craig had gotten too close to turning me into a statistic. I'd busted my butt my whole life to make something out of myself and that man almost destroyed it all. That could've been me locked up with him! Worse, I could have gotten caught in some crossfire and ended up shot. Punk ass.

I took small comfort in knowing that fool would never walk the streets again. Not for a long time, anyway. Just another black man locked up in a white man's cage, where he belonged. I'm *not* the one.

Don't drop the soap, Craig.

ભ   ભ   ભ

"Hel-lo?"

I jumped, knees banging the underside of my desk. I turned toward the doorway. "Dale, h-hey. How are you?"

Dale walked in and sat on the edge of my desk. "Did I scare you?"

"A little bit."

"I'm sorry, Hot Chocolate. Didn't mean to."

"It's okay."

We sat quiet while the seconds crept by. I guess neither of us knew what to say. I know I didn't.

"Oh," I said, springing to life, "I'm sorry I didn't call you back yesterday."

He had called me sometime in the afternoon the day before. At that moment, I just didn't feel like talking to him. He replied, "it's okay. I just wanted to let you know I had a great time last Friday."

I smiled. "Me, too."

He looked over his shoulder, then leaned closer to me. "Do you have any regrets about...you know."

Regrets. I'd asked myself that same question as I drove away from his hotel that morning. No, I didn't regret what I did. Dale gave me what I needed...at that moment. But deep down, I knew we could never be anything more than friends with benefits. Too many hang-ups in me. I guess I wasn't ready to abandon ship just yet.

Of course, that's easy to say considering he lived a thousand miles away. That thought crossed my mind, though, him living in or near my area code. I wondered if I could still maintain my racial barrier just to stay true to my own, possibly at the sake of happiness.

I patted his leg. "I have no regrets, Dale. I'll always cherish that night."

"Me, too. Makes me wish I lived closer."

I swallowed. "Yeah."

He stood up from the desk. "By the way, what was the deal with that guy you saw at the movies?"

"What guy?"

"Aww, you know who I'm talking about."

I frowned. "I do?"

"You know, the black guy with the blond girl. I saw you two staring at each other. I could tell he wanted to say something to you, and you were definitely uncomfortable after seeing him."

Damn, nothing got past him. "I wasn't uncomfortable," I said, playing dumb.

"Hey, it's okay. I get a little unnerved when I see my ex with her new guy, too."

"Dale! That man is *not* my ex-boyfriend! He's just a guy my girlfriend knows."

"Suuuuuure," Dale said with half-shut eyes. "Not a bad lookin' guy, I'll admit. I don't know why he's with that girl when you look ten times better. She was shaped like a mop."

Laughs erupted from me. "You're right!" I said, wiping my eyes. "She did look like she could wipe the floors, huh?"

"Yup. I swear I smelled Pine Sol when she walked by."

I cracked up so hard I almost knocked my Starbucks cup off the desk. "*Pine Sol?* Boy, you are stupid!"

"I know." He looked at his watch and sighed. "Only have two hours before my flight. Well, Hot Chocolate, can I at least get a hug before I go?"

"What? Where are you—oh, damn! You're going back to Florida today!"

"You forgot? Tsk, tsk. Oh, how you hurt me."

"I'm sorry," I said, hugging him.

Dale's long arms folded around me, his hands rubbing my back. "Well, I guess I can find it in my heart to forgive you. Especially after...well, you know."

I squeezed harder. His warmth felt good. "Oh, hush."

He kissed my cheek. "I hope to see ya next year, beautiful. Maybe sooner. Who knows? Maybe I'll just fly out here to visit."

"That would be nice. Call me when you get home."

"I will. Bye, Hot Chocolate."

"Bye, Dale." One last super-bright smile blessed my eyes. Then he disappeared.

I sat down, staring at the multi-colored fish swimming in a digital ocean on my computer screen. It seemed we had a lot of promise, Dale and I, *if* I could somehow hurdle the black-white wall. Or maybe with another white boy like Dale, someone who could tap my funny bone and didn't live on the other side of the country. Dale was the anti-Craig—light years away from the black men I'd dated.

But jumping that hurdle seemed too high, too hard. I couldn't imagine a guess-who's-coming-to-dinner moment. Didn't want to. Only a fool would self-sabotage a shot at bliss solely because of skin color. A fool like me, apparently.

After a long day of drowning myself in loan docs, I left a little after four and headed to my car. While snapping on my seat belt, I glanced at the adjacent courtyard and saw a short black man sitting on one of the stone benches. I recognized him. He was a manager in Sales.

I frowned at the sight of him, my new kneejerk reaction for men in the same skin. I had decided to remain loyal to my own after my brief encounter with Dale; yet, I still found it hard to trust men that looked like me. I never thought of myself as messed up in the head, but for the first time, I felt like it. Just so damn confused.

As I stared at the brotha on the bench, I couldn't help thinking about how he probably wrecked the life of some poor sista, like Craig almost did mine and Kevin's sperm donor on Miki. Then I bet he ran off to some white bitch with golden retriever hair, living the white bread life near some golf course or the beach.

As I jammed the key in the ignition, I noticed a dark-skinned sista strolling toward him. A coffee-skinned little girl broke from her side to rush toward the man, black tap shoes rapping against the sidewalk.

"Daddy!" she screamed. She looked about seven years old, her wide smile stretching from ear to ear.

The man lifted the brown angel high above his head. "Wooo-weee!" she screamed. I couldn't refuse a smile even if I tried. A burst of high-pitched giggles exploded from the little girl's pretty brown face.

He kissed the woman, then they sat down. They seemed like a nice, wholesome black family. Shoot, picture-perfect. I've always respected a man standing strong and proud in his role as husband and father. I hadn't seen many brothas holding it down like that lately. Or...maybe I wasn't paying attention.

The brotha set the little girl on his knee and she rattled off the events of the day. The man never turned away from his daughter, didn't interrupt, just nodded and dropped his jaw once or twice, soaking in her elementary school stories. From the look on his face I could tell that no meeting, deadline, report or presentation was more important than hearing about the multiplication tables his daughter had learned that day.

I knew that look. My father used to share the same look with me. He always made his little girl feel more important than anything in the world.

I rested my head against the seat. Staring at the hood, I said, "What the hell is wrong with me?"

My conscience flooded guilt. Why had I judged that man when I didn't even know him? I looked in the rearview mirror and saw the strained face of an angry woman. No way Daddy would stand for this version of his precious Tammy.

"Daddy."

I reached into my purse. Unzipping the small compartment that held my pendant, I fished it out. Hadn't seen my father in so long. I kissed his face, then looped him around my neck...where he belonged...next to my heart.

Then he spoke to me.

I closed my eyes. *I know, Dad. You're right. I need to let go of the hostility and stop judging. Especially toward my own. And I should be thankful I didn't end up like Craig.*

Channeling my father's words, I felt my demons fading, the hate lifting off my chest. Letting it all go felt good. When I opened my eyes, the family was gone.

Refreshing my lungs with a big swoosh of air, I dug in my purse for a saline dose. My dry eyes needed their daily drops.

Once I found the small plastic bottle, my finger brushed a business card. I pulled it out. It said, "Dr. Terrell D. Jackson, Optometrist" on the front.

Hmmm, I thought, *I do need an eye exam.*

Chapter 15

Penelope

"This sentence is kinda vague, don't you think?"

Mike, my new team member, studied the page. "Yeah," he said, coffee breath twitching my nostrils. "It doesn't say much about collecting flight data. Highlight it. We'll fix that."

I highlighted the paragraph with a marker. Since Tuesday, Mike and I had been working out of a small office at one of the naval schools in Meridian, Mississippi. The same naval school I'd attended years before, actually. Time sure does fly.

The other team members were in an office across from us, while Dedrick worked in the computer room down the hall. He was only fifty feet away, but I hadn't seen or spoken to him all day.

I stretched my arms high and circled my neck. Eleven minutes to ten—almost time to leave.

"Say, shouldn't you be on the road?" Mike asked, reading my thoughts. "Your family lives near here, right?"

"Yes, about four hours north. Greg granted me special leave so I could spend some time with my folks. My father's sick."

"Sorry to hear that. Hope he feels better soon."

"Me too." I slipped on my leather coat and grabbed my purse. "See you Monday after next."

"Okay, drive safe out there."

"I will."

I stopped across the hall to say goodbye to the rest of the team, then headed down the long empty hallway toward the exit. Classes were in session and chitter-chatter faded in and out as I passed closed doors with small square windows. Then I approached the computer room.

I paused. Since my run-in with his sister and her "girlfriend," friction had driven a wedge between Dedrick and I. I thought I could handle smart remarks and stare-downs from racist blacks, but that bitch took things to another level. She reminded me that a white woman "stealing" a black man had better prepare for random psychotic episodes in public places.

My anger toward Sheryl eventually shifted to Dedrick. On the way home that night, I'd said a few choice words about his sister and the rift began. Too much standing up for her; not enough for me. Well, that's how I felt, anyway. We hadn't spoken in a while, and neither of us made any attempts to patch things up. Both too stubborn to make the first move, I guess.

Oh well, it didn't matter now. After the blow-up in the car, our undercover affair had all but flat-lined.

I passed the computer room. As I pushed the exit door, icy air brushed my face, my chilly reminder of winter in Mississippi. I folded my arms against my chest and headed toward the rental car.

When I got back to my room, my cell phone buzzed in my coat pocket. It was my brother Larry.

"Hey, Larry. What's up?"

"How ya doin', sis? All set to come home?"

"Yup. Leavin' in a bit. Got off work a little early so I could get a jump on traffic."

"Good." I could see his lopsided grin taking shape. "Finally away from Mexico."

"Oh, be quiet. You know I live in California."

"Just another oversized Mexican city to me. Anyway, can't wait to see ya, sis. It's been too long. Gotta warn ya, though. Dad's got a bad cold."

"Cirrhosis *and* a cold? He must be really grumpy."

"Yup."

"Well, I hope Mom finally convinced him to take his meds and stop drinking."

"He's taking them. No more whiskey, either."

"Good. I'll be home soon. Looking forward to it." Some truth in that statement.

"Maybe when you come back we can play another game like we did when you were in school. What cha' think?" He laughed.

I frowned. "Huh? What do you mean?"

"Aw, sis. You know what I'm sayin'."

It took a sec, but I figured out what he meant. My brother referred to one of my most shameful moments, a "game" Larry had tricked me into watching. It involved me, Larry, Rick and a fifteen-year-old black boy. So shameful I had blocked it out.

I stopped that hurtful flashback. "I'm not getting into that, Larry. You always make it seem like I was a willing participant. I *never* was and you know it."

"Aw, c'mon. It's one of my fav'rit memories." I heard a few slurps. Mississippi mud beer, probably, or Jack Daniels—his two best buddies. "Anyway, how ya gittin' here? Ya want me to come get ya?"

The last thing I wanted was for Larry to DUI his way down here. "No, I got a rental."

"A rental? No, imma come get ya. Ya shouldn't be drivin' on dem roads by yerself."

I smiled. My brother, the He-Man protector, always looking out for little sis. I missed that.

"Larry, one day you'll realize I'm not a little girl anymore. I can drive myself. I do it all the time."

"Well, promise you'll go slow and watch for ice."

"I promise."

Three knocks tapped the door. Housekeeping usually announced their presence in broken English. Not this time.

"Gotta go, Larry. Someone's at the door. See ya soon, hon."

"Okay. See ya." We hung up.

When I opened the door, I had expected a middle-aged Filipina with a pushcart. Instead, Dedrick towered in front of me, a grin strapped across lips I hadn't tasted in a while.

"Hmmm, trying to leave without saying goodbye?" he asked.

My heart rate sped up. "I...um...I was going to call you."

"Yeah, right. Can I come in for a bit? We need to talk." He shook. "Cold as hell out here, too. You know black folks ain't used to this weather."

I checked my watch. If I wanted to make it to Starkdale at a decent hour, I needed to leave soon, especially with traffic and the slick roads. But with Dedrick in front of me, I didn't want to leave at all.

I stepped to the side and motioned for him to enter. "Um, sure. I've got a few minutes."

He walked in. "Nel, you've been avoiding me since that night at the club. Let's stop this tap-dancin' around each other."

I sat down on the bed. "I just don't know what to say to you, Dedrick. I guess I felt you weren't on my side that night. Like you made your priorities clear."

He sat down beside me and took my hand. "Babe...look. I'm sorry I made you feel that way. But, you know, it's just me and my sister now. We all we got. Even though she gets on my last nerve, that's my heart right there."

"I thought *I* was your heart."

He huffed. "C'mon, girl. That ain't the same."

"Then why don't you go find yourself a black girl or something?"

Dedrick stared at me, his mouth stuck open, eyelids fluttering. I don't know where that response came from. The words flew out of my mouth so fast.

"What are you talkin' about?"

I pulled my hand from his and stood up. "I don't know," I said, sighing. "All this racial crap bugs the hell out of me. Just seems like you'd be better off with a black woman."

I was about to walk away but he reclaimed my hand. "No. I'm better off with *you*."

I stopped in my tracks. Wow, that sounded so *real*. Like he really meant it. I was trying to push him away, but with those simple words, Dedrick mended a tattered part of me that had almost come completely undone. Refilled the gaps in my heart his absence had created. I felt whole again. Calm.

I sat back down next to him, our fingers interlocked. "I feel the same way, babe. But...why does your sister hate me so much? I didn't do anything to her."

Dedrick eased out a long gush of air, like he was deflating his lungs. "Well, let's not forget, people in your family hate me and they don't even know a brotha, either. But, with Sheryl, it's more about me than you."

"What do you mean?"

He stared at the floor. After a few seconds of silence, he said, "Remember when I said my father wasn't around much?"

"Yes."

"Well, the deal is, my father used to mess around with other women. But Ma always took him back until she caught him in *her* bed with a white chick."

"Oh," I said, connecting some of the dots. "Wow."

"Yeah, and his ass wound up marrying her. She had bank, too. Guess he thought he'd hit the jackpot. I think they moved to Canada somewhere."

"Geez," I replied, a little discombobulated. "So *that's* it. No wonder your sister hates me. I bet when she sees me, I remind her of that woman."

"Any white woman with a black man reminds her of what happened to our family. Ma and Sheryl took it pretty hard when my father left for good."

"I don't blame them."

"Me either, but what's not fair is *I* suffered for what my father did. Ma was real bitter about being left to raise two kids by herself. Then she got on me, talkin' 'bout '*if you ever bring home some white bitch, blah, blah, blah.*' " He shook his head. "Sheryl joined in and they never let up. But bein' the rebellious type, when I finally left home, I dated whoever I wanted, including white females."

"I see. Your father never contacted you and Sheryl again?"

"Naw. I admit, even though he wasn't around much anyway, when he left for good, it hurt. As time went on, I convinced myself if a black man could dip out on his wife and two kids for a white woman with money, she must damn sure be worth it."

"Wow, you thought that?"

"Yeah, I did." He stared at the floor again. "And I got so tired of Ma and Sheryl gangin' up on me about who I dated, I convinced myself my father had good reason to bounce. Kinda believed things would be easier with a white woman. Apparently Pops thought that, too." He ran both hands down the side of his face. "Shoot, I just prefer white women, really. I like what I like. Like father, like son, huh?"

I knew about sons Xeroxing the habits of fathers. Larry did it well enough, and not for the better, either. I also understood the power of stereotypes, those made-up generalizations about a group of people, mostly based on a false or small piece of information. I struggled with them, too.

"Well," I replied, "Sheryl has a right to be angry. I guess going out with someone like me is like a slap in the face to her and your mother's memory. But 'cha know what? That doesn't make you *exactly* like your father. He's not as loyal as you are. You wouldn't do what he did, just up and leave for good."

He shook his head. "No, I wouldn't."

"Did you patch things up with your mom before she passed?"

"Yeah. In the end, who I dated wasn't worth breaking up the mother-son bond. She made peace with me *and* my father...even though his punk ass couldn't be bothered to come to the funeral."

I stared at the blank TV. "That's awful."

"It is what it is."

I edged closer to my honey, resting my head on his shoulder. He kissed my temple.

"Why does it always have to be about race?" I asked. "Why can't two people just love each other and not get harassed for it?"

Dedrick placed his hand under my chin, turning my head toward him. "We won't please everybody, Nel, but I don't care. That's their problem, not ours. They can't define our relationship."

He had a point. Why let anyone define us?

With his lips a breath away, we ended all conversation. We kissed, hugged, kissed a little more, rubbed parts of each other under our coats. Did the things I missed so much.

I tried to lean back toward the bed but he stopped me. "Hold on," he said, digging a hand in his coat pocket. "I wanna show you sumn'."

I noticed that slick grin. I'd seen that look many times, as if he hid a naughty secret. He opened his palm to reveal a gold bracelet.

I raised a hand to my mouth. Jewelry has a funny way of making a woman forget why she exiled her man to the doghouse in the first place.

I recognized the bracelet as the same one that had pulled me into Kay Jewelers in Fashion Valley mall one Saturday night. Dedrick, anxious to get to a movie, protested but followed me in anyway. After suffering for a few minutes, he dragged me away. Thought that was the end of it.

But apparently he pocketed that memory and brought it to life today. So sneaky. But in a good way.

"We saw this bracelet together," I said, still staring.

"Yup. You was like, 'this is sooooo nice!' Mouth all wide."

I blushed. "So...um, what's the occasion?"

"Does a guy need a reason to buy his girl a gift?"

Boy, that charm of his. It could make a female drop her strongest defenses *and* panties.

As he clipped the bracelet around my wrist, tears bubbled in the corners of my eyes. I swore a day wouldn't pass without the bracelet clamped on me.

Raising my head, a tear slid down my face. Dedrick massaged my wet cheek with his thumb, wiping away a thin stream. His brown eyes were so tender, so sincere.

No more fooling around. Time to reclaim what I thought I no longer wanted. I pulled him toward me. "Com'ere."

Like a good boy, he did what I told him, easing back on the bed while slithering between my parted legs. Like a *bad* girl, I stabbed my tongue between his lips, driven by the fever between my thighs. I ran my nails down the back of his neck and cheeks. I missed him. So much.

I found his zipper and pulled. He grabbed my wrist. "No, Nel," he said, yanking his mouth from mine.

I wiped the side of my mouth. "What?"

He rose off me. "As much as I want to do this, you have a long drive ahead. You should get on the road."

"Aw, babe, you got me all hot and bothered, now."

"I'm not goin' no where. I'll be here when you get back."

"You sure you don't want some?"

"Nel, I don't want a hit it and quit it. I'd rather us have a full day make-up marathon. Mess around with King Dingaling and you'll never make it home."

I laughed. "You're right about that, Mr. Dingaling."

Although I wanted nothing more than a little nookie for the road, his hormone control impressed me. I realized I was worth more to him than just a rump session.

Dedrick picked up my bag. I got myself together and grabbed my purse. Before opening the door, Dedrick asked, "So, we cool?"

I smiled. Tugging his coat, I pulled him toward me for another kiss. "What do you think?"

"Mmmmm, I'm thinking you need to get your fine ass in that car. Let King Dingaling walk you out."

"Yes sir, Mr. Lingaling, Dingalinga, whatever," I replied, giggling. "My other bags are in the car already."

"Cool. Easier on me."

Dedrick opened the door, looked right, then left, and stepped back into the world where secret lovers roamed. We walked toward my rental, bundled up in oversized jackets, frozen air off our lips trailing us. I saw no one we knew in the vicinity, just a big truck by the base cafeteria unloading supplies and a few sailors walking by.

We hugged and kissed. His warmth draped around me like a blanket to take home. I didn't care who saw us.

I started the car. Waving at Dedrick, I backed up and headed toward my old area code. In a few hours, I would arrive in my old hick town where I-hate-blacks-and-Mexicans rhetoric spewed from tobacco-stained mouths. I would have to endure every hateful word, on top of the sight of my sick father.

And Rick. My brother's best friend. One of the dirtiest, most racist pigs I knew. As far as I was concerned, he was no better than a roach under my boot.

With such good times waiting for me at home, I wondered why I was in such a hurry to leave Dedrick's embrace.

Chapter 16

Terrell

"Mornin', ladies," I said, walking into my second home.

"Good morning, Doc," Luna replied, a big smile slapped on. She placed the large appointment book on the counter and I took a quick look at the list of names littering the page.

Shaundra sat silent, tapping the keyboard, her head down. No words of greeting for the boss.

"Good *morning*, Shaundra," I repeated with a little "umph" in my tone.

"Mornin'," she mumbled.

Still copping an attitude, I see. Time to put a halt to this nonsense.

"Hey, Shaundra," I said, "let's rap for a minute in my office, please."

I finally saw her eyes. Almost forgot what they looked like.

"Why?"

Boy, my mouth almost got hot on her, the same way my mother would when I back talked. Instead, I eased in a breath. "Because I think we should talk. Shouldn't take long."

She stood and slipped around the counter. Luna quietly watched the show.

In my office, I dropped my gym bag in the corner. Shaundra followed me in.

"Please close the door," I said, taking a seat. I gestured for her to sit across from me. "Is everything okay?"

"What do you mean?"

I crossed my ankle over my knee. "It's obvious you're upset with me. The question now is what are we going to do about it?"

She blinked a few times, twisted her lips once or twice. "Well, I used to love working here, until recently." Gold-painted nails from her right hand caught her gaze. "It's hard working for someone who doesn't like you."

My forehead tightened. "Doesn't like you? Shaundra, you know that's not true."

"Let me rephrase: It's hard working for someone who hates black women. I mean, you expect that from a white boss, but from you..." Her voice trailed off.

My head shook. *Hates black women?*

I knew my preference for marshmallows was the root of it all, but I never imagined she'd flip it like that. Yeah, I was sampling from the white girl buffet, but I didn't *hate* sistas.

Still jarred, I scratched my cheek, my gaze taped to the flat screen monitor. "I-I don't hate black women at all," I stammered. "I just... you know...date whomever I choose. How does that translate into me hating sistas?"

"Well, doctor," she said, sighing, "sistas in here flirt with you all the time. I'm not gonna lie, me, too."

"I know."

"And you're definitely not bad on a sista's eyes, comin' in here, smellin' all good and stuff. Not too many young, black doctors on the market, so of course you're in demand."

A grin creased her lips for the first time. I smiled in return.

"Thanks, Shaundra. But you know you can't do that anymore, right? Not very professional. Neither are these moods of yours."

She looked down, inspecting her nails again. "I know, but you have to understand where I'm coming from. Some *very* attractive sistas have been through this office, but it's like you don't even *see* them. But get a blond-haired, blue-eyed flag pole up in here..." She stopped, apparently to seize her loose tongue. "Well, it's sad."

Silence. Me nodding, her staring at the floor. "Flag pole" didn't sit well, but I swallowed the curse word on the tip of my tongue.

My little spat with Tammy and Sheryl flashed through my mind like a rerun. Once again, I felt myself on the hot seat. *Forget that.* Nobody, *especially* someone who received checks with *my* name on it, would micromanage my personal life.

"Well, the bottom line is who I date is *my* business, not yours. My life, my choice, end of discussion. Understand?"

Shaundra's eyelids dropped halfway. She didn't move, just zoomed in on me. She never seemed the type to start pandemonium, but most black women I knew carried hot blood and a short fuse. I fully expected a fired employee screaming "Uncle Tom" or "sellout" to materialize before me.

Didn't happen, though. Instead, in a calm voice, Shaundra said, "Yes, I understand, but it's not about who you date, but who you *hate*. Remember that old white man who was in here a few days ago?"

"Yes. What about him?"

"He took one look at you, then walked right back out. I could tell he pissed you off. Talkin' 'bout 'doin' my business elsewhere.' Ignorant, right?"

I stared at my fingernails, too. I'd caught Shaundra's bug. "Yes, he was."

154

"Well, you're doing *your* business elsewhere, too, doctor. One look at women like me and you run away. Why some brothas judge a whole race of women because of one or two bad break-ups, I don't know. 'Black women this, black women that.' Damn." She shook her head. "You're just like that old man, but worse. Why? 'Cause you ignore your *own* women as if you hate us. Women who look like you...who can identify with a black man. You won't even give us the time of day. I think that's sad." She drew in a breath, eased it out. "You wanted to know what's been buggin' me? Well, there it is."

Ouch. That hit hard. Once Shaundra stepped off the soapbox, back to the nails she went.

Except for Luna walking up and down the hall outside my door, silence divided us again. I didn't know what to say. Shaundra's civil tone had smashed my ego in a way a bitchy attitude couldn't.

I tapped my fingers against the desk. So many words mangled in my head, but couldn't reach my mouth. Was Shaundra right? Was I prejudging sistas the same way that old man had prejudged *me*?

I tried to shrug it off. "Look Shaundra, I date who I want. Just because you don't see me with black women doesn't mean I hate them. Either way, it's really none of your business. If you have a problem with that, well..."

"A problem with you disrespecting sistas? Yes, I do. Consider this my two weeks notice."

Double ouch.

The best optometric technician and personal assistant in San Diego had dropped the bomb on a brotha. I couldn't believe she was willing to walk over a...misunderstanding.

I didn't know what else to say except, "Okay. If that's how you feel."

155

She stood. "Is there anything else?"

I turned away from her. "No."

Shaundra walked out, closing the door behind her. To my relief, the tension went with her, though the exchange left a stain of guilt.

My leather office chair became the throne of a man in need of a deep search within his soul. I rocked back and forth, my gaze fixed on the wall. Solace lay inside my office, but things didn't feel so rosy inside *me*.

With both hands folded under my chin, I faced a harsh reality: I was no different than that old man. One look at a sista and I blocked advances my hungry eyes yearned to pursue. Didn't matter what she looked like, what she said, how she carried herself. A black woman? Nope. Not right now.

So maybe a part of me *did* hate sistas. Damn, Tasha messed me up. Guess I didn't realize how much. Why else had I placed America's Apple Pie of Beauty—white women—on such a pedestal?

Shaundra and I didn't speak for the rest of the day. She worked the front desk while I stayed in my office helping patients fix their visual impairments. Although we entered a sort of cold war with no words between us, I could still hear Shaundra lecturing me. I couldn't shake it. The harder her words latched onto my conscience, the more my own eyes changed. I stepped into Shaundra's shoes and saw things from her point-of-view. For the first time in a long time, I questioned my ban on women who, as Shaundra said, "looked like me."

After my last scheduled client left, I sat at my desk to finish paperwork. I heard a tap on the door.

"Come in."

Luna popped her head in, curly strands of brown hair draped over ringed glasses. "Doc, someone's here to see you."

"A patient?"

"No. She asked for you by name, though."

"She" did, huh? A female. Hmmm. "Okay. Be out in a sec."

Luna closed the door. I figured the mystery person was probably a potential client. Clock on the wall read ten minutes to five, so she would have to come back another day.

When I stepped into the main lobby, I paused. My small crack of a grin dropped into a wide gape. Not many women could do that to me, but this one qualified. Her presence jiggled my face harder than any word or punch.

Tammy.

"Hi, Terrell," she said, gripping my stare tighter with those cute-ass dimples. "Nice to see you again."

"H-hey," I replied, losing cool points with my stutter. "Nice to see you, too, Tammy. I see you took my advice."

"Yeah. Thought I'd stop by, make an appointment, check out the place." She looked around. "Pretty nice. You know I'm way overdue for an eye tune-up."

I chuckled. Still didn't take my eyes off her, especially with my nose caught in rapture, thanks to her flowery perfume.

"Well, you've come to the right place," I said. "Um, my assistant Shaundra can make that appointment for a later—"

"I can stay a little longer," Shaundra said from behind the counter. She wore a kilowatt smile. Where the hell did that come from? "I'm sure you can squeeze in one more patient, doctor."

I tried to hide my surprise, but the way my eyebrows shot skyward, it didn't work.

"Oh...um." I checked my watch. Don't know why; I knew the time.

"We don't have to do it today," Tammy said.

She swiped a thread of hair over her ear. Nice style, with the curled ends touching her shoulders. Her glasses topped off the sophisticated look.

Crazy how I noticed the little stuff. I repeat: Cute as hell.

I tried not to drop my eyes below face level. Hard, though, since dark-brown cleavage peeked from beneath her red V-neck blouse.

With a stolen glance, my hormones pumped like an NFL player before the Super Bowl. The crane-lift rise of my fifth limb clogged my khaki pants.

"You know what?" I said, grabbing a clipboard and questionnaire. "I *do* have time. Just fill out this form first and I'll be happy to give you an exam." I turned to Shaundra. "I'll leave the paperwork on your desk and you can start her file tomorrow."

Shaundra nodded. A soft look of pride warmed her face. "That's fine."

"You sure?" Tammy said. "I can come back if—"

"No, no. It's okay."

She nodded, wearing a small grin. Even then, her dimples teased me. Hate those things!

"All righty, then," Tammy said. "Can I see that form, doctor?"

Chapter 17

Terrell

"All right, now," Tammy said, easing her healthy onion into the exam chair. "As you can see, I'm blind as a bat."

I took some notes on her chart. "Well, I'm not quite finished with my exam, but with you barely able to see the big 'E' on the eye chart, I might have to agree with you."

"Oh, stop it. I wasn't that bad."

I laughed. Tammy's dimples blessed my stolen glances for the umpteenth time.

Although my shot at humor proved somewhat successful, small talk didn't come easy. With other patients, I had no problem. But Tammy was different. I guess our brief yet unstable history damaged a casual link. Hormones urged me to press on, though.

I dimmed the lights and slid my stool closer to her. As I eased the phoropter in front of her face, I thanked myself for popping a breath mint. With our bodies within comfort zone violation, my X-rated mind drew images of me examining more than those pretty brown eyes. I was trying to keep it professional, but failing at the task. Her perfume definitely didn't help.

After an awkward pause, she said, "Dang, been a while since I did this. You're getting my prescription with this clunky thing, right?"

"Right. I just need you to stare at the chart on the wall. I'll do the rest."

"All righty. Hope you can hook a sista up. With my glasses on your desk, I'm handicapped."

I lowered the phoropter, blocking her Grade A face. "I can hook you up."

"Good," she said. Her voice dropped to a whisper. "I need to be hooked up. Bad."

I smiled. *She needs it, huh?*

I stole my gazillionth glance at the slit between what Dedrick calls "tig-o-bitties." I noticed she wore a gold pendant.

Damn. Somewhat strange...our interaction. My visual thefts on her figure, hers on mine, the mutual smiles. Hadn't done that with a sista in what seemed like eons. But I couldn't deny it, her brown beauty had amped up my hormones in a way Barbies hadn't. With Tammy, the attraction felt natural, even with a shade of tension still cloaked over us.

Small talk faded to a pause again. She cleared her throat; I continued my eyeball tune-up by showing her a series of lens choices. Back to professional mode.

After flipping through about eight lenses, Tammy broke from eye talk. "You know, Terrell, I have to confess: I'm here for another reason."

Caught me off guard with that one. "Oh yeah? What's that."

"I wanted to apologize. I started on the wrong foot when...am I talking too much? You probably want to concentrate on that thing, huh?"

"No, no, we can stop for a sec." I moved the phoropter away from her face. "Go on."

She sighed. "I shouldn't have gone off on you when we first met. That was wrong."

I nodded. Tammy's surprise revelation lifted the tension cloud quicker than I thought. It also forced me to face my own guilt.

"I appreciate that, Tammy. But..." I looked down, twiddling my thumbs. "I admit, you had a right to be mad. Damn, I barely knew you two minutes and I went flying off at the mouth. You have nothing to apologize for. *I'm* the one who's sorry. Especially for... you know...that dumb comment."

Her juicy lips flipped upward. That's all it took for Tammy to chip away at the brick wall I'd put up to keep sistas at bay.

I continued. "Besides, you really didn't go off on me. I was actually impressed at how composed you were. You definitely could've cursed me the hell out. Thanks for keeping Sheryl from hanging me by the you-know-whats."

She chuckled. "No problem. She really wanted to, though. Don't get her butt started."

The ice officially broken, we shared a laugh as I moved the phoropter back into position. "So I've heard. Shoot, Sheryl can cut a grown man down just by the way she cuts her eyes. Kinda like what you did when I saw you with your boyfriend the other night." I flipped two more lenses. "Can you see with these two?"

"A little better, but...wait, excuse me? I did not cut my eyes at you! You did that to me!"

"No, I didn't and yes, you did! I don't think your boyfriend noticed, though."

"Oh, boy, please. That wasn't my boyfriend. Just a guy from work."

Yeah, right, I thought.

We paused. The only sound was the phoropter lens clicking into place. Like clockwork, she asked, "So, did your girlfriend like the movie?"

"I don't have a girlfriend," I said. "That was just a platonic collaboration."

"*Platonic collaboration*? Interesting choice of words. I might have to use that one day."

"Use it how?"

Despite the phoropter covering the top half of her face, dimples one and two still snatched my gaze.

"Well...um...I'm an aspiring writer. I'm always looking for unique ways to twist words around. Getting in touch with the artist in—oh, stop! That's perfect!"

"Here? Okay." I moved the phoropter away and jotted down some notes. "So, you're a writer, huh? What do you write?"

"Short stories, mostly. Essays, some poetry. Tryna do my *thang*."

"I hear ya. I have my little thing on the side, too." I scooted back to my desk and pulled a CD marked "Mixtape 8" from my middle drawer. "Believe it or not, I like to deejay."

"Really?"

"Yeah, I'm an old-schooler, though. Got turntables in my garage, gazillions of vinyl records. Dedrick calls me DJ Scratch-n-Sniff sometimes."

A volcano of laughter erupted so fast she slapped the back of her head against the chair. The usual reaction when folks hear my goofy DJ name.

I played the CD. A hard drum beat cranked from the speakers.

Tammy froze, the ends of her feather-like eyebrows damn near kissing each other. Her crooked grin and hard gaze fell on me, like she was trying to figure out what the hell an eye doctor knew about mixing Hip-Hop music.

That look didn't last long, though. Tammy's head eased into a side-to-side bob; then she injected flavor in her shoulders. The twin bubbles poking from her shirt seemed to follow the same "lean back" rhythm.

I dipped into a groove, did my rock-a-way bit for a hot minute. Never pictured Tammy to be so friendly and open. She got me open, too. I definitely didn't feel like a doctor conducting an exam.

During my session with Tammy, an hour blinked by and I barely noticed. Luna and Shaundra had left long ago, leaving Tammy and me alone. Once I wrote up the order for Tammy's new prescription, we headed out.

I locked up and Tammy and I snail-walked into a fresh swish of winter air under a darkened sky. Our verbal tempo flowed like the steady breeze grazing my hot cheeks. We had skipped and glided into different subjects, yapping with no pauses in between. When I found out Tammy played basketball in high school and college, the conversation turned to our workout routines. An athlete. I liked that. A lot.

I let Tammy step in front of me toward her car. Sneaky move on my part—men do it all the time. Our way of taking advantage of the glutes.

And I did. Under the laser beam shine of the parking lot lamps, I caught an up-close glimpse of jelly blessing and pressing the tight fabric of her jeans.

Tammy clicked her car remote. "So," she said, turning to me, "you go to 24 Hour Fitness, huh? The one up the street?"

"Yeah. Dedrick got me hooked on that place." I blew a breath. Cool air wafted from my mouth. "But he's in Mississippi for the next couple of weeks. Down one workout partner."

She opened the door. I held it for her. "Yeah, I know. That boy's always on the road. Well...I'd planned on going this Thursday. Have to maintain my six-pack. Maybe I'll see you there."

Six-pack, huh? I smiled. "Maybe you will."

Our gazes stuck. The pause in our eyes inched to the point of crossed boundaries. A steady rise in body heat bloomed inside my chest *and* a few inches below my own six-pack.

"Well," Tammy said, "I appreciate you squeezing me in, doctor." She slid into the driver's seat. "Thanks for the contact lens kit, too."

"No problem." I closed the door. "All right, then. See you soon."

She didn't reply, just fired her two-dimpled artillery at me one last time. Starting the engine, Tammy waved, drove off, then turned onto Balboa Avenue. She sped through a yellow light toward Highway 163.

I smiled. Love a woman who's not afraid to test the laws Highway Patrol imposed. I did it all the time.

I pressed the keyless remote; two beeps chirped from the only ride left in the lot. Didn't feel alone, though, especially with Tammy playing hopscotch in my mind.

Couldn't deny it. Her apology opened the doors for two adults to share oral elation and the sparks rained on me. My short moment with her seemed like a long summer walk through Balboa Park. Jill Scott couldn't have sung it better.

But a part of me couldn't let it go. The "sista injunction" part.

I stared off into space, flashed back to my last encounter with Tasha. Ironically, I stood in the same spot where she and her unknown sidekick cussed me out. Bitch called me "sellout."

Yes, I knew the book well. Why read the book when I knew how the story would end? I'd thought Tasha was like Tammy, too—in the beginning. *Before* we got deep. But the memory forced me to remember the eventual drama from the common dedramanator—a sista. And Tammy was one.

My session with Tammy had floated my head to the clouds, but I needed to get my head back on solid ground, away from Fantasyland. Despite the hard male piece that yearned to peel away the thin wall between Tammy and me, I didn't want to risk reeling in another angry, black fish. Tammy was fine, damn fine, but it wasn't worth it.

Yeah, our little gym get-together would have to wait.

Chapter 18

Penelope

"Got dammit, this tastes like garbage! I need salt!"

I stopped in the middle of the hall as my father's rants pierced my eardrums. His attacks on my mother had been nonstop since I stepped foot in my childhood home nearly a week ago. In his eyes, Mom never did anything right.

Ever since my father's aged body started deteriorating, he had fallen into a state of unflappable bitterness. A twenty-four hour asshole, basically. Lying in bed all day dying from cirrhosis would dampen even the sunniest of moods, but my dad had always been cranky. Now he was downright unbearable.

"You call this food?" Dad cried. I heard a few rattles. *"What er ya tryin' to do, kill me?"*

Kill you? I said in my head. *You're doing a good job of that on your own, buddy.*

My parent's bedroom door was closed, but it hardly muffled the racket. For a moment, a violent coughing fit interrupted his tirade. Sounded like he was hacking up a lung in there. But sure enough, as soon as he finished, back to the yelling and screaming. I hadn't heard Mom's voice once.

That's when I realized I'd fooled myself, thinking sobriety would have any effect on Dad's temperament. He was still the same abusive tyrant he'd always been and Mom the oh-so faithful wife, suffering in dutiful silence. Nothing had changed.

Facing the wall, I gazed at the endless row of picture frames that littered the hallway. We all looked so happy back then. You'd never know the two females in the photos wore fake smiles. I stared at one picture of the four of us, my ear-to-ear grin as bright as my fuchsia-colored dress. A lump grew in my stomach. Pictures *do* lie.

Leaning against the bathroom door—the same bathroom where my mother once pulled glass from my bloody feet—I closed my eyes. Wasn't sure if I wanted to finish the movie I'd been watching, talk to Larry while he worked on his car or burst through the door to check on Mom.

Dad's voice grew louder. Getting reacquainted with the realities of my home life made me feel guilty about leaving Mom with him. As protective as Larry was of me, he never stepped in on Mom's behalf, so when I moved out and joined the Navy, Mom was left to fend for herself. I sometimes wished I could have taken her with me.

I turned to another framed photo on the wall, this one of Larry and his best friend Rick standing by the river, fishing poles in hand. I cringed at the sight of Rick. I truly despised him.

At fifteen, when my top-and-bottom body parts ripened like grapefruits out of nowhere, all the older men took notice, including Rick. That's when his secret plot to deflower me began.

A few pats on my butt here, comments about my breasts there, even a stolen kiss. I kept it all from Larry until Rick tried to jab his hand inside my jeans at his twenty-first birthday party. Even though his parents had just bought him a used jeep, he cornered me in his bedroom, claiming I'd be the best present of all. I pushed his hand away. I'd had enough.

I told Larry about Rick's advances later that night, and when I saw Rick at a gas station the next day, he had a knot the size of a pinball bulging from his forehead. Of course, Rick blamed it on being drunk and falling. He left me alone after that, though.

Shattered glass jolted me from my short trip through history. I shook away the memories.

"See what you made me do! Pick that up!"

I knocked on the door. I was *so* tired of this. "Mom, is everything all right?"

"Your father and I are fine, dear," she said, still shielded by the door. I heard a few clacks. "I'll be out shortly."

A minute later, the knob turned. Mom cracked the door just enough for me to see her struggling with a lap tray. Broken glass surrounded a plate of half-eaten rice and chicken.

Broken glass. So common in this house.

Mom hurried past me, her red eyes forward, never looking my way.

"Mom, want me to get that for you?"

"No, no, dear, thank you." She disappeared around the corner into the kitchen. Some things never change.

I stepped into the bedroom. It still smelled inside, like stale onions. My father, propped against stained pillows, flipped through the channels. When I first saw him, I was shocked. His skin was the color of an overripe banana and he'd lost a bunch of weight. The disease had accelerated the aging process and turned him into a frail, old man. He looked haggard, run down. But I felt little sympathy.

"Dad, you need anything else?"

He kept his focus on Fox News. "Git me a beer."

I shook my head. Confined to a bed, body a wreck and he *still* wanted the poison that put him there. Unbelievable.

"Dad, you know you can't have that."

"Don't tell me what I can't have! I want a beer!"

I closed the door. His cries fell on deaf ears. Mom could put up with his crap, but I was way past the point of indulging him. He no longer held that kind of power in our relationship.

I walked into the kitchen and found Mom bent over the sink. "Are you all right?"

She turned to me, the corners of her lips inching up. Her smile was worn from years of trying so hard but getting nowhere. "I'm fine, dear. Why?"

"Mom, you know why. I hate how he talks to you. After everything you do for him. He's so...ungrateful." I shook my head. "You shouldn't have to deal with this. Just put him in a home already. Something!"

Her eyes grew wide. "Penelope Ann Miller, what has gotten into you? I cannot and *will* not put your father in a home!"

I blinked. I'd never heard my mother raise her voice.

I reached to touch her shoulder. She backed away. "Mom, I'm sorry. I just hate how he yells at you. At *us*."

We stared at each other, but no words could soothe the strain. I noticed a hint of shame in her blue eyes before she turned on the hot water and grabbed the dish soap. Back to being the quiet housewife.

I studied her for a moment, trying to gather words of remorse. It hurt to look at that face. So pretty, like an unmade southern belle, but battered by twenty-eight years of unreciprocated love. Her grey-blond ponytail had thinned a little, small strands brushing pink cheeks blemished from age and stress. Devotion had drained her. Even in her fifty-five years, no one should look so tired.

Like I'd done many times as a little girl, I grabbed a kitchen towel and stood next to my mother at the sink. She looked over at me, smiled, then handed me a plate. I missed that smile. It could always light up my world, even at times when I thought I hated her for being so weak.

Standing next to her, I jumped back into the skin of my young self again. I'd spent some of my favorite childhood moments next to my mother in the same kitchen we now stood in. Every afternoon, while my father and brother talked man stuff in the living room, we'd escape to the sanctuary of the kitchen, away from white trash testosterone. I don't know if I could have gotten through those years without my mother.

"I don't think I've told you since I got here, but I've missed you, Mom," I said, overcome with emotion and nostalgia.

Her smile grew wider, but she didn't look up. "I've missed you too, dear."

"And I'm sorry if what I said about Dad upset you. I just want you to be happy. You shouldn't have to deal with this day in and day out. No one should have to live like this."

I stopped. The tears in her eyes kept me from saying more.

"I've upset you again."

Mom handed me a plate, then wiped the corner of her eye with the back of her hand. "No, I understand. And I appreciate your concern, honey, I really do. But I've been with your father for so long...I mean, really, can you see me without him? With another man?"

"Yes, I can," I shot back. "One who doesn't talk down to you. Somebody who respects you, the way a man should."

She tilted her head. My quick response had shocked her.

"My," she said after a short pause. "I didn't know you felt so strongly about this."

"I do. I mean, how would you feel if I was dating a man who yelled at me all the time and treated me like his personal slave?"

"Oh, I'm not a slave," she replied in a dismissive manner. After a short pause, she said, "Speaking of that, I've noticed you being a slave to your cell phone, lately."

Changing the subject. That bugged me a little, but I decided to entertain her. "What do you mean?"

"Well, I've seen you looking mighty pleased with yourself after getting off the phone. Only a man can make a woman smile like that. Are you going to tell me about this fella who's got my daughter's head in the stars?"

I blushed. "Is it that obvious?"

"Penelope, please, I am your mother. I can tell when my daughter's in love. So, what's his name?"

Part of me wanted to spill the beans; the other part stayed on-guard. Even though Mom didn't share the same racist redneck mentality as my father and brother, I didn't know if I was ready to talk about Dedrick. His name alone would raise flags.

"Well, he makes me happy and treats me really nice. Very much a gentleman." Dedrick's face flashed in my head. "Never met anyone quite like him."

"Does he always make you smile like that?"

"Huh? Like what?"

"Like you're smiling now."

I dropped my head again. "I didn't realize I was smiling."

Mom chuckled. I hadn't heard that sound in a while. "He give you that bracelet, too?"

Geez, mothers notice everything. I raised my wrist so she could inspect it more closely.

"Oh, very nice," she said. "He must be a fine young man."

"He is. He really is. I hope you get to meet him one day."

She handed me a cup. We stood quiet for a moment. I could hear the faint chatter of Dad's TV down the hall. It seemed the old man had finally calmed down.

"Sharon? What er ya doin', woman? Git in here!"

My father's cries sounded like a whisper, but were still loud enough to sabotage my moment with Mom. Should've known. He had a gift for ruining things.

Without saying a word, Mom turned and walked out of the kitchen to answer her summons. My father's voice was like a magnet that pulled her toward him, whether she wanted to go or not. As I dried off the last dish, I heard the front door open. Larry's laughter rang through the room, but he wasn't alone. I shuddered. I knew it was just a matter of time before I'd see that man.

Rick.

Chapter 19

Penelope

"How ya doin', Nel? Good to see ya."

I shredded Rick's response with a few choice words…in my head. Out loud, I replied, "Hello, Rick. How ya been?"

"Well, ya know how it goes." He took off his Marlboro cap and scratched his buzz cut. "Still driving my Semi, workin' long hours. Got back this mornin'."

"That's good." I picked up my book, *When Love Isn't Enough,* from the coffee table. I figured I'd retreat to my room and read until it was safe to come back out.

"How ya likin' Califo'nia?" Rick asked.

"Love it. Better than 'round here."

"Yeah, whatever, sis." Larry unpacked a bag from KFC. "You won't see me there. I really don't like *you* there, either. Wetbacks and niggers everywhere."

"Shut up, Larry."

Larry smirked. "Mom and Dad in the bedroom?"

"Yeah," I replied. "I think they're taking a nap. Finally a little peace and quiet."

"Yeah, I know. Well, we fixin' to eat, have a few drinks. Want some?"

"Not right now. But leave a few pieces of chicken for me."

Larry grunted. "You'd better git it now! Might not be any left over after me and Rick git through."

I decided I'd rather starve than share a meal with Rick. "In that case, never mind. I'm not that hungry right now, anyway." Rick had a way of making me lose my appetite.

Rick stood in the hallway, blocking my way. "I'll save you a coup'la pieces. No big deal." He smiled.

"No, thank you," I replied.

I pushed past him. Rick didn't fool me. He was still the same old Rick, just flabbier and fatter, especially around the waist. A keg with two legs and a walnut for a brain.

"Good to see ya, Nel," Rick called after me.

"Yeah."

I went into my bedroom. After reading a couple of chapters, I nodded off, but loud laughter and chatter from the living room jolted me awake.

"Look at 'em!" I heard Rick say. "Like a pack of monkeys, kickin' and screamin' at each other!"

I frowned. *What is he talking about?*

I got up to see what the fuss was all about. Rick and Larry were watching TV, still shoveling chicken and biscuits into their mouths. I noted two pieces of chicken still in the bucket.

"Hey, sis," Larry said. "Check out my new favorite show."

After grabbing a plate, I sat down in front of the TV. A news reporter detailed the crazy events of a riot at a Hip-Hop awards show involving a rapper I liked. They caught everything on video. Pure chaos. Elbows and fists everywhere.

A chair flew from the side of the TV screen, smashing a cameraman's head. Four bouncer-sized black guys rushed the stage, then punched and kicked some poor fella what seemed like a million times.

Larry chuckled. "I knew dem niggers could make a show I'd watch. Can't wait to see the next episode!"

Their laughter pierced through me, but I missed the joke.

"These niggers, man," Rick said. He turned to me. "What 'cha think, Nel? You don't got some pet monkey stashed away in yer 'partment back where ya at, do ya?" He laughed.

"Shut up, Rick."

Larry finished his chicken and washed it down with a swig of Jack Daniels. "Course not. I taught her better than that, didn't I, Nel? Unless she's got 'im out back in her shed." Larry and Rick doubled over in laughter.

Larry's reference to the shed incident made my stomach turn. *Why the hell did I come out here?*

Having lost my appetite, I pushed away the last pieces of chicken. "I need some air. I'm going outside."

"You nuts?" Larry asked. "It's freezin'."

I didn't care. I grabbed my coat off the coat rack, wrapped myself up and stepped onto the front porch. Cold air blanketed me, but I'd rather freeze than sit in a room with those two knuckleheads.

The winter breeze brushed against my hot face, making the southern California sunshine seem a million miles away. Despite the high cost of living and traffic from hell, I missed San Diego.

And Dedrick.

His bleach-white gappy smile popped into my head. For a second, I forgot about the cold. Dedrick. My baby. Nel's ray of light.

I hadn't spoken to him since yesterday. I was trying to keep contact to a minimum so I wouldn't have to deal with Larry asking about the new man in my life, but Mom's sixth sense busted me. As far as Larry and Dad were concerned, I was man-less. I planned to keep it that way. But still, my body ached for Dedrick's voice.

I retrieved the cell phone from my coat pocket and scrolled the "Last Called" list. Dedrick's number appeared on the small screen.

He picked up after the second ring. "Hey, babe."

I smiled. His voice was like warm cocoa for my tummy. "Hey, you."

"What da dilly down there?"

"Not a thing. Ugh, I'm so bored. I need to get away from my brother and his redneck friend. What's going on up there? Still having problems with the computers?"

"Yeah. Couldn't upload the database for some reason, but I think we got it now. I stayed until midnight last night after I talked to you."

I smiled at a couple walking down the sidewalk with two kids. "Wow. That's a long day."

"Yeah. Which is why I need a break, so guess what? I got us a motel for Friday and Saturday."

"Really? Where? How far?"

"Damn, you all excited." He laughed. "It's close to your parent's house. The Budget Inn."

"The Budget Inn off Route 195?"

"Yeah."

"I know exactly where that is. And Friday is perfect. Then I can follow you back to the base on Sunday."

"Coming back early, huh? I figured you'd want to spend your last days with your family before we head back to Cali."

"I'd rather spend my last days with you. I'm ready to get out of here."

"You sure?"

"Yes. Mom will understand. How 'bout—" I stopped. Someone rustling the doorknob cut into my love connection.

"Hey, babe," I whispered, *"let me call you back. My brother's coming. Love ya."*

He said the same in return. I shoved the phone into my coat pocket. Rick stepped onto the porch. "Hey."

Damn it. "Hey."

He leaned against the railing. Though I was looking off into the distance, I could feel his stare drilling into the side of my head. "Where's Larry?" I asked.

"Doin' the number two. We're headin' up to the bar. Comin'?"

"Think I'll stay here."

After a pause, Rick said, "So, ya ever think 'bout movin' back here?"

Where the heck did that come from? "No way. Can't stand this place."

"Why's that?"

"'Cause. Ain't nothing to do up in here."

He chuckled. "'Ain't nothin' to do *up* in here,' huh?" He dug his hand in his pocket and pulled out a pack of Marlboros and a lighter. "I see the city done changed you, Nelly."

"Whatever you say."

Rick lit a cig. "Guess I can understand. Wanting to get out of this hick town away from yer family." He blew a cancer cloud. "But I'm guessin' that nigger of yours is the main reason."

I froze. *What?*

A ball of fire seemed to explode in me, but I maintained self-control. Clearing my throat, I said, "Excuse me?"

"Ya heard what I said. Who woulda thought Larry's little sister would grow up to be a nigger lover? Never woulda believed it if I ain't seen it ma' self. Yup. So much for good upbringin'."

I sucked in a big swoosh of cold air. My heart rumbled at a speed that seemed inhuman. A dozen answers couldn't keep pace with the hundreds of questions swirling in my head.

I checked the door. Rick had not closed it all the way, just cracked it.

My heart pumped so fast I thought it would split in half. No use beating around the bush. I tried to stay calm, despite a state of mind bound to turn unstable.

Masking my fear with a straight face, I confronted him. "How did you find out?"

"I saw ya. Had a delivery on base last week. Small world, ain't it?"

Too small. What were the friggin' odds? I thought I was going to throw up.

"So there I was," he continued, "deliverin' sodas to the base cafeteria, thinkin' maybe I'd git lucky and see ya. Well, I *saw* ya, all right." He took another puff. "Saw ya standing in the parking lot, kissin' a got damn chimp."

I went back to that moment. Dedrick and I hugging, kissing. Saying our goodbyes. A truck in the distance, unloading boxes. Just my luck.

"He's not a chimp," I said, my temperature near the boiling point. "Does Larry know?"

"Not yet. Father, either. I didn't tell 'em."

Rick stepped closer. The space between us shrank as he penetrated my comfort zone, still gaping at me. His face was inches from mine.

I didn't budge. "So, are you gonna tell 'em or what?"

He sucked his teeth. "Well, that depends on you."

"What are you talking about?"

"You know what I mean, Nel. We can make"—his gaze shifted toward my hips—"arrangements."

My stomach dropped farther. His hungry stare violated my body, dark eyes molesting me. "Just one time. Larry won't know a thing."

Bastard! He had his hand on the handle and the blade deep in my brother's back.

"Rick!" Larry cried from behind the door. "Ya out there?"

Rick stepped back, pulling himself from my private space. "Yeah, on the porch. Just talkin' to baby sis here."

Larry opened the door and walked out. His stare swapped between Rick and me, sizing us up.

"What's goin' on?" He pushed his arm through his coat sleeve.

"Aw, nothin'," Rick said. "Just chattin' 'bout California and all. Right, Nel?"

I swallowed, trying to smother steam on the brink of erupting in a volcano of rage. How I managed a grin, I really don't know.

I could tell the truth and expose Rick for trying to blackmail me. Or keep quiet and handle the situation my way. As much as I would have loved to watch Larry kick Rick's ass seven ways to Sunday, I knew revealing my love affair with a black man would unleash a hailstorm of fury on me as well. I was screwed no matter what.

"Yup," I replied. "Just talkin'."

Larry zipped up his coat. His glare on us held a few seconds longer, then he said, "Okay. Goin' with us?"

"No," I said, shooing them on with the sweep of my hand. "I'm gonna stay here."

"With *them?* Be my guest." He descended the steps. Rick followed. "Probably for the best, anyway. I'm not in the mood to kick anybody's ass 'cause of you." He winked at me. "See ya."

As I grabbed the doorknob, Rick turned around and winked behind my brother's back. "See ya."

Chapter 20

Tammy

"I should've known," I mumbled under my breath, stepping off the treadmill.

I'd come to 24 Hour Fitness after work the past two days, the same gym where Terrell supposedly got his workout on. Even though I had a gym two blocks from my apartment, I hauled my butt across town on the chance I would run into Terrell. A man who was turning out to be a huge flake. I felt like a damn fool *again*.

While on the treadmill, I would look toward the glass front doors any time they opened. Same old thing, though, folks stepping in with skin way paler than mine. No Terrell.

Wiping sweat off the back of my neck, I walked toward the dumbbells. Other than one sista and a sprinkle of tore-up brothas, I didn't see much of "us." One brotha tried to push up the moment he saw me. Homeboy interpreted the fact that I picked out a pair of dumbbells next to him as an invitation to holla. Wasn't in the mood, though. I'd come here for Terrell *and* a workout, of course. Not some random meathead.

"You need a spot, sista?" He curled 50-lb dumbbells.

I shook my head. "No, I got it. Thanks."

I found a space a few feet away from him and curled my 10-lb dumbbells while facing the mirror.

"Cool. Let me know if you need my help, aw'ight?"

"Okay, thanks." He walked away. End of that.

With an iPod strapped to my arm, Hip-Hop music muffled the Techno knocking from the gym's surround sound. Shaking off thoughts of Terrell, I slipped into a zone, working on my fitness.

As I worked up a sweat, Terrell trespassed into my thoughts again. Damn. How could I have been so wrong about him? I thought I felt a spark between us, something more than just the usual chitchat. A *connection*. Yeah, Mr. Nice Guy put on a nice charade, just some role to retain me as a future customer. Obviously I wasn't pale enough to make the cut for any off-duty attention.

Why was I tripping off that fool, anyway? Up in here rearranging my routine, hoping for another shot at a man supposedly hell-bent on disbarring sistas? Doctor or not, Terrell Jackson was *not* worth it.

"Tammy!" someone cried, loud enough to cut into my music. "What's up, girl?"

Fate must be a comedian.

Terrell had appeared out of nowhere. For a moment I thought my crazy ass was hallucinating.

"H-Hey!" I stammered, pulling the headphones out of my ears. "How are you? I didn't know you were here!"

He stood by a weight bench. "I've been here for a minute. I was talking to one of the personal trainers about a shoulder routine I'd like to try. Gave me some tips."

"Like you need tips."

I meant that. Terrell was toned up like one of those hard bodies on a Mr. Fitness magazine.

He stretched both arms behind his back. "Shoot, I'm always looking for better workouts. I'm getting old, so I gotta work even harder to keep this body tight."

"I hear you on that one. Same reason I'm here. Working on my fitness and you're my witness."

He chuckled. "Well, not quite. You're not doing anything."

"Psst, whatever. You can't see these weights in my hand? And you call yourself an eye doctor."

He smiled. Our gazes held for a few seconds before he said, "So, how are the contacts?"

A woman reached behind me to pick up a pair of dumbbells. I stepped out of her way and stood closer to Terrell.

"The contacts are fine. I can definitely see better than my old ones."

Terrell nodded. "Good, good. Well, I didn't mean to bother you. Just wanted to say hi."

I set the weights back on the rack. "You're not bothering me. Not at all."

For a moment, I thought Terrell would venture off about his business. Then he tilted his head, holding a pensive look, as if trying to figure out what to say next.

"What you working out today, anyway?" he asked.

"My arms, mainly." I flexed my biceps. "See?"

"Not bad. I see what you got going on."

Our conversation paused. Still some level of discomfort between us; I felt it. The look in his eyes seemed to ride the curves of my chest and backside, though, colliding with my hard-body stare down.

"So," he said, "you want to work out together? I mean, if you don't have anything going on right now, routine wise."

"No, no, that's fine. I just started, actually."

"Cool. I'm doing shoulders today, obviously. That fine?"

"Not a problem. I can do that."

"All righty, then." He stepped away from the bench. "Let's see if you can keep up."

No, he didn't. That fool dared to throw a challenge all up in my face? Apparently, he didn't know me very well. "Whatever," I replied. "We'll see who'll need to 'keep up.' "

He reeled his head back. "Oh, it's like that? Okay, then. I'm going to do a few pull-ups first."

"Okay. Let's see what you got. Do your thing, playa."

He laughed. We walked to the pull-up bar and Terrell jumped to grab it with an overhand grip. He dangled for a second, then pulled himself up. His chin rose above the bar.

I swallowed. Cuts from wrists to shoulders, sliced within brown melanin. A truly beautiful specimen, I won't lie. Lean body mass, leaving no room for fat, muscle fibers strained from the tension of competing with gravity. Damn. *Dayum!* He looked like an animated figure of the human anatomy in a medical book.

At eighteen reps, he slowed, teeth clenching.

"C'mon," I said, "you can do it. Two more." I itched to touch his waist and push him up, but didn't. Mr. Muscle Milk did it on his own.

"You got it," I said. Terrell's chin barely rose one last time above the bar before he dropped.

"Wooo," he said, slapping his hands together. "Twenty."

"Barely." I winked.

"Whatever." He circled his arms, stretching them out. I peeked at the lines and dips in his triceps.

"So," he said, "you ready to do shoulders?"

"Yes, but hold on." I stepped under the pull-up bar, edging him out of the way. "My turn."

"What? *You're* going to do pull-ups?"

"Yeah, don't look so surprised. This is part of your workout, right? Help me up."

"Damn, okay." Guess I shocked the hell out of him. Not every day you see a sista on the pull-up bar.

He stood behind me and placed his hands on my waist, his front inches from my back. I glanced at us in the mirror. We didn't look half-bad together. Not bad at all. Good genes, nice bodies, skin barely a shade of brown apart. For a hot second, I escaped to a chocolate-covered Dreamland, then reeled myself back in by jumping toward the bar.

"You got it?"

"Yes, thanks." I stared at myself in the mirror again, my Reeboks hanging about a foot above the floor. Gripping tight with an underhand grip, I pulled myself toward the ceiling.

"Six...seven...c'mon...eight. Go 'head, girl!"

At "go 'head girl," a sista's arms didn't want to hear it. But even though my shoulders were burning and neck veins popping through skin, I refused to stop until I heard him say ten.

"You got it. Nine...one more."

With my upper body screaming, my face about to split while oozing sweat beads, I mustered the last remnant of strength and pulled myself up. My chin tapped the bar.

"Ten!"

I dropped to the floor. "Wooo," I said, heart pounding, trying to catch my breath. "I haven't done that since high school."

"I'm impressed," Terrell said, hands on his waist. "Shoot, you right. I might have to keep up with you."

"Thought I told you." I circled my arms. "So, what's next?"

Terrell stared at me but didn't answer, a small grin stretching his brown cheeks. I smiled back. He knew he had underestimated a sista.

We worked our muscles for about an hour, chatting about all kinds of stuff, from politics to the economy. While helping each other lift weights, I felt the same vibe as when I stopped by his office and he checked my eyesight. Laughing and carrying on, throwing little flirt signs here and there, stealing glances at body parts. To a pair of eyes unfamiliar with us, we probably looked like a couple in infancy.

I kept up with him on the weights, too; I think he liked that. I wasn't about to play sissy. It had nothing to do with trying to impress a man. A sista loves her fitness.

Okay, *maybe* I wanted to impress him a little. Let him know I could work it, too. Besides, I enjoyed his company.

But I admit, the whole I-don't-do-black-women thing hung over me. It stung, like a flame I couldn't douse, knowing once he got enough of being around me and all my "sistaizms," he'd run away to some lily white blonde or brunette.

But I hid that side from him. Although the hurt stayed deep in my gut, I pushed away that sore spot, along with Lady Intuition and all her red flags to the back of my mind, allowing myself to enjoy the moment.

After his third set of shoulder presses, Terrell put the 80-lb dumbbells back on the rack. "Damn, Tammy," he said, wiping his forehead, "I'm done. You trying to kill me?"

"Well," I said, stretching my arms high over my head, "we're even. My shoulders will probably be sore for a couple of days. I loved the workout, though. Thanks for showing me those new exercises."

"No problem." He checked his watch. "We started around five something, I think. It's almost six-thirty, now. Not bad."

I picked up my water bottle. "Yeah. Great workout."

He nodded. That stare again. It stuck on me like Velcro, then would peel away and come right back. But it didn't bother me at all.

"Where are you parked?" he asked. "I'll walk you out."

"That would be nice. I'm parked a few spots down in front. You ready?"

He threw a towel over his shoulder. "Yes. We need to get out of everybody's way."

I looked around. A few Muscle Fitness wannabes stood around us, eyeing the adjustable bench we occupied.

"Yeah, you're right. Let's go."

Chapter 21

Terrell

Did I just work out with this woman for over an hour? I definitely did. Now I'm walking her to her car again. I'm going against everything I'd promised myself just a few days ago.

Again, my defenses had crumbled. Whatever hard shell I'd structured to fend off Tammy, those damn dimples, soft voice and hard body had busted in and knocked it down. *Man!* Wearing a sports bra that cuddled her "twins," I concurred on her six-pack. Not ripped or anything, but washboard. Her hard abs would retract against her brown belly as she breathed in and out during each shoulder exercise. Body of an athlete, but it didn't taint her soft curves. *Very* nice.

Almost as nice as those glutes packed against grey sweatpants. The two most important muscles on the human body. Way better than my biceps.

But what *really* got me, the cherry on top of an already sweet package, was her GI Jane workout prowess. That girl busted out chin-ups and handled dumbbells in a way some men couldn't. Impressed the hell out of me. Man, I couldn't stop staring.

As we stepped outside, Tammy noticed my car right out front. "Well, didn't you get the VIP parking spot."

"Yeah." I donned my sunglasses. "Got lucky. Some guy pulled out as I was driving up."

She walked up to my car and scoped out my baby again. "This is so nice. All slicked out. Clean."

"Thanks," I said, my grin loud and proud. "Washed Lexy before I came to the gym."

"*Lexy*? You call your car *Lexy*?"

I flashed a grin. "What can I say? She's my girl."

"Uh huh." Tammy peeked inside. "I see you got a ball back there."

"Yeah." I snapped my fingers. "Hey, I forgot, you played ball, right?"

"Yup. I haven't shot in a while, though."

"Is that right?" I asked, grinning.

"Why are you smiling like that?"

I grabbed the ball from the backseat, then bounced it between my legs. "Time to get back into it. I want to see what you got, Sheryl Poops."

Her mouth dropped open. "No, you didn't!" She stepped toward me. "You tryna challenge me *again*, Slobe Bryant? Haven't you learned?"

"Apparently not. You're good with the weights, but I don't know about your B-ball skills. Let's see you—"

The ball slapped against my knee. I swerved my head, still dribbling air, then realized Tammy had jacked the ball.

She now bounced the ball between her legs, mimicking my pose with handles like a point guard.

"Now what?"

I won't lie; that freakin' turned me on. More so than I already was. I liked the spunk she had packed into her tight little frame. A cocky spark that matched my own.

She dribbled the ball around the parking lot. I saw the skills evident in her moves—the way she dribbled, kept her eyes on and off the ball, the crossovers. And somehow, she retained a feminine grace, even as she Allen Iverson-ed the ball between her legs. Whatever mojo she sprinkled on me, it made me want to delve deeper into her world.

"Tammy, are you challenging me to a pick up game?"

"I sure am. Unless you're scared of getting beat by a girl."

"Oh really? There's a court not too far from here."

"Let's go."

"Damn, okay. What about your knee? Bad knee, right?"

"Don't worry about it," she said, still dribbling. An SUV approached, riding a speed bump, so she stopped and walked back to my car. "I can still move, but not as fast. I have better shoes in the trunk. And I'm wearing shorts underneath. I'm fine."

Not bad. She came prepared. "All I needed to hear. I want to see what you got. Stealing the ball from me and what-not."

"Well, I'm ready." She handed me the ball. "Let's go before it gets dark."

Damn. No hesitation, no second thoughts, no backing down. I didn't like it; I loved it.

CB   CB   CB

She got game. Made a believer out of me.

As luck would have it, four teenagers were playing a game of 21 at one end of the court when Tammy and I arrived, one of them female. As soon as we set foot on the asphalt, the challenge was obvious—two teams, each with two guys and a splash of estrogen. I didn't give a damn that the youngsters were half my age with rabbit energy; I could keep up with them, especially with a spring chicken about seventeen on my side. I mainly wanted to witness Tammy relive her WNBA hoop dreams.

"All right," I said to Tammy while warming up with a few shots. "You on my team now. I'm not trying to lose."

I missed a shot. Tammy caught the ball, shot about ten feet from the basket with perfect form and *swish*. "I'm not trying to lose, either. So keep up." She winked at me.

When she said "keep up" this time, I definitely believed her. Wearing MJs, a NIKE T-shirt and baggy shorts that hid all her lady lumps, she reeked "baller."

We won the first game by four points. Tammy, clearly schooled in the fundamentals, relied more on technique than speed and flashy street ball skills. The Britney Spears look-a-like guarding her had skills, too, no doubt a starter on some varsity team. I had rebound on lock under the rim; Spring Chicken would slice through the lanes for lay ups; and Tammy took care of the outside shooting. That's how our roles fell.

The defeated wouldn't stand for the "L," so we ran it back. Same intense drive from all of us, but this time, they edged us by two points. I noticed a frown on Tammy's face for the first time. Despite making four points out of nine, a loss is a loss. And Tammy wasn't having it. Me, either.

"You know we're runnin' this back, right?" Tammy said to the Kobe Bryant of the other team, a lanky kid with a short Afro and headband.

"Shoot, it's getting dark. We ain't got lights out here."

Right about that. With sunlight fading and no court lights, the sprinkle of beams from the street posts provided a weak source. Grey skies cloaked darkness around us. Light enough to see, but not for long.

"All right," I said. "Let's go to five. It's tied up, so best outta three."

We went back to battle. Since they won last game, their ball.

We tried not to give up jack this game. The hustle for supremacy caused more body bumping, hand slapping and blocked shots. All the while, we fought the clock of the night. Took more time to tie up at four than it did the last two games.

They had the ball, their chance to win. The blonde took a shot; Tammy tried to block, but missed. I cursed under my breath because it looked like a clean bucket, but the ball bounced around the rim and flew back out. I jumped before my defender had a chance and rebounded the ball, dishing it out to Spring Chicken. Cutting the ball through his legs, he drove through the lane and jumped. Both guys leaped with him. A guaranteed blocked shot stuffed in his face, but he fooled them both by kicking it out to Tammy.

The blonde had gone after my teammate while he powered in for a lay up, leaving Tammy by herself. When she tried to run back to block the shot, the ball flew out of Tammy's hands. Too late.

I knew it the moment the ball went airborne. *Swish*. Game over.

Tammy pumped her fist. "Yes!"

I pumped with her, smiling. I gave her a pound. "Nice shot."

"Thanks," she said. "Good game."

Although the two guys on the other team cursed, they shook our hands before dipping out. The blonde waved at Tammy, told her "nice game." Then they disappeared into the night.

I picked up my ball. "Man, I'm glad you made that shot. I was getting a little winded."

"Me, too." Tammy wiped her forehead with her T-shirt. "Felt good, though. Haven't played in a while, but I still ran with those Energizer Bunnies."

I chuckled. I knew what she meant. If you're two times as old as your opponent, and can still hang with him or her on the court, you must be doing something right. I felt good, too. Not time to pop the Geritol pills just yet.

We walked back to our cars. Lexy's hood almost kissed Tammy's bumper. Street lamps lit up the sidewalk we now stood on.

"Well, I should be getting home," Tammy said, unlocking her car. "I'm beat. Thanks for the workout, though. I had fun today."

"Hold on a sec."

She closed the door. "What's up?"

"Are you going to the gym tomorrow?"

She glanced up the street. "I don't think so. I'll probably just relax. Let my body recover from all the torture today."

I nodded. "Oh. Okay. Well...um..."

She tilted her head. "Well, what?"

"What are you doing Friday night?" Didn't even think about the question. Just came out.

She stared at me, then leaned against the window glass. "I don't have any plans. Why?"

"Well," I said, heart hammering away, "I was thinking about taking you to dinner."

Her head reeled back. "You're asking me *out*?"

"Yes."

She crossed her arms. "Seriously?"

"I wouldn't ask if I didn't mean it."

She blinked, eyelids flapping like a loose shutter against a window. Before she could shoot me down I said, "Look, I know we got off on the wrong foot, but I had a great time with you today."

"I did, too, but I didn't think I was your type."

Man, she wasn't going to make this easy. I wasn't going to let her push me away, though. The first time I saw her at Sheryl's house, I'd felt a flutter in the pit of my gut. Well, the flutter was back, and this time around, I could tell it was more than lust. I'd tried to deny it, but everything became crystal clear today.

"Tammy, what I said at Sheryl's house was ignorant and stupid. You are nowhere near what I painted you out to be and I would love to make it up to you. If you'll let me."

She nodded. I noticed her eyelids lower, cutting me in half it seemed. I couldn't read her at all.

Damn, I'm embarrassing myself.

I almost said forget it, but a slight grin returned and she unfolded her arms. Dimples "winked" at me. "Okay. All right. Let me give you my number."

I'll be damned. "So...it's a date?"

"It's a date."

Chapter 22

Penelope

How dare he? Who the hell does he think he is, giving me an ultimatum like that?

Every time I thought about Rick and his proposed "arrangement" a few days ago, I had to suppress homicidal thoughts. I wanted to harm him in the worst way; something that culminated in castration. I had no doubt that if I didn't agree to his plan, he'd go straight to my brother. Dirty, filthy pig. I'd give anything for him to just...disappear.

Mom's voice shook me away from Rick's invisible stranglehold. "I need to get more medicine for your father. That cough has gotten worse."

"What?"

She reached for cough syrup on the top shelf. "More medicine, I said. What's wrong with you, honey? You seem a little out of it."

An older couple approached. I pushed the basket from the middle of the aisle so they could get by. "Nothing. Just distracted, I guess."

"You're thinking about your man friend, aren't you? What time are you meeting him tonight?"

Not soon enough, I thought. I needed Dedrick to whisk me away from the small-city boredom and murder fantasies I'd harvested, even if that meant being camped in a motel for a couple of days. "Probably around eight or nine. He's been working late."

"Well," she said with a sigh, "I enjoyed having you here, honey. Seems like it went by so fast."

"I know. Maybe you can visit me in California? I'll buy your ticket."

"That sounds nice. Depends on your father though. Not sure if he's well enough to travel."

"No!" I said, my voice raised. "I don't want him to come!"

My mother frowned. "Nel, honey, I really wish you'd try harder to get along with him. Like it or not, he's your father."

"I know," I said, rolling my eyes.

She crossed a few items off her grocery list. "He probably doesn't have much time left. It would mean a lot to me if you made an effort to resolve your differences." I kept a few choice words to myself. Leave it to Mom to refer to a lifetime of abuse as "differences."

"I don't have anything to say to him, Mom. We have *nothing* in common."

"You have blood in common. That should be enough." She leveled me with a look that made me feel about four years old again, caught and scolded for making too much noise and disturbing Daddy. "It just breaks my heart that you're not close."

And whose fault was that? Maybe I could have focused more on bonding if I hadn't been so afraid of him.

I wanted to be a smart ass, but clammed up. I didn't want to fight with her. Especially on my last day home.

"Okay, Mom. All right. I'll talk to him before I leave. For you."

A grin creased her soft face. She didn't say a word, but her eyes told me everything.

196

The lines around her eyes and cheeks told stories—the emotional damage, verbal abuse. My heart ached for her. She was so loyal to that man she had sacrificed everything for him—her life, her dreams, happiness. And for what? Love? I wondered if my father even knew what love was.

We left Food Max and headed toward my rental. While strolling through the parking lot, Mom asked, "When are you saying goodbye to your brother?"

"After he gets off work, I guess. I'll probably stop by his place on my way out of town."

"You'll probably have better luck trying to find him at the bar. I swear that place is his second home. I'm surprised they haven't named a bar stool after him."

I laughed. "Good point. I'll look for him there if he isn't home."

We loaded our bags into the trunk. All this talk about heart-to-hearts had me aching to have one with my mom. It didn't feel right to keep her in the dark about Dedrick.

I took my car key out, but didn't put it in the ignition just yet. "Mom, I need to talk to you about something."

"What, dear?"

I took in a breath and tried to remind myself that my mother did not share the same bloodlines of hate as my father and brother. But before I could get the words out, she asked, "Is this about your friend? The young man you're meeting tonight?"

I smiled. Moms always knew. "Yes. There's something I need to tell you about him."

"Is everything all right?"

"Everything is wonderful." I pulled my cell phone out of my purse. "If you choose to meet him, I'm sure you'll understand why."

"Why wouldn't I want to meet him?"

I clicked the little camera icon on my phone. "Well, here is a picture of him. His name is Dedrick."

She took the phone from me. I'd pulled up one of my favorite pics of Dedrick, a close-up that I'd taken while he watched a football game. Before I snapped the pic, he glanced my way with a smile that could light up the darkest room.

"Well?" I asked, unsure of what to expect from her. "What do you think?"

To my surprise, she said, "Nice looking young man. I love his gappy smile. Great teeth."

I tilted my head, mouth open. "Yes, you're right. He *does* have excellent teeth."

She smiled. "Well, if he makes you happy, I'm happy."

I paused, staring at my mom's pretty face, trying to peek into her mind. No disgust in her eyes, no signs of guilt about a daughter who loved outside her racial zone. I'd prayed for a moment like this, with the one person in my family who I felt would understand.

I let out a breath. "I can't tell you how relieved I am to hear that. I was hoping you would be okay with him being black. You are... *right?*"

"I'm not your father, Nel. I love you no matter who you date. As long as he treats you well."

"Thanks, Mom. You have no idea how much that means to me."

She stared out the window, deep in thought it seemed. "I've been thinking about what you said the other day. Do you really think I could find another man? At my age?"

"Are you kidding? As hot as you are?"

She frowned. "Penelope, I'm being serious."

"So am I! See, that's what I mean, Mom. You've spent so many years being put down and taken for granted that you don't even realize your own worth. Any man would be lucky to have you, Mom. Dad does *not* deserve you."

She sighed, a far-off look in her eyes, as if contemplating what life might have been like if she'd taken a different road. "I can't leave him now, though," she replied. "He's so sick."

"Like I said, put him in a home! He can be someone else's problem."

My lack of sympathy for the man who gave me life surprised me. In some ways, I was happy about the cirrhosis, especially if his death was the only way my mother could be free.

"Stop saying that about your father, Nel. Besides, those places cost money. Even if I wanted to, I couldn't afford it."

"Then come to California and live with me! Larry can take care of Dad."

"No, Nel. And, please! Stop it!"

I faced forward, resting my head against the seat, tapping the steering wheel. No more words. Not from me.

I started the car, backed up and headed home. I couldn't control my mouth very well, so we sat quiet for a moment.

Mom broke the silence when she asked, "Speaking of Larry, does he know about Dedrick?"

Mom sure knew how to change a subject. "No."

"Good. Keep that to yourself, honey."

My thoughts flashed back to Rick and his threat to out me to my brother. *I can't believe Rick actually thought he could blackmail me. What did he expect, that I'd just say "you win" and slide my panties off?*

"Do you remember what he did to that black boy?" Mom asked, breaking into my thoughts. "The one who was harassing you when you were in high school?"

"Of course, I remember." How could I forget an incident branded into my memory? Larry reminded me of it all the time. The boy had been a classmate of mine. Fifteen years old. I'd always blamed myself for what happened to him.

"I don't want your brother and Rick to try and do the same thing to your friend. Larry really did a number on that poor young man. Only thing I remember about him is what I saw when Larry pointed him out to me in a store one day."

Yes, they did a number on him, but Mom didn't know the whole story. I never told her what really happened. Never told anyone.

I didn't say anything, but I swear I was trying to crush the steering wheel under my hands. Mom made me realize I'd had enough.

I'm a grown woman. No more of anyone, especially a man, dictating how I lived my life. I was tired of being scared, wondering what Larry and Rick would do to Dedrick and all. What would Larry *really* do, anyway? Shoot his own sister?

Screw 'em. Both of 'em, damn it.

I shoved all fear aside. Why have it, anyway? No more worries, no anxiety, especially with Dedrick on the near horizon. I'd pop into the bar for a while to see Larry, hang out a bit, maybe ride the mechanical bull. Then I'd say goodbye to my brother and a one-fingered F-you to Rick. And if Rick decided to open his ugly mouth, I'd deal with it.

I'm not scared of those two anymore.

CB CB CB

After I packed up my things, I made my way to my father's bedroom. I promised Mom I'd try to make amends and didn't want to let her down. I knocked three times on the bedroom door. "Dad? It's me."

"What do you want?"

I should've known he'd throw a smart-ass remark. I opened the door. "I'm leavin' tonight. Just wanted to see you before I leave."

"Um."

Typical Dad reply. "Um" meant "yes," "no," or in this case, "okay." I figured that out as a kid.

Ignoring the onion smell, I asked, "So, how ya doin', Dad?"

He sneezed, then wiped his nose with a cloth. "Got damn cold fixin' to kill me."

Won't be the cold. "Mom bought more cough medicine."

"Um."

Adjusting his head against the pillow, he stared at highlights from a hockey game.

"Well, Dad, like I said, I'm getting ready to leave."

"Um. Goin' back to that earthquake state, are ya?"

"In a few days. Got some stuff to wrap up at the base before we head out."

No reply. We sat quiet, watching ESPN. I really had nothing to say to the old man, but I was trying. Part of me wanted to get up and run, but another part didn't want to disappoint Mom. Hell, a small part actually *did* want to put things on the table and clear the air, maybe click with him in some way.

A black man's face appeared in the upper left-hand corner of the TV screen next to a commentator. I recognized him as a ball player involved in a sexual assault case.

"Serves that nigger right. Lock 'em up, I say."

I shook my head. So much for finding common ground. He couldn't go five minutes without some I-hate-black people speech.

I couldn't hold my tongue any longer. "What is your problem with black people? Are you still mad about the black man they promoted over you? Dad, c'mon. That happened when I was what, eight?"

"Monkey wasn't qualified!" he cried. "We should go back to hangin' 'em, like we did in my day. That'll teach their uppity asses."

"Teach them what?"

"Teach 'em to stay in their place! This is a white man's world!"

White man's world? Yeah, right.

I glanced at the TV, watching how the "white man's world" crucified black men. Before dating Dedrick, I never understood this whole thing about the media lynching black men in a public forum. How the media became prosecutor, judge and jury all rolled into one. But the examples on TV always jumped out at me now. Once I became sensitized to the issue, I saw it everywhere.

I watched my father curse at the screen and thought he showed signs of senility; then I realized he acted the same way when I was a kid. Pathetic. He was stuck in some kind of Jim Crow time warp.

Racist rhetoric constantly spewed through cracked yellow teeth and chapped lips.

What good did all that jibber-jabber do? He should've been more concerned about how to stay healthy.

The more he rambled on, the less I saw him as my kin. All I saw was some sick fogey stuck in an ancient decade where black men and *all* women played second fiddle to the All Mighty Whitey.

"Dad," I said, trying to open his mind, "we live in a multi-ethnic society, now. Even our president is black."

"Ain't my president."

"Maybe so, but you see white-black couples all the time, especially in California. That's the world we live in now and I have no problem with it."

"I got a problem with it!" he yelled, his pink forehead so crumpled I could barely see his eyes. "Stay with yer own kind!"

"Whatever." I stood up. To hell with a peace talk. "People can be with 'another kind' if they want. Get used to it."

"What do ya mean 'get used to it?' " he asked with a phlegm-filled grunt. "You're not messin' around with a monkey, are ya?"

My fingers squeezed the doorknob, stifling a violent itch. I cracked the door.

"I told ya I'd kill ya if you let a monkey touch ya!"

I froze. Painful memories flooded my head—me standing in broken glass, his hand locked on my arm, me crying. He *had* said he'd kill me, and his threat followed me all through high school and into adulthood. What kind of father says that to his own child? And the saddest part of all? I knew he meant it.

But I didn't care anymore. My breathing sped up, same as the thumps inside my chest. "Well," I said, "I guess you'd better get your shotgun, *Dad*." I swear I saw the eyes of the devil.

"Ya little bitch! Git out! Don't you...you..." He coughed what seemed like a dozen times. I thought he was going to yak up a lung. Not my problem, though. I slammed the door and shut him out of my life.

Mom hurried to my side from the kitchen. "Nel, what—"

"You need to leave that asshole," I said, pushing past her. I grabbed my bag, determined to flee the toxic environment. "I'm outta here."

Mom followed me to the front door. "I'm so sorry, honey. I shouldn't have forced you to talk to him. I don't know what I was thinking."

I could still hear my father cursing up a storm. "Listen to him. Did you hear what he called me? I shouldn't have to put up with that kind of abuse and neither should you. I don't care how sick he is."

She looked down the hall, her gaze locked on the bedroom door. A tear slid down my mom's cheek. "So, he knows about your friend?"

"I didn't plan on saying anything, but he pushed the wrong button."

She nodded. "I guess I should've known it would come out sooner or later."

"It did." I hugged her. "I love you, Mom."

"I love you, too, honey."

Mr. Motor Mouth cut between us. "*Sharon! Git in here!*"

Mom released me. "I'm going to try and calm him down. You go on."

"Mom," I said, taking her hand, "please don't."

"It's okay, dear," she said, putting on a brave face. "I'll be fine. I can handle myself."

I searched her face. I'd never heard anything like that before. Not from her.

But a part of me didn't want to leave like this. I was escaping again and leaving Mom alone with a monster.

"Are you sure?" I asked.

"Yes, yes. Go on. I'll be just fine, really I will." We embraced again. "Thanks for coming home. It was good to see you."

"You, too." I pulled the front door open. "I'll call you when I get to the motel. And remember what I said about California."

She nodded. No words. Brave face still on.

Stepping outside into the dark, cold air nipped my bare face, colder than just an hour before. But it could have been the Ice Age and still wouldn't have cooled the flames feeding my spiteful conscience.

I started the engine and let it run. Shutting my eyes, I replayed dear old Dad's reaction the moment I planted the possibility of his daughter's retreat to the dark side. Literally.

I smiled. I felt good, strangely enough. Like I'd broken the power he had over me. All my life, a cloud of fear hovered over the females in the house. In Dad's twisted mind, anyone with a vagina equated to servant and dark skin meant less than human. Well, I showed him. He couldn't control what I do, who I see. *No* man had that kind of power. I could only hope Mom saw the light soon, too.

I checked the dashboard clock. I still had two hours before meeting Dedrick. Just enough time for a cold one and someone else to tell off.

Chapter 23

Penelope

"No thanks," I said over the voice of country singer Trace Adkins booming through the speakers. I leaned back against the bar, a can of Miller Lite in my hand. "Not in the mood to dance. I'm leaving in a bit, anyway."

"Ya sure? This song was made for backsides like yours."

I moved my head to avoid the potential suitor's Stetson hat. With his face inches from mine, I held my breath to block the Jeff Foxworthy look-alike's chew-polluted breath. "I'm fine right here. Thanks."

Unlike most men, he knew how to take no for an answer. After tipping his hat, he made his way onto the dance floor and joined the sea of oversized hats and cowboy boots, toe-tapping to the Honky Tonk Badonkadonk line-dance.

Nance, the bartender, set another beer in front of me. "That's what, the fifth guy you've shot down? Don't you wanna git out there?"

"Not really. Just came in for a coupla beers. Not lookin' for company."

"I hear ya," she said, wiping a glass. "Sometimes, I'd rather have a cold one than a stiff one, too. Easier to get rid of, if ya hear what I'm sayin'."

"I do," I said with a laugh.

I watched a dozen or so leather boots tap the wooden floor. I hadn't been to a honky tonk in a while. Cowgirls and cowboys in tight denim swayed to the rhythmic twang in the center of the dance floor, while couples two-stepped around the perimeter. Dedrick once said if a beat was a virus, white people *still* wouldn't catch it. I didn't agree. White people can move; we just dance to a different beat, that's all.

I was never much of a line dancer, but as I tapped my fingers on the stool next to me, humming the lyrics, I realized I missed my southern roots. Around Dedrick, I traded my CMT lifestyle for a little of his BET. But I had to admit, something about a good country song just soothed the soul. Had a way of bringing you back down to earth. I guess a part of me *did* miss the South.

Too bad Rick had to walk up and ruin the moment.

He slapped a ten-dollar bill on the counter. "Git me another one, Nance."

I felt a burn around my face. My stomach dropped, but I didn't say a word. Just stared ahead.

Rick nodded towards the dance floor. "S'prised you ain't out there."

I didn't reply. I listened to Tim Mcgraw because he had better things to say.

Looking past Rick to the pool table area, I saw a few guys standing around with sticks in hand chit-chattin', but no Larry. "Yer brother went out back for a smoke," Rick said, reading my mind. He inched closer, invading my personal space.

"You know Larry don't like you talkin' to me when he's not around," I said, putting some space between us. "Remember what happened the last time you tried to put your hands on me?"

Rick grinned. "I'm not tryin' ta cause no trouble, Nel. Thought I'd get a game a pool outta ya, that's all." He took a sip. "You already beat yer brother. I wanna play ya, too. Got a coupla balls I'd like you to knock down for me."

He laughed. I didn't. What the hell? He would not give up.

"What is wrong with you, really?" I set my beer on the counter. Nance had a front row seat to our little show.

"Nothin'. Just wonderin' 'bout our little 'rangement."

"Are you kidding? We never had an 'arrangement.' Get away from me. Pig."

Red flushed his face. "You little...so you're gonna keep screwin' that nigger boyfriend a yers?"

Nance walked away to attend to another customer. An old man seated a few seats down stared at me. Rick had said the N-word loud enough for everyone at the bar to hear.

"Whatever, jackass. You won't get any of this. *Ever.*"

"So ya won't do it?"

What an idiot. No wonder he dropped out after the ninth grade. "Let me make this clear since you obviously don't understand English." I leaned toward him. "I'd rather sleep with a donkey than you, you got that? Huh? Good. Now leave me alone."

Rick eyed me for a moment and I noticed a tic in his left cheek. I thought he would deck me, but instead he turned and walked away. "Donkey" was the best animal I could think of, but it worked.

I released the breath I'd been holding back. I finally did what I came to do—told Rick the Roach to kiss my ass. Damn, that felt good. Even better than telling off my father. I was on a roll.

Tail between his legs, Rick went back to his cubbyhole near the pool table. And right on cue, my brother reappeared from a back hallway with two other guys.

My cell phone buzzed against my waist. A text from Dedrick.

I'm about twenty minutes away. I wanna see ass and tits when I open the door!

Laughing, I finished my beer and gathered my things. Time to say goodbye to Larry and get back to my real life. As I buttoned my coat, Larry and I made eye contact across the bar. He stumbled toward me, bulldozing his way through the crowd. The nape of my neck tingled, like small pricks from a needle. I guess I'd tried to forget this moment would come.

Larry set his hand on the bar. Blood red colored the whites of his eyes. That always happened when he drank too much. This time, though, I don't think the red came from the alcohol.

"Who's this nigger Rick's talkin' 'bout?"

I didn't respond, just glared over his shoulder at Rick, a thumb tucked in his jeans, the other hand wrapped around his brew. He wore a satisfied smirk, clearly enjoying the scene about to unfold.

"You just couldn't keep my business to yourself," I said to Rick.

Rick shrugged, winked and knocked back a swig. Ugh, I *hated* him.

"What the fu—!" Larry screamed, slamming his beer bottle on the floor near my feet. The sound of broken glass triggered flashbacks. I stepped back, bumping the stool behind me. More heads turned to us.

"Is it true or not?"

Sprays of spit slapped my cheek. He leaned toward me, face twisted, eyes on fire.

I wiped my face with a napkin. "What I do in *my* life is *my* business!"

More heads turned. Larry paused for a moment, looking at my wrist. "Did the monkey give ya dat bracelet? Huh? Are ya messin' 'round with one er what?"

"Yup," Rick said. "Saw 'er ma' self, kissin' on 'im."

I rolled my eyes. Screw Larry and his toad friend. Who were they to question what *I* do? Yelling at me like I'm a damn eight-year-old. I didn't owe them any explanations. Hell no.

"You know what, Larry? I don't have to put up with this. If you don't want to say goodbye to your sister, then fine. I'm outta here."

Larry grabbed my arm. "Let go of me!" I pushed against his chest, knocking him backward into Rick.

"You little bitch!" Larry yelled, stepping in front of me, blocking my forward progress.

Bitch?

Déjà vu all over again—first Dedrick's sister, then my father and Rick. Now my own brother.

"Nel, I swear if I find out you're—"

"Well, it's true!" I shot back. "My boyfriend is black, all right? Happy, now?"

Jaws dropped. Tim Mcgraw still screamed in the background. Chatter echoed around me.

Larry's cries reduced to a blank stare. That look...like I'd sucked the soul out of him through his eyes. Embarrassed him in front of his hometown crowd.

Then it happened.

I never saw it coming, his palm slamming into my cheek. I stumbled against a table and fell to the floor, landing in a puddle of beer and broken glass. The contents of my purse spilled under a pool table. My brother had never hit me before.

210

Larry's voice became a clutter of noise, muffled by a sharp ring in my ears, pain shooting through my elbow. My head froze in a daze before I realized what happened actually *happened*.

Once my brain registered the fact I was lying on the floor, I rose to one knee, swiping hair away from my face. Two guys held Larry back as Rick looked on.

Nance appeared by my side and wrapped a towel around my bloody hand. "Are you all right, sweetie?"

I collected my belongings from the floor and shoved them back in my purse. "Yeah, I'm okay." She helped me to my feet. "Thank you."

Larry sat on a stool, his back against the wall while two of his friends tried to calm him down. Rick placed a hand on his shoulder and said something in his ear. I held my cheek, shot him a glare, but didn't say a word.

Spectators stood around me like flies, but other than Nance, no one else offered to help. Their eyes said I deserved it. I no longer belonged.

"No sister of mine's gonna be with some nigger!" Larry yelled, pointing at me. "Hey! Ya hear me?"

I ignored him. My feet couldn't carry me fast enough toward the door. They all became a blur; the front door became my escape.

I yanked out my keys. Bundled up in my coat, fast-walking through the parking lot, I found my car. Slipping into the comfort of peace and quiet once again, I placed my forehead on the steering wheel, trying to ease the rumble of my heart with deep breaths. A knot found a place in my throat. My strong woman front folded and tears finally slid down my cheeks.

I rubbed my face, still hot from Larry's attack, replaying the whole episode in some crazy slow motion haze—him confronting me, his hand across my face, me falling to the floor. And Rick's smug self lovin' it all.

I used to think an interracial fling wasn't worth it. Constantly having to defend myself. Standing up to idiots and their snide remarks, black and white. The stares. The hate. Confrontations.

But *they* had the problem, not me and Dedrick. I dried my tears. Larry and Rick didn't deserve the luxury of making me come apart.

I checked myself in the rearview mirror. Hair all over the place. Cheeks red, but no scratches. I decided not to tell Dedrick what happened. I'd handle it on my own.

As I finger-combed my hair, a loud screech alerted me to a truck speeding out of the parking lot, pebbles spitting into the air. It disappeared down the street.

I frowned. "Was that Rick's truck?"

Chapter 24

Terrell

I turned Lexy off. "Here we go."

Unstrapping my seat belt, I popped an Altoid and conducted my necessary pre-inspection. Wallet. Check. Car keys. Check. Breath. Check. I glanced at the mirror, smiled, then winked at the flawless face staring back.

Definite check.

Clicking the car remote, I stepped up the stairs that led to Tammy's apartment. Although the sun turned in for the night a few hours ago, lamps lit up the parking lot and sidewalks around each building. On the way in, I heard giggles. Two snow bunnies, all dolled-up for a night on the town, had turned the corner, blabbing away. When I came into view, they paused all flap, then flashed flirty smiles. I smiled back.

That's how I usually got 'em—the twinkle in my eyes, perfect teeth. They liked what they saw; I could tell. Tall, clean-cut brotha, GQ-ed in a sport-coat, button-down shirt, jeans. Bathed in Giorgio Armani cologne. But I hadn't put together my Fly Guy style for them, so I kept it movin', hoping Tammy would react the same way.

I stepped up another flight of stairs toward apartment 312. As I got closer, my heart kicked up a bit. I'd talked to Tammy twice since we made our date. After that B-ball game, Tammy kidnapped a bigger chunk of my mind, more so than when we first met. I thought about her all the time, night and day, like some hardwired daydream. Man, I thought I could play it cool, but apparently my nerves didn't get the memo.

When I reached her door, I knocked three times. A few seconds later, Tammy answered.

"Hello, Dr. Handsome," she said, reintroducing her dimples.

"Hey, sexy," I replied, my gaze stuck on her face. The same gold pendant lay around her neck, just above the plunging V-neck of her blouse. I felt a wiggle in my pants.

She wrapped her arms around my back. Our cheeks brushed against each other. Skin so warm. Man. Scent like a flower garden. I looked over a shoulder, peeked at her booty pressing Apple Bottom jeans. It occurred to me we'd never embraced before.

Cuter than ever, too, a slight contrast from the hoopster I saw a few days before. Hair parted in the middle, the ends caressing her neck and shoulders. Light on makeup, little lip gloss. A smooth touch.

She closed the door, then wrapped her purse around her jacket sleeve. "Thank you for picking me up. It's nice seeing you again, Terrell."

I smiled. "Good to see you, too." Like a gentleman, I extended my forearm. "Shall we?"

"Oh," she said, looking surprised. She cuffed her hand under my arm. "Yes. We shall."

And like that, I embarked on my test drive with Tammy, eager to figure out this itch I had for her. Part of me hoped we would last until the sun came up again.

We headed downtown. Tammy looked good sitting in my ride, an extra ingredient of sexy for my Lexy. We rapped about the work week, really feeling each other out on a formal level. As we talked, the butterflies in my gut subsided. She made it easy for me.

I parked in the Seaport Village lot, a tourist complex with good grub and steady entertainment near Coronado Bay. Patrons buzzed around shops and arcades, their hot fingers strapped to credit cards, no doubt. Tammy and I strolled by face painters and balloon sculptors, enjoying the carousel of weekend fun. A trumpet's seductive whine serenaded us, courtesy of a free jazz concert near the plaza. We headed to Edgewater Grill, a restaurant overlooking the bay.

"Not bad," Tammy said, staring at a ferry passing by. "I see you listened when I said I love the water. I can't believe I work right up the street and have never been here."

"First time for both of us," I said. "I'm just glad you like seafood."

She smiled at me. I smiled back. So far, a brotha was on point.

The hostess led us to a table on the patio. We had a postcard view before us, despite the big-ass plant by my seat. Folks came and went on the waterfront boardwalk. Lights were all around, from the sailboats near the Coronado Bridge, to the bright red, white and blue "76" on the USS Ronald Reagan, an aircraft carrier moored at the naval base across the bay.

The cool seawater breeze was just right and I was glad I'd reserved a patio seat. I helped Tammy remove her jacket before removing mine.

"Nice view, huh?" she said, reading my mind again.

"Yup. Glad I reserved this spot in advance."

"Good job. You get an A."

"Thank you."

Tammy "dimpled" me again. My "wiggle" turned into a growth spurt down below. I had to peel away my stare. Crazy what a smile can do to a man.

I ordered two glasses of Chardonnay and the Seafood Fettuccini. Tammy ordered a grilled Mahi Mahi. Our plates arrived within fifteen minutes.

"Is it good?" Tammy asked, between bites.

"Uh-hum," I replied, chewing. "Yours?"

"Yes. By the way, keep getting those nutrients. I don't want to hear any excuses when I beat you on the court next time."

I froze, my fork stuck in mid-air. "Oh, it's like that?"

Tammy nodded while sipping her wine. She eyed me, wearing a sly grin. Confidence. I liked that.

"I won't lie," I said. "You shocked me on the court. You got skills."

"Thank you. Felt good being out there again. I'd like to play more often." She did the shoulder-bob dance. "Yup, I still got it."

I chuckled. "Yes, you do. How's the knee?"

"It hurts a little. I don't know what I was thinking playing basketball after working out with you. It's a good thing I had a massage scheduled the next day."

"Yeah, I was sore, too. Can't lie. Hey, you said you messed up your knee in college, right?"

"Yeah. Tore a ligament. Boy, did it hurt. I ended up quitting the team because I couldn't compete at the level I wanted. I don't consider myself a quitter, so that was a particularly bitter pill to swallow."

"I hear you. You can still do your thing, though. I bet brothas trip off a fine woman posting them up on the court."

She nodded. "I get my share of propositions. My ex in Dallas would have a fit when I played. Even with no make up, baggy clothes and hair all tied up, he still had problems. Men have such weak egos. It wasn't about me showing my body or anything. I just wanted to play."

"Like my girl Sanaa Lathan in *Love and Basketball*, huh? Interesting."

Although I commented on B-ball, what I *really* wanted to hear more about was this dude in Dallas.

"So, this ex, how long have you been broken up? If you don't mind me asking."

"I don't mind. Close to a year. Like a fool, I spent way too long playing 'down ass chick' with him."

"What do you mean?"

"Well, for starters, he got fired from his job, but wasn't trying to find a another one." She shook her head. "Lazy ass."

"That's what broke you up? Him being lazy?"

"No, I broke up with him because he cheated. And I'm glad I caught his ass because I later found out he was part of some illegal arms ring, selling guns to ex cons."

"*What?* Are you *serious?*" I tried to keep my voice down.

"Yes, unfortunately. I haven't spoken to him since I left Dallas, but my friend Miki told me he got busted after a gun he had sold was used to kill his best friend."

"*Whaaaaaaat?*"

"Yup. *And* the girl he was messing around with got busted with him, too."

"*Whaaaaaaaaaaaaaaaaaat?*"

Tammy nodded, then took another bite from her plate.

"Dayum," I said, trying to recover. "Talk about a boomerang effect. A cheating, unemployed, arms dealer? No wonder you gave up on brothas."

She frowned. "What are you talking about? I never gave up on brothas."

"Aw, c'mon! You know Peter Brady was trying to claim ownership of you at the theater."

She rolled her eyes. "Oh, here we go. No, he was *not*." She swiped a strand of hair behind her ear. "Pssst, Peter Brady. You a fool. What, did it bother you?"

I paused. *Did it bother me?*

It did. No use denying it. No different than when I saw a black actress I'd loved for years on the arm of a white boy. Married to a brotha for a long time, divorced him, then she fled to the other side. It seemed to me she flat out gave up on brothas. Like Tammy.

As bad as I wanted to know if he hit it, I didn't go there. Not my business. Shoot, maybe I really *didn't* want to know.

After a short pause, I replied, "To be honest, a little."

Tammy tilted her head, then crossed her arms while leaning back against her seat. I felt an imminent attack.

"Now, ain't that the pot calling the kettle black! What about you, Mr. Jungle Fever? I do recall Betty Crocker under your arm!"

I cracked up. She had jokes. No attack. I felt relieved.

"I know, I know. You got me," I said. "It's a double standard. Most brothas don't want to see a fine sista jump the fence."

"Please, black men do it all the time. Though it's not entirely your fault. Women of all races throw themselves at brothas because you are the finest men on earth." She raised her index finger. "But! The one or two sistas I know who dated white men did it as a last, *last* resort. Black women are definitely more loyal. But where has loyalty gotten us? Alone."

To some degree, I agreed with her. Her tone was firm, but I never felt like I had to Bruce Lee a defense.

"Before I went out with Dale," Tammy continued, "I said to myself 'why not try it?' Especially after what you said at Sheryl's house. I was so pissed."

I dipped my head. "I know. I apologize again for that."

"Apology accepted, but I would like to know the story behind it. Why did *you* give up on *sistas?*"

I glanced at the people around the restaurant, smiling, laughing. A soft jazz melody wailed in the background. Amid the chatter, Tasha popped into my head—the rants, the yells, the over-the-top jealousy.

I told Tammy about Tasha and some of the other black females before her, and how Tasha was the last straw. After my psycho ex run-down, Tammy said, "Wow. You and I have more in common than I thought."

"Really? How's that?"

"Well, bad break-ups drove us to date outside our race. Like we just got fed up. We went about it in different ways, of course, but still."

I couldn't believe we were discussing such a hot topic so...calmly. "Damn, you're right. I never thought about that."

"Crazy coincidence, huh? Your last sista girl definitely seems like a difficult woman, though. You were a good man to put up with her."

"And you were a good woman to put up with Mr. Arms Dealer."

She shrugged. "Yeah, I guess I was."

Again, Tammy surprised me. I expected her to chastise me for using my history with sistas as an excuse to ban *all* sistas. Instead, she found another link between us.

I said, "You know, I guess a part of me kinda believed the hype that white women are easier to deal with."

"Do you still think that?"

"I mean, not really. Every woman has their issues. Doesn't matter the race. I guess I was experimenting, seeing what the fuss was about. Saw Dedrick with a white girl and being all happy about it, so I said the same thing as you did—'what the hell?' "

"And you see all these celebrity brothas, too, huh? Walking around with white women."

"Yeah."

"You was just being a man trying to sample another flavor."

I nodded. "Pretty much."

"Well," she said, wiping her cheek with a napkin, "I understand people have their favorites, but I hope you realize Tasha was the exception, not the rule. And even though you had so-so experiences with other black women, it doesn't mean we're *all* like that. We just want to be treated with respect and be loved, you know? We already have to deal with the media portraying us as bitches; we don't need brothas beating us down, too."

"I feel you." Crossing my arms, I mocked the same on-guard pose she still held. "What about you? You don't think *all* brothas are jacked up, do you?"

Tammy stared...so damn focused...her gaze digging into me, but no reply. Instead, she dug a fork in her food, then slid it through her lips...slow. Sipped wine while gaping at me, a spark in her eye. Sneaky, but sexy.

I really didn't know how to react, though. Tammy made it hard to read her, but a few seconds later, the rise of her plump red lips creased her soft brown cheeks.

Then she leaned forward and said, "Well, doctor, I'm here with you now, aren't I?"

I smiled. "Yes, you are!"

So slick, this woman. We chuckled, sipped on more Chardonnay, stole glances at each other. I liked what I saw every time.

As we sank into a new groove, I realized my comfort with her. I sensed a strange kind of warmth, one I hadn't felt in a while. Damn...*ever*.

Time ticked on, but I didn't notice. Plates wiped clean, replaced by two strawberry cheesecakes. One glass of Chardonnay turned into two more for each. People around us became ghosts of the night. Except for a few couples, we held it down alone.

Man. The devil in me sparked. My mind became a playground, first molding PG-13 snippets of her, then full-length X-rated video clips with me as co-lead.

But I also recycled other moments with her. Like when we embraced, her cheek pressed against mine. The smell of her. The first time I experienced that deadly smile at Sheryl's house. Even our time in the gym...I remembered how my gaze wandered, appraising her prime real estate while getting our "swoll" on. Body of an athlete, sculpted by years of dumbbells and a knack for handling the ball.

Tammy went on about her friend Miki back in Dallas. Part of me lost track of her words, though. I blame the curve of her breasts.

And those freakin' dimples. Was I drunk? No, no, I didn't need alcohol to ignite my fire. Had to be the lips…like ripe strawberries. I saw myself absorbing the leftover taste of wine left on her tongue.

In no time, I became a man of steel.

But I played it cool, smiled, nodded as she spoke. A brotha couldn't stand for at least five minutes, though.

After destroying our cheesecakes, Tammy offered to pay half the bill, but I refused. With more small talk, I bought myself a few extra minutes to "deflate." Then Tammy and I stood and stretched, my bones popping. We'd chained ourselves to the seats for a little over two hours.

While donning her jacket, Tammy turned to the water and said, "I'd love to see how far this boardwalk goes."

"Me, too. Let's find out."

Chapter 25

Terrell

We strolled at a snail's pace, my hands cuffed behind my back. I loved how the bay looked at night. Calm waters smoother than sheet glass, lights flickering off soft waves like a sea of pearls. I usually found this kind of scene on local San Diego magazine covers and in art galleries.

As Tammy and I conversed about the view, a cool ocean breeze blew around us, the air soaked in the bay's salty scent. Peaceful around here. We stood a world apart from the party-til-you-drop jungle of the Gaslamp Quarter, the main artery of downtown, packed with bars, nightclubs and X-rated shops. I understood why Tammy loved the Feng Shui qualities of water.

Dude in a bike cab eased toward us. Tammy and I stepped onto a patch of grass, giving the couple riding in the small carriage some room.

As they rode by, Tammy asked, "Hey, am I walking crooked?"

"Doesn't look like it. Why?"

"Wooo," she said, blinking, "I think that wine is kicking in." She linked her arm through mine. "What, I had like *three*? Please don't let me fall in the water."

We angled around an older couple. "I'm watching you, so don't worry. You're safe."

She blessed me with a grin. Tingles spread through my belly and I sensed the chemistry of a Harlequin moment. I could see the light brown hue of her eyes. Lips curved like wings, only a taste-test away.

But I punked out. Turned my head forward and followed the cobblestone path.

Damn. Why am I so nervous? Never had a schoolyard crush like this on anyone in my vanilla-coated assembly line.

We headed toward Embarcadero Park, a small grassy area in front of the sky-high Marriott hotel. San Diegans of all flavors wore their chill hats, some lying in the grass, others wrapped in a lover's delight on park benches, staring at the water. I noticed Tammy stroke her pendant and realized I'd seen her do it a few times before.

I asked, "Is that pendant a good luck charm? You like touching it."

"You can say that."

We stopped for a moment and she flipped it open. A clean-cut gentleman held a little girl's ankles as she perched on his shoulders. The oval-shaped photo seemed too small to contain their hi-beam smiles. No one could mistake who DNA'd Tammy's dimples.

"Look at you, all cute and stuff. Your dad?"

She nodded, still staring. "My favorite picture of us."

Tammy seemed rapt in the mini pic, almost cut off from the world around her. I let her have a moment with her father.

She looked up. When our stares connected, *I* became cut off from the world. The short space between us presented another opportunity to savor her flavor. But I held back the impulse. *Again.*

"Um, yeah," I said, breaking my gaze. "I see why. You were a little heart breaker, I bet."

Tammy shook her head. "I'm sure that was *you*." She closed the pendant, winking at me.

I grinned. We continued our slow motion by the ocean. Curious, I asked, "So...what was your father like?"

"My father?" She paused, then said, "He was a good man. Funny as all get out, always making me laugh. I just loved being around him. My mother passed away when I was a baby, so he was pretty much all I had."

"I'm sorry. I had no idea."

"It's okay. He did his best to keep her memory alive for me. Dad was always telling me stories about her and stuff. He adored my mother. Shoot, worshipped her. He never remarried."

"Really?"

"Yeah. In nineteen years, I can't remember him having a meaningful relationship with another woman. He once swore to me no one would ever take her place." She sighed. "That's old-school black love for you. Seems like you don't see that anymore."

I lowered my head. In a sense, I felt somewhat at fault for the so-called collapse of black love. After Tasha, a black woman couldn't even *pay* me for conversation, much less blocks of my time. I'd deemed them "too this, too that," none of them worthy of my devotion.

But Tammy? In a league of her own.

Before I expressed my thoughts, Tammy said, "I know I'm partly to blame. I was tired of all the negative mess about black men, so I said, 'eff 'em. White men have to be better than this. Let me call Dale.' So we went out and had a great time, but...I don't know... ultimately, it just didn't feel right. Does that sound racist?"

225

"No, no," I replied, staring at the Coronado Bridge. Its lights stole my gaze for a second. "You just weren't comfortable with him. Interracial dating can be hard. Believe me, I've had my share of uncomfortable moments."

"I bet. I also felt guilty about how I was stereotyping *all* black men. I mean, by doing that, I lumped my father into the same category as my ex and all these other tired, lazy, no-goal havin' Negroes. But all black men aren't the same. I'd forgotten that."

That hit my heart. Truth resonated in her statement. So easy to lump us into messed-up categories, as she said. Most black men don't audition for the nightly news crime report.

But that's what *I* had become—a judge of black women with one glance. I was just as ignorant as that racist old man who'd spat on my competence with one glance of my brown skin.

"You know, I'm guilty of the same thing," I confessed. "I said a lot of mess about sistas, too; you already know that. But...I was wrong. *Way* wrong."

"How so?"

Go for it, man. Now. "Because none of the women I've dated come close to having what you've got going on, black *or* white."

She smiled. Dimples...boy, damn. Killed me every time.

We stood face to face again. I couldn't take it anymore. I stared so deep I swear I scorched my hunger for her into those pretty brown eyes. My gut tingled, but I refused to detach from this moment. I leaned toward her and dove in. The scene around me... it all faded away.

Tammy didn't resist.

I tasted Chardonnay. Our mouths grooved like two hips grinding to a slow-dance. Loved the bubblegum-smack melody our lips made. Been a while since I savored lips as thick as mine.

226

I slid my hand down her sleeve and locked our fingers. As our tongues bathed each other, tingles became jolts that shot though my belly and inflamed my loins. It didn't take long for the hard effect to press my pants.

Our lips parted. "Damn, boy," Tammy said. Her eyes seemed to roll in the back of her head. "I've been wanting to do that all night. I didn't know it would be like that, though! What are you trying to do to me?"

I chuckled. "Just trying to get a little taste of what I've been missing."

"Oh, is that right?"

I didn't answer. Again, our lips met. My tongue probed for leftover zest I might have missed the first time. After about thirty seconds of Heaven, I came up for air, then replied, "Yup."

She buried her face in my chest, giggling. Her hair tickled the tip of my nose. When she raised her head, my lips grazed her temple. And that's when I saw her walking toward us, one of my one night hit-it and quit-its. Christy, the same Barbie I took to the movies the night I saw Tammy with what's-his-face.

I cursed under my breath. Tammy gave me an odd look, then turned around to see what made my eyes swell. Christy killed my natural buzz the moment she pulled her magic trick and appeared out of nowhere, but I chilled. No need to feel all flushed over an old blip on my female radar screen.

"Well," Christy said, walking up with a shorthaired marshmallow, "now I know why you didn't call me back."

Man. Just my luck I'd run into a been-there-done-that. My heart picked up a notch, but I kept my nerves in check. I felt Tammy sizing me up, probably wondering what I'd do or say, so I put my arm around her.

"Hey, Christy. Good to see you."

"Well, apparently, not *too* good," Christy said, while her hair blew in front of eyes that I knew despised what they saw. "I guess you got what you wanted from me, huh?"

Christy's friend stood in the background, tugging her arm. Still trying to play smooth, I said, "Christy, this is my date Tammy. Tammy, Chr—"

Whack! "I never should've gone out with you! Prick!"

I didn't just see stars; I saw the whole solar system for a split-second. Senses all jacked up. I didn't know a woman's hand could move so fast and hit so hard.

Christy's friend dragged her away as she screamed at me. She topped off her retreat with a one-fingered salute. Shocked, I stared at them as they walked away, my mouth like an open manhole. I rubbed my cheek while suppressing the part of me that begged to get all 300 on that ass. Out of the corner of my eye, I could see Tammy struggling to keep her smirk from turning into a full-blown laugh-a-thon.

A couple with two kids walked by. One of the little boys looked at Christy, then back at me, eyes wide like he saw the greatest thing ever. People lying in the grass near us had no problem figuring out the asshole Christy was yelling about.

"Well, well, well," Tammy said, "as you can see white females can act the fool, too." She pulled away from me, crossing her arms. "You know, you have an interesting effect on the women you go out with."

Tammy was right; I sure did know how to pick 'em. Embarrassed, I tried to regain some composure. "Yeah, I guess I do. Damn. Only went out with her once."

"It looks like you made quite an impression."

I took in a big breath, blew it out. Like many of the other one-nighters, I got what I wanted and never called her back. "I knew she liked me and I pretty much dissed her. I guess I deserved that."

Tammy nodded. We stared across the water, the breeze brushing against our faces. Cool air massaged my hot cheek, easing away the pain.

Tammy said, "Well, at least you can admit you were wrong. I was checking to see if you'd raise a hand to her, but you didn't. Good on you." She paused, then said, "I feel her, though. Sometimes you men deserve to get smacked up. I think every woman has felt like her at some point."

"Yeah," I said, sliding my hands in my pockets, the sting in my face fading. "Can't argue that."

I watched the waves crash against the rocks. Saw two teenagers sitting on the bottom of the embankment, lips glued to each other. I enjoyed that same moment with Tammy just minutes before. Now I felt like my time with her was doing the same as the waves—crashing.

But being the Queen Bee of surprises, Tammy cuffed her arm under mine, continued our stroll and said, "Little Miss Mop and Glow got some heat behind that swing, huh?"

"What?" I cried. "Did you just call her *Mop and Glow*?"

"Yes. I remember her from the movie theater. Big head, long stringy hair and a tooth pick for a body? Dale and I thought she kinda looked like a mop."

I think the whole 619 area code heard me roar. Tammy did the same. Mop and Glow. So wrong, but *high*-larious.

With us doubling over from laughter, we rode over the speed bump Christy had placed between Tammy and me. The two of us

229

kept it movin', left it all behind. That's what I liked about Tammy...
well...among so many other things. She could flip a tense situation
into a comedy show and look fine as hell while doing it. I wanted
to hold steady on her frequency, definitely not willing to switch
channels on her just yet—as long as she allowed me to stay tuned
in.

As we continued our quest to reach the end of the boardwalk,
arms interlocked, then holding hands, I realized running into
Christy symbolized a death to old ways. Nothing in me yearned
to make Tammy another notch in my belt, despite the little head
trying to convince my big head to bend Tammy over tonight. I
saw her as much more than booty to conquer on the first date. I
wanted to dig deeper into her *mind*, not between her legs. Not yet,
anyway.

We walked until we reached our destination. I had to work in
nine hours, and I noted a few yawns from her, so I took Cinderella
home. Of course, I endured more jokes about Christy bitch-
slapping the black off me, but it was all good, all in fun.

We got to Tammy's door, her hand in mine. The bulge in my
pants was like a crouching tiger, hidden dragon ready to pounce on
its next victim. I tried to use Jedi-mind tricks to chill my little man
of steel, but with Tammy's jelly teasing to get up on it, he pushed
forward against my zipper. Though I longed to handle my business
like a man should, I held strong and said, "Tammy, I had a great
time with you tonight."

"I did, too," she said, her dimples forcing another wiggle under
my belly button. "A very nice time."

"That's good. I would love to come in and all, but I have to
work."

"Whoa, slow down, Action Jackson." She crossed her arms, tightened her forehead. In a true sista stance, she said, "What makes you think I was inviting you in?"

Oops. "I mean, I...um...I was just saying, uh—"

"Spit it out, doctor!"

I let out a hearty chuckle. "What I'm *trying* to say is...well... I think you're special. I really like spending time with you. I just don't want to ruin anything by coming in and maybe moving too fast, you know."

"Oh, okay." She nodded. "I respect that. I think you're special, too. But don't get it twisted. I wasn't going to invite you in, anyway. Not tonight."

"Okay, then. Guess that's settled. Fine."

"Fine, then!"

"Fine!"

We watched each other, waiting to see who could hold it together the longest. Then we blew up at the same time. Damn, we acted so much like pre-teens, all crushed out on each other.

She placed a hand on my shoulder, steadied her balance. "Woo, I think I'm still a little tipsy," she said. "I'm gonna sleep good tonight."

I took her hands in mine once again, rekindled the feel of her soft brown skin, pulled her to me. "Oh, really? Well, before you do that, I need to do something real quick."

Our lips danced to a familiar melody, one I could groove to all night. My tongue in her; her tongue in me. Perfect symmetry. Prickly little tingles around my body amplified, skipping down the back of my neck, my chest, my gut—everywhere. Before long, I truly thought my zipper would no longer contain the dragon within the cage of my pants.

"All right, now," Tammy said, pulling away and looking down. "Somebody down there has a real hard head, pokin' my stomach and everything."

"Oh, my bad," I said, backing away, but not at all embarrassed. "Better roll before Superman busts through."

"You crazy. Superman." We kissed one last time, one more taste for the road. Then parted ways.

As I walked toward the steps, I said, "I'll call you tomorrow. Maybe we can work out again."

"I'd like that," Tammy replied, dimple-lating me. She pulled her keys out of her purse. "I have a writing class in the morning, but I'm free after that."

"Cool. Have a good night."

"You, too."

She waved. I watched as she walked in, her jelly taking a few seconds longer to disappear than the rest of her body. Then she closed the door, the image of her burned in my head now, swimming in a sea of fantasies I hoped would come true. One part of me damn sure couldn't wait. But that would all come later, naturally, not forced. The way it should be.

As I descended to the bottom level, the floral scent of Tammy now a part of me, I thought about my partner Dedrick. Man, oh, man. I knew he would love to hear about this.

Chapter 26

Penelope

"Damn it! Where is he?" I cried, wearing a hole in the rug. I surveyed the motel room for the billionth time. Traces of Dedrick lay everywhere—two gym bags at the foot of the bed, bottle of cologne on the bathroom sink, Styrofoam carton of food on the nightstand. Even the TV was still on. But no Dedrick. His cell phone was on the dresser with three missed calls from me. That really got me scratching my head.

But seeing his rental car sitting empty in the parking lot disturbed me more than anything. Where could he have possibly gone *on foot*? Damn it. I know I'd taken longer than expected, but he knew I was on the way. If I hadn't stopped at a hole-in-the-wall store to get a pack of beer for him I would've gotten here sooner.

I glanced in the mirror. My face was so twisted, half-buried under strands of hair. In and out of the cold had left a red and pink tint, but I still looked like that woman smacked to the ground less than an hour ago.

I'd hoped Dedrick's presence would abolish that painful episode out of my head, if only for tonight. But no. There I stood, kicking the nightstand. Alone.

I needed answers. Like right now.

I stepped outside into the winter air and headed for the lobby. The clerk at the front desk hadn't helped much the first time I'd questioned her, but I was going crazy in that room. Someone had to know something.

The clerk looked up from her magazine when I entered. "Hello again. Did you find your friend?"

"No, I didn't," I snapped. "Are you sure he didn't leave a message for me?"

She flipped through a small Rolodex. "Let me see...room 128. Dedrick Davis. African-American gentleman, right?"

I nodded.

"Um...no, I'm sorry." She adjusted her glasses. "No other messages. Just the one saying you could have a key to his room."

I beat the counter with my fist. Unstable nerves made my face twitch.

I swiped hair from my eyes and said, "I'm sorry. He's my boyfriend. I'm just a little frustrated." *Where the hell is he?*

"I understand. If my boyfriend wasn't here, I'd be mad, too."

My slight chemical imbalance subsided somewhat with her show of empathy, so I adjusted my tone. But before I could apologize, she said, "It's been pretty quiet around here tonight. Well, with the exception of those drunks in the pick-up truck."

I thought my chest would cave in. "What pick-up truck?"

"Silver Dodge. These guys drove up about fifteen minutes ago, making all kinds of noise. Then they went tearing out of here in an awful hurry. They almost sideswiped my car on the way out. Damn hillbillies."

Her words faded somewhere around "fifteen minutes ago." I took a step back, reeling. *Silver Dodge?* Couldn't be. How?

I hightailed it back to the room. Grabbing my cell phone, I dialed the only number that made sense.

Larry picked up after the second ring. "Hey sis. How ya doin'?"

"Where is he?"

"Where's who? Speak up. Can't git what ya sayin'."

"Damn it, Larry, stop messin' around! Is he with you or not?"

I heard chuckles in the background and the faint voice of Travis Tritt on the radio. Larry was still in the truck with Rick. He had to be.

"Larry?"

"Oh, sorry 'bout that, sis. Rick was shuttin' up that pet monkey we just picked up."

Every muscle in my jaw malfunctioned. I couldn't speak, couldn't move. That kind of audacity shoved me onto deadly terrain with muddy surfaces. I had no idea what lay ahead, paralyzing my will to fight.

"Larry...please tell me he's all right," I said, now struggling to talk. "Please."

More laughter. This whole thing was nothing to them; just two country boys hunting for new game. "Oh, ya mean...Deidre?" Larry's voice was slurred. "Uh, Deer...drick? That his name?" He chuckled. "Couldn't understand him much. Slang and all."

I swallowed. "His name is *Dedrick*. Did you do anything to him?" My voice cracked.

"C'mon, sis. He's all right. Just tryna git 'quainted. Me and Rick wanted to show our new friend here 'da hood.' " Drunken laughter filled my ears.

I grabbed my purse and headed to my car. "Let me speak to him."

235

"Aw, ya can't do that. He's a little tied up right now."

My stomach sank further. I couldn't tell a sick joke from the truth. Stabbing my key in the ignition, I kicked the engine to life. "Larry, Christ! You'd better let him go right now or I'm calling the cops!"

No response. A little chatter on the radio. That's it.

Then Larry said, "Wouldn't do that, sis." His voice was so calm. Nonchalant. "Call the cops and yer nigger friend might be wearin' a new neckpiece when they find 'im."

"You...if you hurt him, I...ugggh!" I threw the phone. It bounced off the glove compartment, then fell on the mat.

I drew in deep breaths, trying to avoid a colossal breakdown. Tears filled my eyes.

This can't be happening. Dear God, this cannot be happening.

My mind flashed through a series of horrific scenarios. While I didn't want to believe Larry and Rick would hurt Dedrick, I'd lived in the South long enough to know that hatred was an ugly, unpredictable thing. Not too long ago drunk rednecks strapped a poor black man to a truck and dragged him to his death.

My stomach turned. No more Dreamland; this was real. As I raised my head, wiping away wet stains from my face, my bracelet brushed my lips.

I reached for the phone and dialed Larry's number again.

Larry answered. "There ya are. Lost ya for a sec."

I strapped on my seatbelt. "All right, you win. No police. Now, what do you want? What is this about?"

"Awww, don't play dumb. I git it! Ya got me more bait to skin!"

"Huh? What are you talking about?"

"It felt good kickin' that boy's teeth in," Larry said. "When was that, Rick? Ten, fifteen years ago?" I heard more laughter. "We git ta do it again!"

My bottom lip fell, chest on the verge of imploding. I'd figured out his plan. The "boy" he was talking about was Damon, my former high school classmate. The one my brother and Rick had ambushed years ago. In Larry's eyes, Dedrick had become another Damon.

And I still had no idea how they'd found him.

"We're almost there, sis. Ya know the spot, so hurry up. We'll save a front row seat for ya."

He was right—I *did* know the spot. As much as I'd tried to banish the memory, it all rushed back to me. I'd vowed never again to return to the scene of the crime, but Larry was determined to drag me down memory lane.

I threw the car into reverse. "I'm on my way. Don't do anything until I get there."

Chapter 27

Penelope

I parked behind Rick's truck and shut down the engine. Street lamps granted the only source of light as I pounded the pavement toward the house. I wore a thick coat, nothing for my hands or face, but couldn't worry about that now.

Mom and Dad were already asleep, unconscious to the crimes committed in their own backyard. I opened the side gate, my heart on a warpath. Tip-toeing across the grass, my hands reached out for the fence to guide me through the thick black of night. Despite my blind trail, I knew this route well.

I finally reached the shed in the backyard and heard hushed voices inside. Hinges creaked as I opened the door. A weak trace of moonlight crept in with me, casting light on the scene inside.

I stopped the door midway, then gasped, falling into some kind of full-body arrest. My eyes and brain refused to sync together, muddled by the surreal scene in front of me—straight from the pages of a Stephen King thriller.

What was I thinking to not call the police?

Rick stood in the back corner, gripping a shotgun, the barrel pointed at Dedrick's head. I couldn't see my baby's hands.

"Close the door," Larry said, his frame like a shadow a few feet from Dedrick. He held a flashlight. "Hurry up."

I reached for the door and shut it behind me. Streams of outside light shrank, until Larry's flashlight was the only thing left, its glow now on Dedrick. As my eyes adjusted in the dark, I noticed his legs stretched across the oil-stained concrete floor, back against the wall. Black tape reached from ear-to-ear across his mouth and wrapped around his ankles. His wrists were banded with rope.

They had tied him down like a got damn slave.

"Welcome to the party," Rick said, now a silhouette.

I tried to calm my shivers while scraping bits of inner strength together. As much as my body throbbed to reach out to my love, I held back. No sudden moves. Didn't want to give Rick any reason to accidentally-on-purpose pull the trigger.

But I had to get Dedrick outta there. And *fast*. I just didn't know how.

"Rick, please. Get that gun away from his head."

"What for?" he asked, his face masked by the black. "Scared of a lil' monkey brain gittin' on ya? Already cracked his head with the butt end of this here shotgun." He laughed.

"Please," I repeated.

"Do it, man," Larry said.

I heard a snicker, then saw the barrel rise. It now pointed toward the ceiling. My sighs dissolved into an icy fog of exhaled breath.

Larry pointed the flashlight in my direction, blinding me. I raised a hand in front of my face.

"Tell 'im why we're here," Larry said. "Tell 'im 'bout our little game, Nel."

I shook my head. Tears bubbled. "Stop it, Larry! And get that light out of my face. Please!"

"Why, sis? You're in the spotlight! Tell da monkey 'bout what happens to guys like him that touch my sister."

239

I didn't answer. Silenced by shame.

"Let me help ya out." Larry knelt down next to Dedrick, shining the light in his face. Dried blood was caked on the side of his cheek and neck. I saw a large gash above his ear.

"Ya see, boy," Larry continued, "when Nel was in high school, there was this black kid who used ta always mess with her. He was 'bout fifteen, sixteen years old, tryin' ta git a taste of some vanilla ass, know whatta mean?"

"Yeah," Rick chimed in, "you know y'all like white meat."

Warm tears slid down my cheeks. I hugged myself tighter, the shaking like one big rumble now, my teeth clamping down on each other. I couldn't tell if the trembles came from anger or the frigid air.

The cold didn't seem to bother Rick or Larry one bit. They had *become* the cold, like the steel that encased the hate in their black hearts.

"Larry," I said, eyes flooding, "Please. If you—"

"Hold on a sec." He pointed the light at me. "I'm tryin' ta tell a story."

Then he told Dedrick everything...

When I was in high school, I had a secret crush on this black boy named Damon. He was in my Algebra class, and we would sometimes hang out in the school library where he'd help me with word problems, being a math whiz and all. We'd also talk about books, movies and how we planned to get the hell out of Starkdale after graduation. I liked him. Damon was my friend.

But when Rick saw us talking in the school parking lot one day, he told Larry. I was so afraid of what my brother would do, I threw my friend under the bus. My father had already warned me what would happen if I let "one of them" touch me. Figured Larry would make do on my dad's promise.

"What's this I hear about you hangin' out with some black kid?" Larry had asked.

Like a coward, I replied, "I wasn't hangin' with nobody. That boy keeps following me around. You know I would never let some nigger touch me."

I had no idea my cowardice would set in motion an unspeakable horror.

Rick somehow convinced Damon I liked him so much I wanted him to take my virginity—in this shed, of all places. So Damon, an innocent black kid stirred by teenage hormones, came to the shed alone one afternoon shortly after school...thinking he'd get laid.

Rick had dangled a carrot in front of Damon and Larry did the same to me. I arrived home from school when Larry greeted me, saying he had a present for me in the shed. Initially, I was ecstatic. Someone had stolen my bike the week before and I assumed Larry had found it. But my joy died the moment he opened the shed.

Damon lay on the concrete floor, beaten, bloodied, crying. While balled up in a fetal position, clutching his chest and stomach, I could see fear burned in his eyes.

I couldn't speak. Larry grabbed my hand, pulling me toward Damon. Larry knelt down next to him and said, "See her, boy? That's my sister." He pointed at him, poking his forehead. "If you *ever* follow her around again, I'm gonna bury your black ass under this shed, got it?"

Damon nodded. Tears mixed with the blood that covered his face. "And you ain't tellin' nobody 'bout this, right?" Rick said. "'Member what I said I'd do to your family?"

241

Again, Damon nodded. Then they let him go.

Damon never told anyone what really happened and he never spoke to me again. Since then, I could never shake away my guilt, knowing I played a part in Damon's assault. If I hadn't befriended him, and then lied about it, Damon wouldn't have ended up with a broken eye socket.

Deja vu. Nearly fifteen years later, we all stood in the same spot, playing the same "game." And again, I was the bait. Just like before, I held a robotic stance, not knowing what to do, what to say.

"Can't tell ya how much fun that was!" Larry said as he finished his graphic recap.

"We shouldn't a let him go so easy, though," Rick said. He leaned toward Dedrick. "But, we ain't makin' the same mistake again. *Boy.*"

"Got that right," Larry said.

"Stop!" I cried.

"Shhhh, keep your voice down, sis. Don't wanna wake up the folks."

I stepped forward. "*Are you serious?* Don't wanna wake...no! Stop it, now!"

Wiping my cheeks with the back of my hand, I said, "Larry, enough is enough. Like it or not, I love this man. What does it matter if he's black?"

Larry paused for a second, staring like a man unsure what to do or say next. Rick tapped the shotgun barrel in the palm of his hand.

"Told ya, man," Rick said.

"Shut up," Larry snapped.

Larry stepped over Dedrick's legs and came toward me until we stood face to face. He reeked of whiskey.

"Sonofabitch," he said, turning his anger on me. "You *are* with this primate, ain't ya? Don't you remember what me and Dad said we'd do to you?"

They drew closer, cornering me in front of a small window, blank faces like zombies in the dim light. I reached behind me and wrapped my fingers around the handle of a shovel, preparing myself to come out swinging, kin or no.

"Rick," I said, "since we're revealing secrets, why don't you tell Larry about what *you've* been doing behind his back?"

Larry turned to Rick. "What the hell she talkin' 'bout?"

"Nothin', man. She ain't sayin' nothin'."

"Oh really?" I said, fixing my glare on Rick. "Afraid to tell him about the deal? You know, trying to blackmail me into sleeping with you? 'Larry doesn't have to know about it,' remember?"

We stood still. Dead silence...except for crickets chirping somewhere in the shed. Nothing burned my brother more than a Benedict Arnold. Especially when the traitor was family or a "best" friend.

"That true, man?" Larry asked, stepping toward Rick. "Huh? You still tryin' to mess around with my sister? You did this behind my back *again*?"

Rick backed up. I noticed Dedrick trying to loosen the rope around his hands, so I added fuel to the fire, keeping the focus on me.

"You know it's true, Larry," I said. "Just think of all the crap he's done behind your back over the years. You know how sneaky he is."

"She's lyin', man," Rick said. "Ya gonna take the word of this little whore over—"

Larry shut Rick up with a fist to the mouth, knocking him back against a metal cabinet. The shotgun fell to the floor.

Rick lunged at Larry, knocking the flashlight out of his hand. The flashlight cut off when it hit the ground, but I could still see a little from the moonlight shining through the window. They stumbled over a lawn mower and fell to the floor, disappearing into the pitch black of night somewhere in the corner of the shed.

Finally, I had my chance.

I rushed to Dedrick's side and ripped the tape from his mouth, then tried to loosen the rope around his wrists. "I'm so sorry," I said, fumbling with the knot. "I'm so, so sorry. Are you okay?"

Dedrick looked out of it, but wiggled his hands, pulling the rope. He winced and said, "W-w-we need to get outta here. I— Nel!"

"Arrgh!" I cried. My head and neck snapped back, a clump of my hair wrapped in a tight fist.

"C'mere, bitch!" Rick grunted.

My elbows scraped the floor as he pulled me backward. I kicked the shotgun while struggling, but couldn't reach it, couldn't see it anymore. I grabbed Rick's wrist, digging my nails into his hand. Didn't work, so I reached back, gripping his nuts as hard as I could.

"Awww!"

He pulled my head down. In the blur of it all while clawing at him, he pinned me down. The full weight of him now on my pelvis, crushing me. As he slammed my wrists against the pavement, my knuckles brushed against something...didn't know what at first. Then I realized I was hitting the shin of my brother's still body. Didn't know if he was unconscious or dead.

"Get off me! Get—"

He cuffed his hand over my mouth, my lips pressed against his salty palm, muffling my ability to dig my teeth into his filthy skin. In the faint streak of light that filtered in through the window, I saw his face—twisted, evil—a man determined to force his will on me.

"I'm tired of you telling me no, Nel," he said, unbuckling his belt with his free hand. "If you can spread 'em for that nigger, then ya gonna spread 'em for me!"

His face was inches from mine, beer breath stinging my nostrils. He had me. Trapped. I tried to wiggle away, kick, move, scream— anything. But I couldn't budge, though. Not with someone close to three hundred pounds on top of me.

Part of me couldn't believe what was happening. There I was, in a cold shed, my brother dead or unconscious…my boyfriend beaten and shackled…and Rick…on top of me, yanking my legs apart, finally trying to reclaim what he always thought was his.

But I wasn't going to let him take it without a fight. I pulled an arm free, then slashed him across the face. "Ugh!" he grunted. He did the same to me, but with way more force. My head now in stars, I almost blacked out.

Then I heard a wallop sound. Rick slumped away from me onto the concrete floor. Before I could collect my senses, someone grabbed my hand and pulled me to my feet. Dedrick.

"Are you okay?" he asked.

I stumbled. "Y-yeah, I think so," I said, grabbing my head.

"All right, let's get you out of—watch out!"

Dedrick pushed me aside, my back hitting the wall. My head was still in a cloud, but in the haze of it all, I saw Rick lurch forward with a shovel.

245

Dedrick somehow wrestled the shovel away. I saw flashes of arms flailing back and forth, men grunting, punching. Bodies banging against tools, the cabinet, the wall. I looked to the floor. Couldn't see the shotgun, but I knew where it had fallen. With Dedrick and Rick battling at the other end of the shed, I bent to my knees, reaching for it—but touched a boot instead.

I looked up. Larry had come to. I don't know when, but amid the chaos, somehow he had gotten to his feet.

"Larry?"

"Get out of the way, Nel."

"Larry, what—"

He pushed me back. The moonlight slipping through the window revealed what I had been looking for—the shotgun...in Larry's hands. He pointed at the opposite end of the shed.

Dedrick and Rick came into view. Dedrick had the upper hand. Still, a wave of panic rippled through me.

I reached for the gun. "Larry! No!"

Too late. One gun blast rocked my eardrums, somehow unable to muffle a guttural shriek of pain. A body slumped face first toward the cold concrete floor.

Chapter 28

Tammy

"Hey, girl!"

Tomi wrapped me up like he hadn't seen me in years. It felt like it, really. Last time I saw him was the same day I met Terrell.

"Heeeeey!" I replied, pressing my cheek against his. "Long time no see, pretty boy."

Tomi looked good. Hair all slicked back with a light-brown tint, new silver earring in his left ear. His black T-shirt screamed "Don't Want No Short Dick Man!" in bold white letters. Always the crack-up.

He held the door for me. "Damn, lookin' all cute."

"Thank you. Going to the gym later."

"I heard that. Go 'head, Beyonce."

I smiled. Nothing special regarding what I wore. Pink sweat suit, matching pink and white tennis shoes. Hair pony-tailed, no make up, dressed to get all Bionic Woman up in the gym. Pants cuddled my booty well, though. So did the tight tank top underneath my jacket.

I closed the door behind me. "I figured I'd swing through after my writing class and see y'all. Where's Sheryl?"

"That crazy heifa's in the bathroom." He sat in a chair next to one of Sheryl's tree-sized plants.

A door opened. "No, I'm not." Ms. Thang stomped into the living room. "About time, girl. Sit your butt down and spill it."

I laughed. "Dang, can a sista get a 'hello' up in here?"

"Oh, I'm sorry. *Hello.*" We hugged. "Now let's hear about this hot date."

"You are so damn nosy."

"Yeah, she is." Tomi laughed. "Nose all in people's bidness, like a damn police dog or sumn'. I'm gonna start callin' yo' ass Fido."

Sheryl rolled her eyes. "Whateva."

We sat down on the couch. Taraji P. Henson appeared on the TV screen. A Tyler Perry movie.

"Oh, y'all watching—"

"No, we ain't." Sheryl grabbed the DVD remote and hit the PAUSE button.

"Damn, girl," Tomi said. "You done lost your mind?"

Sheryl ignored him. "So, who is this mystery man?" She looked me over. "And where you finna go? Look at you. Pink sweat suit, titties poppin' out your shirt. Uh-huh. Who you tryna impress?"

"Shut up, girl. Nunya."

"It's another white boy, isn't it?"

"Another white boy?" Tomi jumped in, eyes wider than cue balls. "You went out with a *white* boy?"

"Not just went out," Sheryl said. "More like *turned* out."

I shook my head. Why in the world did I tell Sheryl about Dale? I was never going to hear the end of it.

"No," I said, "not this—"

"How big was it?" Tomi asked. He leaned forward and pointed his index finger. "Finger-length?" He extended his arm. "Or forearm-length?"

"Oh, damn." I put my head down. "Why me?"

"Hmmph, she tryin' to act all shy, now." Sheryl turned to Tomi. "She told me that white boy hit it real good, too. I heard they eat coochie like they at a damn Hometown Buffet or somethin', huh, Tammy?"

"Will you shut up!" I cried, laughing.

"Uh-hum." Tomi cut his eyes at me. "Probably one of them cornbread country boys, hung like a charged water hose. Name like Danny or Bobby, I bet."

"Billy Joe," Sheryl said. Everybody got jokes.

"For your information, I went out with Terrell."

Sheryl's forehead crumpled. "Terrell? I've never met a white boy named Terrell."

"No, I had a date with *the* Terrell last night, knucklehead." I paused for drama's sake. "The eye doctor."

You could hear an ant crawl.

Sheryl and Tomi mimicked Taraji's frozen frame on the screen, like two street mimes, tongues in knots. Terrell's name had become a real-life PAUSE button. I smothered a monster laugh.

"You a damn lie!" Sheryl cried.

"Now why I gotta be all that?" I asked, half-talking, half-howling.

"You talkin' 'bout that fine-ass man who was up in here the other day?" Tomi asked.

I nodded.

"Oh, *hell* naw!" Sheryl damn near screamed, hands waving all over the place, acting the fool. "You-are-a-damn-lie!"

"I'm not lying! He took me to dinner last night."

"You sleep with him, too?" Tomi asked.

"No."

"*What?*" Sheryl cried. "Now, how you gonna sleep with a white boy on the first date and not give it up to the black doctor? Girl, you all mixed up."

Should've known Sheryl would put me on blast. "Damn, is it wrong to take it slow? I'm meeting him at the gym today, too."

Sheryl turned to Tomi, then me. Back to Tomi. Back to me. Somewhere in the last five seconds, she forgot how her tongue worked.

"I thought he only liked white girls," Tomi said.

"Well...I'm reeling him back to the dark side." I giggled at my corny little joke.

Sheryl's eyelids flapped. She searched my lips, my eyes. My face may as well have been a CSI crime scene the way she stared, her gaze prodding for evidence of a lie.

I said, "Girl, stop staring at me."

She shook out of her daze. "Okay, I *gotta* hear this. How he go from 'I don't mess with sistas' to hooking up with you?"

"Yeah?" Tomi asked.

I broke it down for them. I didn't want to embarrass Terrell, so I left out the part about him getting slapped. Then for good measure, I let Sheryl hear Terrell's voice message, the one he left after our dinner date.

"Damn," Sheryl said. "I'm impressed. *Very* impressed."

"Me too," Tomi added. "You worked sumn' on him, girl."

I shrugged. "Well, we just like each other, you know. Got a lot in common. Just had to figure it out."

"Well, I think I figured sumn' out about you," Sheryl said. "Known you all these years, but now I see you must have some voodoo coochie, boy. Make a man do whatever you want. White *and* black."

Tomi and I cracked up. "Girl," I said, "what the hell are you talking about?"

"I mean, damn, you revamped that boy's whole frame of mind, right? He was dead set against dating black women; now he's all up on you. I bet that coochie's good enough to make Tomi a straight man. I know Terrell can't wait to get a taste of that." She chuckled. "Can I borrow it until then?"

Tomi swatted his hand in the air, then crossed his legs. "Shhhh. I don't know 'bout making me straight, now. Dick makes me tick. That's it." He pounded his knee. "Oh! That's my new shirt, girl!"

I damn near fell off the couch laughing so hard. Those two always set my belly on fire.

"Going to the gym with him, huh?" Sheryl asked. "Well, excuse me, Wonder Woman. Damn, Dedrick was right."

"Right about what?"

"He mentioned you and Terrell might hook up. Said that a while ago, just before you moved here. I'll be damned if it didn't come true."

"Sho' did," Tomi said. "Now unpause the damn movie."

"Dedrick said that, huh? Interesting."

"You know what? I'm calling that boy right now. He'd love to hear this." Sheryl pulled out her phone. "We haven't talked since he left for Miss—"

"Girl, I said unpause the movie! Don't be ignorin' me."

Sheryl shot Tomi a pair of demon eyes, then aimed the remote at him. "I'll pause *yo'* ass talkin' all that mess."

"Oh boy." Sandwiched between these two "girls" yapping at each other, my ears suffered blunt force trauma. But they had me rollin'.

After more bickering, Sheryl clicked the remote again, resuscitating Taraji. She threw the remote to Tomi and went back to her phone.

I stood up and stretched. "Ya'll are fools. You got any bottled water in the fridge, Ms. Gossip?"

"Yeah," Sheryl said, pointing toward the kitchen.

"You want anything, Tomi?"

"Yeah, some of that voodoo magic you got. See if you can pour some in a tall glass for me."

"Boy, shut up." I disappeared into the kitchen.

Man, those two. I didn't have some magic potion leaking between my legs. Terrell and I clicked, that's all. Man likes woman, woman likes man. Once we got past the whole no-black-men, no-black-women trip, what happened next came natural. But if Terrell had fallen under some kind of sista hypnotic spell, that was fine with me.

I grabbed a bottle of water from the fridge. I could hear Sheryl on the phone.

"What?" she asked. "What are you..." her voice trailed off. She sounded upset.

When I walked back into the living room, Tomi had muted the TV. The look on Sheryl's face...I'd never seen her so scared. A dark cloud settled over the room, killing the party mood.

"What is it?" I turned to Tomi. Found no answers in his eyes. Only signs of concern.

Sheryl dropped the phone, her hands trembling. I knelt beside her and heard a woman's voice say Sheryl's name several times before the line disconnected.

Sheryl's eyes watered. My God. Dedrick. Something happened to Dedrick.

I placed a hand on her knee, clutching my pendant with the other. "Sheryl, what's going on? Did something happen to Dedrick?"

A tear slid down her cheek. "My brother's in the hospital," she said, her bottom lip quivering. "He's been shot."

253

Chapter 29

Penelope

"The doctor's finishing his exam and then you can see him," the nurse said. "Is there anything else I can do for you?"

I knew she was staring at the scratches and bruise on my face, but I forced a smile and said, "No, I'm fine. Thank you."

Warm gestures had become alien to me. My mental state harbored little capacity for pleasantries. A dead body can do that to ya, I guess.

The waiting room was empty, except for an elderly couple. Still, I chose a seat as far away from them as possible. Old people like to talk. I didn't want to talk. I settled into a hard blue chair next to a long hall.

Finally an escape from the whirlwind. For the first time I was able to sit down without someone in my face, throwing questions at me. It started seconds after Rick hit the concrete.

Lights appeared out of nowhere, all around the shed. Flashlights. Little did I know, Mom had called 911, awakened by the noise from the shed. Once the shotgun fired, Larry panicked and tried to run, but two cops ordered him to the ground, guns drawn. The carnage inside forced them to cuff me and Dedrick at first, until I screamed for them to leave him alone. After they saw his bloody shirt and battered head, they did the right thing and released Dedrick for medical attention.

Although Rick took most of the blast, the bullet tore through him and pierced Dedrick in the side torso. An ambulance arrived and took Dedrick away, but I stayed behind. Handcuffed. I'd never been handcuffed before.

More police cars appeared. So many red and blue lights flashing up and down the street. Mom cried while cops hauled Larry and I off in separate cars. Despite the cold, neighbors stood outside, watching. Medics, cops, men in suits. Everywhere. At least it seemed that way. Fourth Street became one big carnival centered around a dead man, perfect for the primetime news and local papers.

I never cursed my brother the way I did that night. He was at fault and I wanted everyone to know. I didn't hold back; I yelled and kicked at him, let it all out in the open. Cops didn't know who from what, though.

Until Larry told the truth.

The protector, that stubborn part of him that funneled compassion toward me, found its way to the surface. That's the Larry I cherished—my big brother, not the monster who held Dedrick hostage in the shed. He refused to let his kid sister take the fall and confessed everything. Said he fired the shot that killed Rick.

The police let me go and I went straight to the trauma center, praying harder than I'd ever prayed in my entire life that Dedrick was okay. He *had* to be okay.

But a mountain of guilt and anxiety punctured my heart. *If not for me, Dedrick wouldn't be here,* I repeated in my head.

I met the doctor who took Dedrick in. I expected the worse, prayed for the best. With all that blood, more bad than good. But for once, I got the news I'd wanted to hear.

Although shot, Dedrick suffered superficial wounds. Missed all vital organs, thank God. And that cut in the back of his head looked worse than it appeared. No concussion, no brain damage.

Doctors stitched his wounds, but decided to keep him there a couple more days. I tried to stay with him, but the hospital didn't allow overnight visitors, so I went back to my parents' home. Saturday became a series of brick walls, though. Cops stopped by again. Questions on top of questions. Phone calls on top of phone calls. And friggin' news reporters.

Reporters clogged the streets around my parents' house. All the news channels were trying to get the scoop. Apparently, the local gossip machine was fired up, with the neighbors spreading rumors trying to get their five minutes of fame. The words "hate crime" hung in the air.

I didn't get a chance to see Dedrick any part of Saturday, not with all the crap going on. Well past visiting hours when done with the circus, anyway, but I learned his condition had improved. So back the next day, Sunday morning, where I am now. No reporters, no cops, no men in suits today. Whirlwind gone...for now. But after I received calls on Dedrick's phone yesterday afternoon and a few times after, I knew more visitors would arrive soon.

"Miss?" the nurse asked, breaking into my thoughts. "The doctor is done. You can see your friend now."

"Thank you."

Grabbing my purse, I followed the nurse down the hall to Dedrick's room. We passed one or two doors before the pace of my heart hit full-speed, surpassing the rhythm of my footsteps. We turned down another hall. I took in a breath, then eased it out, wiping clammy hands against my shirt.

How would he react to me? Would he blame me as much as I blamed myself?

"Here we are." The nurse opened a door and held it for me.

"Thank you," I said. She walked away. I walked in.

Dedrick lay on an inclined bed. He clicked the TV off when he noticed me. Soon as I closed the door, I lost control of my emotions. The build-up of fear, anxiety, guilt and shame poured out of me in a wave.

"Hey," he said, motioning for me to join him on the bed.

"Hey."

As I drew closer, Dedrick frowned. "Damn, babe, you really look worn down. You okay?"

I sat on the bed. "I am now."

We kissed, then embraced. Pressed my cheek against his, felt his body heat, tried to merge our energy together. Touching him caused more emotional debris to rain from me.

"Babe, um, your hair is in my nose."

"Oh." I moved my head away. "I'm sorry."

Dedrick wiped his temple with the sheet. "Got me all wet, too."

"I know, I know. I'm so sorry."

"It's cool," he said, patting my knee. He handed me a few tissues. "Looks like he got you pretty good. How's your jaw?"

"Still hurts, but whatever. Just glad you're fine."

"I'm glad *you're* fine."

"I am." Wiping my cheeks and nose, I asked, "Dedrick? Um...is it really fine between *us*?"

He didn't respond. Instead, he adjusted his head against the pillow. Sighing, he stared at the ceiling, interlocking his fingers

257

on his chest. It appeared his mood changed when I asked that question. Like he went somewhere else and I wasn't a part of that new place.

"Well," he said, "gettin' shot ain't no joke. And my head still hurts, got stitches and stuff, but...I definitely have a ton of questions about this whole thing." He raised his head. "Oh. The cops said your brother confessed to everything."

"Yeah, he did."

"Good. Well, I guess that's that. Case closed."

"Yeah."

We sat quiet, reflecting, trapped in our thoughts. But I didn't know where Dedrick's mind went; yet, I had an idea. I rubbed my palms together, trying to brace myself for the storm of questions I knew he wanted to ask me.

"Um, you said something about questions. What did you mean?"

Placing his head back on the pillow, he said, "Yeah, I do. Well, first off...okay, when you came in the shed, I was like 'why the hell is she here? Why didn't she call the police?' "

I lowered my head. Same question I'd asked myself. That brought more guilt. More tears.

"I wasn't thinking. I mean, I *thought* I was."

"What?"

I took in a big breath, collected myself and started over. "Dedrick, I thought if I had called the police, they would've shot you. In retaliation, I guess. I figured my best chance was to try and talk them out of it."

He shook his head. "Girl, what the hell? You already tried to take on my sister and her flame boy friend. What, you thought you could take on two men, too?"

I'd never thought of that. Trying to joke, I said, "Yeah, I guess so, huh? Well, you know me. Ms. Fiesty."

He looked at me. His eyes said it all. Like two blades ready to slice me for such a stupid response.

"It ain't funny, Nel," he said stone-faced. "You were messin' around with our lives."

That shook me. Our *lives*.

I turned away, shielding my shame from him. No matter how much I tried to control my tears or forget the nightmare, the tears kept falling, but still couldn't wash away the guilt.

"I know, Dedrick," I said, sniffling. "I thought I was doing the right thing. I just...had to get you outta there."

No response. Nothing at all. Just whatever was going on in our thoughts.

But I didn't need anyone to remind me of who to blame. The gravity it all sunk in. It was *my* fault...Dedrick lying there...shot. If I hadn't tried to be a big badass going to the bar to tell Rick off and all, none of this would've happened. I really should've just left it alone. This was *all* my fault.

Facing away, my back toward him, I asked, "Do you want me to go?"

I felt his hand slip into mine. "No."

My body tingled. The touch of his hand brought me peace. I could breathe now. And smile.

I turned to him. "You sure?"

"Yeah. You might not have gone 'bout it the smartest way, but... babe, you *did* save my life." He pulled me close, caressed my cheek. "Thank you."

259

The flood really came this time. I laid my head on his chest, wiping my facing with the sheets. Dedrick ran his hand through my hair, then kissed my forehead.

"I love you," I said.

"I love you, too, babe. And all this wasn't your fault."

It all faded away—the shame, the guilt. Pain I still felt in my sore back and jaw—gone. At least, I didn't feel it anymore. In that moment, none of that consumed me. With my head on his chest, I rode the rise and fall of his breathing and closed my eyes, my balance finally restored. Him and me together, alive. That's all that mattered.

"Babe," he said, rubbing my back, "I need to know sumn' else, though."

"Yes?"

"What your brother was talkin' about in the shed. Something about some young brotha they beat up. That true?"

I sighed. Raising my head, I replied, "Yes, it is. A boy got beat up because I lied. And I can't tell you how much I've regretted it."

As he digested my words, I tried to read his eyes. I couldn't.

The ceiling became Dedrick's point of focus again. He replied with only one word: "Damn."

I knew that ugly part of my history would maybe drive a wedge between us if revealed. That's why I never wanted to expose it.

"What are you thinking?" I asked.

He blinked several times, still staring up. If I could only read his thoughts.

"Well, when your brother was talkin' all that mess, I was thinkin' 'how much was she a part of that kid gettin' beat down?' Then I was like 'and how did they find me in the first place? Only Nel and

I knew about the motel.' One minute I'm getting something out the car, the next a guy walks up to me, asks if I know you, I say yes, then *bam!* Blow to the head and I'm out. Your boy Rick snuck up on me or sumn'. Next thing I know I'm tied up in the back of a truck, freezin' my ass off, groggy as hell. I don't know how many times I blacked out."

My God. I filled my mind with "if onlys." If only I hadn't tried to handle things my way. If only I hadn't stopped for beer. If only I hadn't kissed Dedrick in that parking lot. If only I hadn't switched teams and traveled to Mississippi in the first place.

But since it happened, I'd yet to feel remorse for Rick. Coming from Dedrick's mouth, it cemented my cold heart. I still loved my brother, but he belonged behind bars. For the rest of his life for all I cared.

"Babe, I *swear* to you, I didn't tell Rick and Larry where you were. I don't know how they found out about the motel."

"Maybe your mom told 'em."

"But I never told her which motel we were staying at. The only time I said the name of the motel was when I spoke with you. Nobody was around, though. I...wait a minute."

Flashback. Me on the phone, standing on the porch. Dedrick telling me about the motel. Me repeating the name and location out loud. Rick walking outside a second later. That was it.

I shook my head. "What a friggin' snake. I think I know what happened."

"What?"

"I was standing on the porch talking to you when Rick walked out the house. He must've been eavesdropping. He's a sneaky ass. Always been."

"Well, he can't get at you ever again, Nel. Not anymore."

A chill rushed through me. I didn't realize I'd said Rick's name in present tense. He was right. Rick would *never* come back again. *Ever*. I'd rehearsed his demise in my head so many times. Like I said once, I wanted him *gone*.

But I never imagined death would knock so close to home. And so soon.

"You know what, Nel?"

"Yes?"

"Part of me feels like your brother shot him on purpose."

"You think so?"

"Yeah."

A lump rose in my throat. I saw Rick again, falling to the ground, a pool of blood spreading around him.

Dedrick said, "He crossed you for the last time. And I really believe your brother took him out because of it."

The side of my head throbbed a bit. Reliving the worst night of my life took a toll. "Okay, let's not talk about this anymore, all right? All that matters is you're okay."

He smiled and reached for my hand. "*We're* okay. And you're right. It's over now."

I pulled his hand to my face, rubbing his knuckles against my skin. "So...are we cool?"

"Girl, I said we were, I—"

His eyes shifted away from me toward the door. I turned in the same direction.

"Dedrick? Thank God, you're all right!"

Oh, boy. The gang's all here.

Chapter 30

Terrell

"What's up, man?"

"What up, fool?"

My boy. All the pieces there. His wide gap-toothed smile flashed me. Aside from noticeable facial scars, he looked fine. Man.

Penelope stood when we entered the room. From the bruise on her jaw and bags under her eyes, I could tell sleep had become a luxury yet rewarded.

While Tammy and Sheryl took turns embracing Dedrick, I gave some love to Penelope. "What's up, girl? Good to see you again."

"Hi, Terrell," she said, holding a smile that seemed strained. "Good to see you, too."

"Thank you for taking care of my boy."

"There's nowhere else I'd rather be."

I turned to Dedrick. As I faced him, I felt myself about to boil over, but bottled it up.

"Hey, man." I embraced my partner. "You don't know how happy I am to know you're cool."

"Thanks, man." He patted my back. "Thanks."

We stood for a moment, quiet, all of us relieved to lay eyes on Dedrick alive and well. Tammy and Sheryl stood on the other side of the bed, tears flowing over happy smiles.

"Oh! Tammy." Dedrick grabbed Penelope's hand. "I don't think ya'll met. This is my girl, Penelope. Penelope, Tammy. My other sister."

They threw up awkward waves at each other. "I was talking to you on Dedrick's phone today, right?" Penelope asked. "Giving you directions?" Tammy nodded.

"You know y'all didn't have to come down here," Dedrick said.

"Boy, are you crazy?" Sheryl said, wiping her face. "We would've gotten here sooner, but everything was booked. I didn't know it was so hard to get flights the same day. I was this close to renting a car to *drive* out here."

"It's okay, sis. Everything's fine."

"*Fine?*" Sheryl cried, her relief giving way to anger. "Boy, you got shot! What the hell happened anyway?"

I knew it. Leave it to Sheryl to get straight to the "dirty." No respect for Penelope at all. Didn't even look at her.

But I admit, I had to know, too.

Dedrick exhaled a breath. "Sheryl, it's...I'm cool. Trust me, everything's cool."

"Babe," Penelope said, "maybe I should go."

"No, no, Nel," Dedrick said, reaching for her. "You don't have to go."

"Yes, maybe she *should* go," Sheryl said, cutting her eyes at Penelope. "This is family business." She turned to her brother. "And what the hell you mean 'everything's cool?' " Her voice jumped, tone rough and rude. Tammy grabbed her arm, whispering for her to calm down.

"Sheryl, get this straight: Nel's not goin' anywhere, so stop talking to her like that. And chill out." Dedrick slapped Sheryl's butt. "Your little brother's fine. Don't worry about it."

"Boy, I don't understand. You're actin' like this is no big deal. You were *shot!*" Her voice got higher. "Got stitches in the back of your head and bruises on your face. Who did this?" She turned to Penelope with an icy glare. "Is that bitch involved?"

"All right, girl." Tammy pulled her arm. "You need to stop. You'll get us all kicked out."

Dedrick didn't say anything, just held onto Penelope's hand. Then Penelope dropped a mega bomb when she said, "I *was* involved. It was all my fault. My...my brother shot him."

My bottom lip fell. I couldn't possibly have heard her right.

Air in the room grew thick, its vapors combustible. Seconds from detonating. All eyes on Penelope.

I heard Dedrick curse under his breath. "Babe, I told you it wasn't your fault. And I wanted to tell her when I was ready."

"She was going to find out soon enough. May as well hear the truth from me."

Silence again. Shoot, I didn't know how to react. Sheryl's face twisted, became that of the devil. Detonation imminent.

Penelope looked so tired. Like a woman spent, resolved to what would come to her. Tammy placed a hand on Sheryl's arm. "Sheryl, honey," she said, her voice low, "calm down, now. Remember, this is a hospital."

A tear slid down Sheryl's cheek. "I'm gonna kill this bitch."

Oh, man. I didn't doubt Sheryl planned to make good on her threat, so I stood closer to Penelope, prepared to intervene if necessary.

"Sheryl!" Dedrick cried. "Chill out, girl! I wouldn't be alive if not for her. Penelope saved my life."

Everything stopped. All eyes on Dedrick, now.

Before anyone could recover from his words, Dedrick said, "Yeah, it's true. Nel's brother and his friend didn't like Nel with a black dude, so they swooped me up, wanting to 'teach me a lesson.' " He squeezed Nel's hand. "When Nel found out what was going on, she risked her life to save mine. I mean, look at her face! You have no idea how much she put on the line for me. What it almost cost her. I was able to get out alive, thanks to her. The other guy...well...he wasn't so lucky. He's dead."

It took all my strength to pull my jaw back up. None of us had any idea all that had gone down. A man *died?* No wonder Penelope looked like she hadn't slept in days.

"Damn, Penelope. Damn, I..." I stepped toward her, wrapped her up. A real embrace. And the runoff came so quick—I didn't expect it. No time to stop my heart's storage bank from overflowing. I didn't even try.

We swapped tears against our chins. I felt the quiver in Penelope's lips against my cheek. Tammy couldn't hold back, either. I watched her squeeze Penelope like she never wanted to let go. We stood together like dams with cracks that leaked tons of water.

Penelope disentangled herself from the group hug. She said, "I'm gonna wait outside. Give ya'll some time alone."

Sheryl's face softened. "You don't have to go," she said, now standing between Penelope and the door. "Please...stay."

"It's okay. You guys are all family."

"No, no, please. You deserve to be here, too." Sheryl's voice cracked.

She placed a hand on Penelope's shoulder. Heartfelt. Genuine. That's what I sensed from her. For a second, I thought I was looking at the Twilight Zone the way she flip-flopped. I understood, though. How can you hate someone who saved your brother's life?

Under a tear flood, Sheryl's lips rose at the corners. "Thank you for giving me my brother back."

They stood for a moment, facing each other. No more words. No hugs. None needed. A silent handshake squashed it all.

"All right," Penelope said, nodding. "Okay."

She reclaimed her spot next to Dedrick, stroking his cheek.

"I'm proud of you, sis," I heard Dedrick whisper to Sheryl. Now on her best behavior, Sheryl sat in a chair by his bed, holding one hand while Penelope held the other.

I fixed my gaze on Tammy; hers met mine. Tunnel vision all over again, stuck on that Ebony Queen face. Damn...so lovely. Hand-crafted by angels. For a second, I disappeared, replaying a sweet moment on the plane.

To get my mind off Dedrick, Tammy let me read a story she'd written. Halfway through it, she placed her head on my shoulder. I held her hand.

Right then, while absorbing that familiar flowery scent of her, I made up my mind. No more taste-testing with loose white women. Scratched *all* women off the menu, actually. I figured I'd see how far Tammy and I could take this thing we had for each other. Whatever that "thing" was, I didn't want it to end.

I noticed tears had wet Tammy's dimples. I found tissues on a corner table, pulled her to me and wiped each cheek.

"What the...am I seeing what I think I'm seeing?" Dedrick asked.

"Huh?" I asked. "What are you talking about?"

Dedrick raised his head. "You two. Starin' at each other all starry eyed. The hell? Are ya'll holding hands, too?"

I found an itch on my neck. Tammy pulled her hand away, turning her attention to a spot on the wall she liked.

"Wow, I love this white," Tammy said, running her fingers down the wall. "So nice. I was thinking about, um, painting my apartment this color."

I pressed a fist to my mouth, holding back chuckles. Nothing nice about the bland color at all, but for some reason, I found it interesting, too. "Yeah, you're right. I love how, uh, 'white' it is. I might have to paint my—"

"Hold up! Stop playin'!" Dedrick leaned forward, pointing at us. "You two hooked up, didn't you? Sheryl! I knew it! I—*ow.*"

"Be careful, babe," Penelope said, trying to push him back down. I could tell Sheryl sat a second away from cracking up.

Back to our normal selves. Tammy's friend Miki called, so Sheryl filled her in. Other than that, we pretty much slammed the lid on any talk about what happened. Figured Dedrick and Penelope would let us know the details when ready.

But of course, Dedrick wanted to know about Tammy and me, so I spoon-fed him the 411. Found out the punk had predicted months ago that Tammy and I would eventually hook up. Well, my boy was right.

A knock turned everyone to the door. "Excuse me," a nurse said. "You have another visitor, Mr. Davis."

"Another visitor?"

A woman walked in holding a plate with aluminum foil wrapped around it. An older lady. Long grey hair and a pretty face.

Penelope stood up. "M-Mom. What are you doing here?"

I felt the woman's discomfort when she said, "I thought I'd bring some lemon pie."

I don't think anyone saw that coming.

Penelope took the plate from her and placed it on a table by Dedrick's bed. Everyone nodded toward the woman, holding gracious smiles. Even Sheryl.

Penelope held her mother's arm. "Mom, you didn't have to do this."

The woman removed her scarf. "I felt I needed to." She took in a breath. I could tell she struggled to speak. "Sir," she said to Dedrick, head down, "I am extremely sorry for what my son did to you."

Dedrick took her hand. "My name is Dedrick, ma'am. Please, no apologies needed. None of this is your fault or your daughter's." He took a whiff of the pie. "This smells fantastic. Thank you."

Dedrick flashed his famous smile. No hate in his eyes, nothing vengeful. She acknowledged his hearty gesture with a smile of her own. Tammy and I stood in the background, savoring the moment.

Penelope's mom pulled her aside. She said something to her daughter in private. I don't know what she said, but Penelope looked like she'd heard the best news ever. They hugged while we watched.

It appeared the storm had subsided. Calm winds, now. No sellouts in here. Only white and black folks wearing happy smiles.

Discussion Questions

1. Tammy is an educated woman who was in a relationship with Craig, a wannabe thug who barely graduated high school. Was she settling? Is this all too common?

2. Even after the perfect date (and a one-night stand) with Dale, Tammy realizes she wants to stay loyal to black men. Yet, she's still angry with black men. Is this a common dichotomy for black women?

3. If Dale lived in the same city as Tammy, do you think Tammy should forget her hang-ups with race and develop a relationship with him? Should she have tried a long distance relationship with Dale? Who's the better fit for Tammy—Dale or Terrell? Was giving up her chances with Dale worth a shot at Terrell?

4. Terrell had a dream about a white woman he's never seen before and had an "accident" because of it. Is that a valid reason to be angry with him, even though he told Tasha the truth about the dream? Should Terrell have lied and said he was dreaming about her?

5. Terrell and Tammy had similar breakups that led to them dating interracially, but Terrell also had shallow reasons for "abandoning ship." He started dating white women immediately while Tammy put *all* men on hiatus for months before going out with Dale. Is this indicative of how black men and women would react in this situation?

6. Terrell was shocked at how much he was attracted to Tammy. Was he so blinded by prejudice that he couldn't "see" Tammy at first?

7. Penelope had a real life once-you-go-black-you-won't-go-back moment. Does this actually happen? Was her relationship with Dedrick based on this stereotype?

8. White women are often portrayed as dainty, meek, trashy, and/ or air-headed. How does Penelope counter these stereotypes? Or does she?

9. Penelope shows her independent, don't-take-no-mess-from-anyone attitude at times. Do you think she got carried away with it when she decided to tell Rick off face-to-face about his indecent proposal?

10. What was your favorite or most memorable moment in the book? Why did it make an impression?

11. Many people agree black women are portrayed negatively in the media, especially in various reality shows. Can the same be said about white women portrayed as trashy, airhead bimbos?

12. Do you think racial stereotypes influence people to date outside their race?

13. Are white women unfairly criticized for dating black men? What about black women dating white men?

14. Overall, did you enjoy this book? Why or why not?

Read on for an excerpt from
WHEN LOVE ISN'T ENOUGH
The debut novel from Stephanie Casher

Available Fall 2010

http://www.pantheoncollective.com

Chapter One

Samantha Merrick had spent her whole life playing by the rules and doing what was expected of her. But even good girls are susceptible to making bad decisions, or a series of bad decisions, as they try to figure out who they are.

She woke up that fateful morning with a hangover and a strange boy in bed next to her. Where was she? Squinting in the darkness, her lover's form came into focus—chin-length blond hair, muscular arms, a perfectly sculpted chest. A thin sheet covered the lower half of his body, and like her, he was completely nude. Her eyes darted around the unfamiliar surroundings until they landed on a surfboard propped in the corner of the room. *Ah yes, the surfer dude.* It all trickled back to her.

She felt around in the dark for her clothes. Regret, combined with the aftertaste of tequila and stale cigarettes, triggered a mild nausea. Determined to sneak away before he woke, she crept out of his bedroom, without bothering to leave a note. She had no desire to see him ever again.

Samantha jumped behind the wheel of her trusty Toyota, the pounding in her head merciless. As if on autopilot, she maneuvered her car toward the beach. The ocean was her sanctuary, and she could sit for hours on the edge of the cliff, releasing her problems into the sea, the waves slowly eroding the layers of regret as they crashed against the shore. She always ended up at the water's edge whenever she felt the urge to run.

As bumpy as her second year of college was starting out, she was glad she had decided to come to school at UCSC. The sleepy, coastal town of Santa Cruz was everything Samantha had hoped it would be, and she often marveled at how blessed she was to have the opportunity to attend college in such a beautiful place, amongst such progressive, liberal-minded people. She'd been having the time of her life.

But the events of last summer changed all that. Her awestruck wonder and sense of adventure had been replaced by a searing cynicism, the quest for knowledge taking a backseat to the more pressing pursuit of finding something, anything, to numb the pain. Samantha was no longer concerned with freeing her mind. All she wanted to do was forget…

She pulled into the deserted parking lot as the sun crept upward in the morning sky, erasing the last traces of night with its ascent. Sunrise was a particularly magical time, the pre-dawn air curiously still, as if the day were holding its breath, waiting to be born. The dew-speckled ground glistened in the morning sun and cast an aura of shiny newness across the landscape. She grabbed a blanket and took a deep breath, drawing in the crisp, salty air. The promise of a new day was one of the few things that still inspired her.

The Santa Cruz coastline had no shortage of scenic vistas, but Samantha was partial to this one secluded ledge off West Cliff Drive. As she made her way down the narrow footpath, she was surprised to find a guy sitting in her spot. He was staring across the ocean, legs hanging over the side, still and motionless like a statue. Tempted to leave and look for somewhere less populated, she decided against it. If she relocated now, she'd miss the sunrise, so she selected a spot on the eastern side of the cliff. Together, yet apart, they watched the sky slowly change from red, to orange, then gold, before finally fading into blue.

Half an hour passed before he moved. When he finally looked her way, a startled expression briefly marred his serene features. He blinked and shook his head, as if she were a mere apparition he expected to disappear. Samantha smiled at him and waved. A simple, casual gesture to assure him she was indeed real.

"Sorry I'm in your spot," he called out. Samantha's heart stopped. How could he have possibly known that?

He pulled a pack of Marlboro Lights from his breast pocket and held one out in her direction. "Smoke?"

Samantha walked over to where he sat. Taking the cigarette from his outstretched hand, she sat down beside him. Their eyes met, and she was struck by this odd sense of familiarity.

"Forgive me if the answer is yes," she began, "but, do we know each other?"

A sly smile played on his lips. He lit her cigarette, then his own, saying nothing.

"Did I say something funny?" she asked, irritated by his non-response.

He took a long drag from his cigarette and chuckled. "Do you often meet people and forget you've met them?"

"No," she snapped. Then her thoughts flashed back to the nameless boy whose bed she had just fled. "Well, sometimes..." She cocked her head and looked at him curiously. "You didn't answer my question."

He smiled at her again. "No, we've never met."

"Then how did you know you were sitting in my spot?"

"Let's just say that I love sunrise as much as you love sunsets," he whispered.

Samantha was intrigued. How did he know she loved sunsets? How did he know this was her spot? Who was this presumptuous stranger?

She examined him more closely. He was very attractive, with an aura of cool that suggested he was much older than the college boys she was used to seeing around campus. His caramel skin tone matched her own, almost exactly, and he had a head full of curls where an afro should have been, betraying his mixed-race heritage. She couldn't shake the feeling that she knew him from somewhere, and wondered if maybe she'd seen him at one of the multicultural functions on campus.

As if reading her mind, he confessed, "I've seen you here before."

She let out a nervous giggle. "What, are you stalking me or something?"

"Not exactly."

Another long pause. Samantha grew more confused by the second.

"Relax," he said finally, sensing her discomfort. He gestured to a large Victorian off the main road. "I live up there. The window on the second floor, with the wind chimes outside of it, is mine." He smiled again. "Watching you talk to yourself is one of my favorite ways to spend the afternoon."

A wave of vulnerability washed over her—this man *had* been watching her! "Oh, I see, you're like a peeping Tom or something."

He laughed and put out his cigarette. "No, I'm a people watcher. You happen to be a very interesting person to watch."

He captured her eyes in a penetrating gaze, as if he was looking *in* her, rather than at her. Samantha felt herself being drawn to him

278

psychically, hypnotically, a level of intimacy present that hadn't been earned. She turned away to break the spell.

"So why do you come out here and sit on the cliff by yourself?" She glanced toward the house. "I mean, you can obviously see the sunrise fine from your window."

He reached into his pocket and pulled out his cigarettes again, offering her another. She declined.

"Don't get me wrong, the view is great from up there. But sometimes I need to get away from it all. When you sit in this spot and look out across the water, all you can see is ocean for miles in three directions. All evidence of life and the city is behind you." He took a drag from his cigarette, exhaling slowly. "When I'm feeling overwhelmed, all that water makes my problems seem so small and insignificant. It's quite humbling really, a great way to start the day, with a fresh perspective."

Samantha's curiosity was piqued. "Do you come out here every morning?"

"Nope. Only when I'm feeling a little lost."

The word echoed in her head. *Lost.* One simple syllable that perfectly described the past four months of her life. Minutes passed as they sat together in shared solitude, looking across the sea.

"So what's got you up and out on the cliff so early?" he asked, breaking the silence.

She smiled at him knowingly. "I guess I was feeling a little lost this morning, too."

Concern filled his dark-brown eyes. "You want to talk about it?"

Samantha drew in a deep breath. It had been so long since she'd confided in someone. She had tried talking to her friends, but they were too busy partying their lives away to be of much help. If she was told to move on and get over it one more time… "I don't want to bore you with my problems."

"I can think of many adjectives I'd use to describe you, my dear, but boring would not be one of them. Talk to me."

Strangely enough, something in his eyes made Samantha feel like she could trust him. "Have you ever had something happen that made you doubt every instinct you've ever had, every decision you've ever made?"

"Sure. Everyone experiences that kind of wake-up call at some point in their lives. It's like a rite of passage."

Samantha picked up a stick and started drawing designs in the sand. "Maybe so, but some days I wonder if I'm going to make it through to the other side."

"Of course you will," he assured her. "Heartbreak and disappointment build character."

"But that's just it—how can any experience build character when I don't even know who I am anymore? Getting up every day and going through my normal routine… It's like trying to squeeze into clothes two sizes too small." She threw the stick over the edge of the cliff in frustration. "My old life just doesn't fit me anymore."

He took a moment to search her face, as if seeing her for the first time. "I know exactly what you mean."

"You do?"

"More than you know. But isn't that what going away to college is all about? We're supposed to be finding ourselves, right?"

"Supposedly, but I only feel more and more alienated from my surroundings as the days go on. Sometimes I don't know *why* I do some of the things I do." Her thoughts returned to the anonymous boy she'd spent the night with, and a fresh wave of shame washed over her. For the first time she felt slightly self-conscious. She had literally just rolled out of bed and hadn't looked in a mirror since sometime last night. She probably looked tore up!

"Don't worry," he said. "You look fine."

Was he reading her mind? She lifted her head and found him looking at her. This time she didn't retreat from his gaze, choosing instead to look deep into his eyes. They were beautiful, he was beautiful. She could have spent the entire day sitting out there just looking at him. A few moments ago, he was just some random guy she'd met on the cliff. Until she felt it. *Click.* It was quiet, and it was subtle, but it was there. *Click.* And she had no words...

She was lost in his eyes when he was suddenly distracted by the appearance of an older couple making their way down the path, hand in hand.

"Looks like we have some company." He collected their discarded cigarette butts and put them in his half-empty pack.

Samantha glanced at the older couple and smiled, but inside she was secretly disappointed they were no longer alone. She wasn't ready to part ways with the mysterious stranger.

Once again, as if reading her mind, he asked, "You wanna get some coffee or something? I'm just about due for a caffeine fix."

Samantha's heart skipped a beat as she tried to hide her relief and excitement. "Sure," she answered, as casually as she could manage. "That sounds great."

He rose to his feet and extended a hand to help her up. She felt a shock of electricity when they touched, and much to her surprise, he continued to hold her hand as they started toward the path. "Wait," she said, pulling away reflexively. "I don't even know your name."

He smiled at her again and she melted. "Tony," he responded, then corrected himself. "Well actually, it's Anthony, but no one ever calls me that. You?"

"Samantha," she replied softly. "Most people call me Sam."

"It's nice to meet you Samantha." He extended his hand again and she took it.

Yeah, she thought. *Nice to meet you, too...*

Chapter Two

They exchanged life stories over coffee. Samantha couldn't get over the instant connection she felt to this stranger. They had both grown up in a predominantly-white, middle class suburb, where they had been one of the few brown kids in their schools. Straight-A students throughout high school, they were both majoring in Sociology at UC Santa Cruz. Children of divorce, neither of them was very close to their fathers. To discover that he shared the same rare ethnic mix—Black and Filipino—was icing on the cake. The similarities were numerous and startling—he could have been her twin, the male version of herself. He was new and familiar at the same time.

Conversation flowed easily, and Samantha found herself revealing more to him about her life, fears, and dreams than she ever had with anyone. It had been so long since she'd had a sympathetic ear that the sentiments poured out of her like water rushing through a broken dam. Tony listened attentively when she spoke, eyes full of empathy, asking thoughtful, probing questions that pushed her to look deeper into each issue. He appeared to have an intuitive understanding of exactly what she was feeling, and on those few occasions when Samantha had to pause to search for the perfect word to complete her thought, he would often jump in and finish her sentence. It was eerie, like he truly had the ability to read her mind.

Coffee turned into lunch, and as the hours passed, Samantha discovered she was able to read his mind, too. Tony was one of those long-winded individuals prone to rambling, as if his tongue could hardly keep up with the speed at which his mind churned out ideas. Sometimes his thoughts would break off into a seemingly meaningless tangent, only to wrap back around and come full circle four tangents later to make a very insightful and profound point. To a normal person, he may have been hard to follow, but Samantha was able to keep up with him through every random turn and subtle iteration. A couple of times, Tony paused dramatically mid-sentence, as if testing their newfound connectedness by challenging her to complete his thought. His face would register amazement, then amusement, as Samantha confidently finished his interrupted sentences, assuring him they were indeed on the same page so he could continue with his profundicizing.

Samantha was captivated. Tony was by far the most interesting person she had ever met—definitely an intellectual, very spiritual, yet refreshingly grounded. She was spellbound by his elaborate narratives and soapbox diatribes, delightfully entertained by his wit and humor, and impressed by his unique perspective on the world. This man had a truly global consciousness! His words resonated so deeply at the core of her being that at times she resisted the urge to pinch him, pinch herself, just to confirm that he was real. She couldn't remember the last time she'd enjoyed someone this much, and as the day wore on, she felt the blossoming of a powerful physical attraction. It made sense—he was stimulating in every possible way. As a matter of fact, Samantha was on the verge of being *over*stimulated.

After lunch they decided to drive up the coast to one of the more remote and secluded beaches. No topic was off limits—they delved into subjects such as politics, social problems, religion and spirituality, women's rights, and racism. With very few exceptions, they agreed on virtually everything. They even shared the same secret fantasy of abandoning Capitalist society altogether in favor of a simple little life on a remote island somewhere in the sea of their choosing. The only difference in their fantasies was that she preferred the Mediterranean, while he dreamed of the Caribbean.

They strolled down the beach side by side, marking a path just above the water's edge, footsteps in sync. Samantha marveled at how easy it was to share silence with him as well. After an entire day of nonstop conversation, they had naturally lapsed into a contemplative silence, both lost in their own thoughts. Talking out her anxieties had cleared her head, and the heavy weight she had been carrying around seemed to have temporarily lifted. She felt steadier and lighter, experiencing peace and contentment for the first time in months.

As they made their way back to the car, Samantha started to tense—she didn't want the day to end. She unlocked the passenger side door for him, but Tony made no effort to get in the car. Instead, he folded his arms across his chest and studied her thoughtfully. "This is crazy."

"Which part?" she asked, relieved that he didn't seem to be in a rush to leave.

"Do you realize we've been together for almost twelve straight hours?" A slight tremble in his voice betrayed a flicker of insecurity. "I can't believe you're not sick of me yet."

"Are you kidding? I can't believe you're not sick of *me* yet," she confessed, mirroring his quiet vulnerability back at him.

Tony reached up to brush an eyelash off her cheek. "To tell you the truth, I can't imagine ever being sick of you Samantha."

Samantha caught her breath. No one had ever said something like that to her before. He turned her head toward him and their eyes met. There it was again, *Click.* Time stood still. Looking into his eyes, she felt a renewed sense of hope, like maybe it was possible for her broken heart to heal. She had resolved herself to a lifetime of loneliness, vowing never again to let someone get close enough to hurt her, but the strength of their connection was undeniable. This man made her want to believe in love again.

"What's crazy to me," she started, struggling to regain her composure, "is that even though we just met this morning—"

"It feels like we've known each other forever," he finished simply.

Samantha looked up to find sad and troubled eyes staring back at her. A dark cloud had appeared in Tony's disposition, and she had no idea what had brought it on. She scanned his face for a clue to what was going on in his head, but the mind-reading thing didn't work this time. "What is it?"

He said nothing. Instead, he took her hand and led her to a bench a few feet away. After they were both seated, he started speaking again. "I have never wanted to kiss anyone more than I want to kiss you right now."

Samantha's heart caught in her throat. "Okay... But why do you look so tortured about it? Kissing is supposed to be fun."

"I have a girlfriend."

The words hung in the air—all her buoyant hopes and blissful feelings instantly deflated. Now she understood why he looked so sad and troubled. She had no doubt that a similar expression had settled in on her own face. Of course she would meet the man of her dreams, only to find out he was unavailable. Of course. Her self-protective walls snapped back into place as she scolded herself for being so foolish and trusting. The disappointment stung and burned much more than it should have, and though she tried to hide it, she doubted she was successful. It was hard to appear unaffected when all she wanted to do was scream, curse, and throw things. But not yet, not in front of the man. That tantrum would have to wait until she was in the privacy of her own home.

"I can't believe that after twelve hours you're just now getting around to mentioning that," Samantha muttered. She grabbed the pack of cigarettes from his front breast pocket.

"I know, I'm sorry. I don't want you to think I was intentionally misleading you—I swear that wasn't it. Honestly, I didn't think about her at all for most of the day, as terrible as that sounds. It wasn't until the chemistry kicked in and I realized you and I were bonding at this ridiculously rapid rate that it occurred to me 'Shit, I have a girlfriend.' But by that time we were having such a great time, I didn't want it to end. I still don't want it to end. I figured the second you found out I had a girlfriend something would change." He searched her face. "I can see in your eyes something already has."

It was her turn to say nothing. She was in a state of shock, speech wasn't even possible at this point.

"Samantha, I have never met anyone like you before. It sounds crazy, but I have this feeling we were supposed to meet, you know, that our paths were supposed to cross. This is some crazy Fate shit, right? I knew the second I turned my head on the cliff this morning and saw you sitting there that it was Fate. All things happen for a reason, right? This had to have happened for a reason, right?"

She lit her cigarette, saying nothing.

"You totally think I'm a jerk; it's written all over your face. See, I was afraid this was going to happen." He stood up and began to pace. "That's the only reason I didn't say anything earlier. Not to make excuses or anything, I just... well... I just didn't know what to do. I mean, this has never happened to me before, you know what I mean? Samantha? Damnit woman, will you say something?"

She ignored him. He pulled another cigarette out of his pack and lit it in frustration.

"How long have you guys been together?" she managed finally. Of all the questions racing through her mind, that was the one that came tumbling out first.

He stared at the ocean, unable to look at her. "Four and a half years."

"God Tony." How could this be? They had hit it off so well. "Do you love her?"

Tony paused for a long while before answering. "It's complicated but... Yes, I love her."

Samantha's heart sank—that wasn't the answer she'd wanted to hear. "Then what exactly is it you want from me?" she snapped, not bothering to mask her bitterness.

He sat down beside her, eyes pleading, but she continued to avoid his gaze and fixate on the ocean, refusing to get sucked back into what she had been starting to feel for him.

"I know this is incredibly selfish of me," he began softly, his expression pained and miserable. "But I can't imagine just walking away from this." He hesitated for a few seconds, and then continued. "I was hoping, for now at least, that we could be friends."

Samantha shuddered. "Friends," she repeated. "Do you know how many traumatic childhood memories you conjured up with that sentence?" A dry laugh escaped her lips. She had way too much pride to let him see how devastated she really was.

He relaxed at the sound of her laugh, the playful twinkle returning to his eyes. "Give me your car keys."

"Whoa." She pulled her purse out of his reach. "You drop that mega-bomb on me, ruin my lovely afternoon, and now you want my car keys? You may be cute, but you're not that cute."

His playful tone evaporated. "Look, I know you feel I've misrepresented myself, and if you decide you want nothing to do with me, I'll have to accept that. But girlfriend or no, I haven't felt like this in a long time, and that's the truth. Please, just give me a few more hours, a chance to end this day the way it should have ended. One perfect day, from sunrise to sunset. That's all I ask."

She should have run screaming in the other direction, far away from this man named Tony and the tidal wave of emotions she was feeling. Her rational mind flashed warning signals, cautioning her to get out while she still could, but her heart wouldn't cooperate. Why was he so irresistible?

"Where are you going to take me?" she asked suspiciously. She didn't have any intention of turning him down, but refused to come off as too eager.

"Will you just give me the keys and trust me?"

Trust. Now there was a concept foreign to Samantha. Her ability to trust had been completely crippled by her last relationship. But for some reason where Tony was concerned, trust was disturbingly automatic. Even with this new revelation about the girlfriend, every instinct she had was telling her to give in and go with him, consequences be damned. She'd finally found someone she could open up to, who understood her, and she didn't want to give that up. Handing him her car keys, Samantha couldn't help but smile at the way his face lit up when he realized she wasn't going to deny his last request. Yup, she was about to board a runaway train. The only thing left to do was hang on and try to enjoy the ride...

About the Author

James W. Lewis is a novelist and freelance writer published in several books. After spending twenty years in the Navy, James retired from active duty and now moonlights as an assistant personal trainer while completing his studies in Kinesiology.

www.ingramcontent.com/pod-product-compliance
Lightning Source LLC
Chambersburg PA
CBHW021509240626
47154CB00002B/560